CRITICAL ACCLAIM FOR LEIGH RUSSELL

'A brilliant talent in the thriller field'
— Jeffery Deaver, bestselling author of *The Bone Collector*

'Leigh Russell is unmissable'
— Lee Child, author of the bestselling *Jack Reacher* series

'Leigh Russell has become one of the most impressively
dependable purveyors of the English police procedural.'
— Marcel Berlins, *The Times*

'Taut and compelling'
— Peter James, bestselling author of *A Twist of the Knife*

PRAISE FOR *JOURNEY TO DEATH*

'Russell evokes the exotic locale beautifully, but readers will be
in the grip of the suspenseful story, too, even as they feel
the island heat and smell the flowers.'
— *Booklist*

The Times/Sunday Times Crime Club pick

'As usual, Russell delivers imaginative plots, perfectly paced.'
— *The Times*

'[Leigh Russell] will have you coming back for more with her
adrenaline-pumping novels, full of adventure, anticipation and
excitement. Be sure to add Leigh to your must TBR list.'

'I found myself engrossed in this tense thriller from Leigh Russell.'
— *Shots*

'Lucy is an attractive and likeable protagonist . . . *Journey to Death* makes the subtle point that those who appear fragile and vulnerable often have unexpected resources of strength and resilience. It is a thoroughly enjoyable read.'
— *Mystery People*

'Russell has delivered another crackling read . . . Lucy is a brilliant new character and I doubt very much you'll put this one down until you're done. I certainly couldn't.'
— *Crimesquad*

PRAISE FOR *RACE TO DEATH*

'Leigh Russell weaves a fascinating tale that had me completely foxed. Whilst the mystery is tantalising the characters also fascinate, so clearly are they drawn.'
— *Mystery People*

'As tense openings go, they don't come much better than this'
— *The Bookbag*

'Another first-rate story by the talented Leigh Russell. Highly recommended.'
— *Euro Crime*

'The tension is built up cleverly until the final, shocking, denouement'
— Ron Ellis, *Shots*

PRAISE FOR *COLD SACRIFICE*

'A top-of-the-line crime tale and a five-star must-read'
— *Take-A-Break Fiction Feast*

GIRL IN DANGER

A LUCY HALL MYSTERY

ALSO BY LEIGH RUSSELL

LEIGH RUSSELL

GIRL IN DANGER

A LUCY HALL MYSTERY

Published by Thomas & Mercer, Seattle

www.apub.com

ISBN-13: 9781503938250
ISBN-10: 1503938255

Cover design by Lisa Horton

Printed in the United States of America

To Michael, Jo, Phill, Phil and Rian

Prologue

WHATEVER HAPPENED, he could not risk drawing attention to himself. Adopting a nonchalant pose, he slipped both hands into his pockets and stared straight ahead. It was important to time it right, but he could not delay much longer. Patrice always strung it out as long as he could, but this time it was going to be over quite quickly. He had to capture Patrice in the act. He made a conscious effort to breathe slowly. Better to miss this chance than screw it up by rushing. There would be other opportunities. If anyone spotted what he was doing, he would be next.

Almost completely shut off from natural light, the cool temperature in the cellar was convenient. Bodies could not always be removed before they began to decompose. Body parts were less problematic. Limbs, even headless torsos, were relatively easy to dispose of, dropped into the river at night in weighted bags. No one paid much attention to them, if they were ever found – there might be a brief mention in the media, and a few questions asked, before they were consigned to oblivion. Patrice joked about taking out shares in chainsaws because, once rigor set in, complete bodies were awkward to shift so if Patrice hadn't constructed a cellar with efficient drainage, they would be knee deep in filthy blood by now.

Even so, the place still resembled an abattoir at times, but they were all used to the stench; it was unavoidable. Sometimes they had to hang on to corpses for days until it was possible to move them safely. But it was worth the effort because although the cellar was hidden away, word got around. No one messed with Patrice and his gang.

But even Patrice was assailable.

Fighting to control his panic, he forced himself to maintain an appearance of composure. He prayed his paranoia was uncalled for, but the way Patrice had been looking at him recently had been making him feel uneasy. Any sign of nerves and he might arouse suspicion. Patrice could scent fear. He thrived on it.

After all his apprehension, it went like a dream. Preoccupied with the spasms of the dying man, no one took any notice of him. No one even glanced in his direction. As Patrice laughed and stubbed out his cigarette, the dying man let out a thin scream. A delicate whiff of burning flesh permeated the stuffy cellar. Patrice turned to grin at his audience and the massive diamond on his ring seemed to wink in the electric light.

'Nice one, boss,' he muttered, joining in with the general murmur of approbation.

Careful not to sound too enthusiastic, he looked down at the floor so his face could not betray his feelings. The slightest irregularity could arouse suspicion.

He imagined Patrice turning on him. 'What are you looking so happy about?' he would yell. 'It's only a stiff.'

Scuffing the toe of his shoe on the dirty concrete, he suppressed the laughter threatening to bubble up from his chest, because it had been ridiculously easy.

From the way Patrice banged on about it, his cellar could have been locked away in the vaults of a Swiss bank. 'They all think they're so clever, but no one's ever going to find out what goes on down here,' he liked to boast about the place he called his play room. 'As long as we're careful, we can do what we like. No one can stop us.'

Only that might not be true for much longer.

What Patrice liked to do usually involved inflicting pain. Each to his own. As a rule, his victims had it coming. But Patrice was right about one thing. It never did any harm to be careful.

He continued to stare at the floor, avoiding meeting anyone's eye. He had been asking around lately, trying to find out who was new on the scene, looking for a reporter hungry for a scoop. Someone arriving in Paris from overseas would be best. Anyone who knew Patrice's reputation would be afraid to touch it. In the meantime, he would keep his treasure safely locked away.

1

'What do you mean? What sort of information are you talking about?'

'You've been asking questions.'

Lucy glanced around to check that no one was listening. The anonymous caller was right. She had been questioning fellow journalists and police press officers about a variety of crimes since she had arrived in Paris three months earlier. With her childlike features and slim build, she was often mistaken for being much younger than her twenty-four years. Determined to be taken seriously as an investigative journalist she was hoping to establish her reputation with a scoop, but so far she had not managed to unearth a single story of her own. She spent most of her time proofreading other people's articles and updating the website. Impatient to start making a name for herself, she did not want to share this potential lead with anyone else, at least until she knew what was on offer. It could be a lucky break for her.

'How did you get my number? What's your name?'

Her informant refused to answer any questions over the phone.

'Meet me on the Quai de Jemmapes by the bridge on Rue Louis Blanc at half past seven on Sunday evening.'

Lucy would have felt more comfortable meeting indoors in a public venue, but the streets alongside the canal were always busy. On summer evenings they were packed. It could hardly be dangerous to meet a stranger there.

'How will I know who you are?'

'You won't. I'll find you. Wait for me at the end of the bridge.'

'But—' Lucy began to protest that she needed to know more about what her anonymous caller wanted before she agreed to meet him.

'If you don't come alone, I won't approach you, and don't tell anyone about this. People's lives are at stake.'

Before she could respond, he hung up.

Lucy stared at her screen, doing her best to hide her excitement and wondering whether the caller's parting comment was true. She thought he had sounded frightened, but he could have been issuing a veiled threat against her own life. Armed with this new lead she went to speak to her boss, hoping he would finally be impressed by the consequences of her research.

'Lucy, I've been meaning to speak to you,' he said by way of greeting before she could open her mouth. 'Sit down and listen carefully. I hear you've been pestering people for stories, and it's got to stop. It's not professional.'

Removing his black-framed glasses, the editor rubbed his eyes with the back of his hand. Lucy started to reply, but he raised his hand to silence her. When he resumed speaking, he sounded exasperated.

'I don't want you running around hunting for stories any more. It can take years to establish good relations with a useful source, and no one appreciates junior members of the team trying to jump in before they've even learned how things work here. It just doesn't do to go rushing around, blinded by enthusiasm. We all need to exercise a certain degree of diplomacy. It's naive to think otherwise.'

Lucy frowned. 'What if a story comes to me?'

The editor shook his head. 'Don't try to run before you can walk. We're a responsible news agency. The public trust us to get our facts right. Nothing else matters.'

'Not even if people's lives are at stake?'

The editor gave a tired smile. 'Don't be melodramatic.'

'But—'

'You're letting your imagination run away with you, and that's unacceptable. Our job is to report the facts. If you want to tug at your readers' heartstrings, go and work for a women's magazine. News reporting is a tough business, Lucy, and if you allow your emotions to cloud your views, you'll be out of a job before you know it. We report the news. We don't make it. Stick to the facts if you want to carry on working here. I'm warning you because you're inexperienced. But you need to learn fast. So, no more stories. Stick to keeping the website up to date for now.'

Lucy returned to her seat worried by the warning she had received. She considered going back and telling the editor about her planned meeting with an anonymous informant. Once he knew what was happening, his opinion of her might change. Sitting at her desk, she reviewed her options. If the tip-off turned out to be a waste of time, it was best kept to herself. Her editor already appeared to regard her as empty-headed. She could not afford to make a fool of herself in front of him. On the other hand, if she had been offered a genuine lead to a serious story, she suspected the editor would want one of his more experienced reporters to follow it up. But the informant had chosen to contact her. With any luck she would turn up to work on Monday morning with a genuine scoop of her own. She was not about to give it away.

She had been wildly excited when she had accepted a post as a reporter in the Paris office of the UK-based Current Affairs International, and the experience of living in a foreign capital had exceeded her expectations. Although the job was nothing like as sensational as she had anticipated, she had fallen in love with Paris. From elegant buildings along stately avenues, to the warm smell of baking and the bustling pavements of the Marais district, where she lived, and the magical views of the Seine after dark with lights glistening on the water, it was a city of contrasts. She missed nothing about London except her friends. Now not only had her best friend Nina come to stay with her for the rest of the summer, but she had been given a lead for a potential story. After making a note of the time of her rendezvous with her anonymous informant, she settled down to work, doing her best to put the phone call out of her mind.

'I've got to go out this evening,' she told Nina on Sunday.

Nina raised her eyebrows, grinned and nodded her head, her mouth too full to speak. They were sitting on a bench in a peaceful walled garden off the Rue des Rosiers, eating a late lunch of massive pitta breads crammed with hummus, tahini, mouth-watering crispy falafels and a generous portion of salad. The garden was beautiful, but it hid a tragic past. Dedicated to the memory of the children of the Marais who had been deliberately slaughtered by the Nazis during World War II, the place invited quiet reflection. Lucy often came to sit here by herself, soaking in the tranquillity. She was pleased that Nina liked it too. Sitting side by side, they gazed at the overflowing flower beds as they chomped.

'It's only work,' Lucy added, as she finished a mouthful. 'Nothing very exciting.'

With luck, that would not prove true.

'Working on a Sunday evening?'

'News can break at any time.'

Nina laughed. 'You sound like a real newshound.'

Lucy smiled. 'I'm working on it.'

'Don't worry about me,' Nina reassured her later when Lucy was getting ready to leave. 'You go and do whatever it is you have to do. I need to wash my hair anyway, and it'll give me a chance to touch up my roots.'

Lucy smiled. Nina bleached her mousy hair so that it was almost as blonde as Lucy's natural colour. They were sometimes mistaken for twins, although their features were quite different. With blonde hair cropped very short, Lucy looked younger than Nina, who had a darker complexion. While Lucy's huge eyes gave an impression of childlike innocence, Nina's narrow hazel eyes made her look shrewd.

'I should be back by nine and we can go out for a drink, if you like,' Lucy said.

'Sounds good. It won't take long to do my hair.'

With a flutter of excitement, Lucy set off to meet her anonymous informant. Hoping it would not be a wasted journey, she took the Metro from Saint-Augustin to Chaussée d'Antin–La Fayette, where she changed line and took a train to Louis Blanc. From the station it was only a short walk across the bridge to the Quai de Jemmapes. The streets along the Canal Saint-Martin were packed with people, mostly Lucy's age or younger. The majority of them looked like students. As well as the crowds strolling along the pavements, people were sitting all along the canal bank, smoking and chatting in the warm summer evening.

Lucy waited on the pavement at the end of the bridge. Several minutes passed without any sign from her informant. Watching a stream of pedestrians crossing the bridge on their way to an evening out, she began to feel annoyed. Instead of coming all this way on the strength of what was probably a prank message, she could have been at the flat, having a laugh with Nina. She was about to turn round and make her way back over the bridge to the station, when a voice muttered her name. She spun round. A man in a grey baseball cap was standing right beside her, his eyes fixed on the canal.

'Don't look at me,' he murmured, still staring at the murky water.

Out of the corner of her eye she studied his long thin nose and gaunt cheeks. He had a small, crooked scar on his chin, and there was an unhealthy sheen on his pasty face.

'Stop staring at me,' he hissed through clenched teeth, without turning his head. 'They're watching. They're always watching. If they see you talking to me, we'll both be dead before the night's over.'

2

LUCY LAUGHED NERVOUSLY. Taking her lead from the man in the grey cap, she turned away from him and gazed down at the dark water.

'Who are you?' she asked.

'Get your phone out.'

'What?'

'Pretend to be talking to someone on your phone. That way they won't know you're talking to me.'

'I'm not sure—'

'Just do it.'

'OK, I've got my phone. I'm pretending to talk to someone. What now?'

'Now you shut up and listen.'

She glanced around. Still looking down at the water, the man in the grey cap was holding his phone to his ear.

'I got something that's going to interest you.'

'What makes you think that?'

'You're here, aren't you?'

'Yes.'

'So do you want the story or not?'

Lucy hesitated. Despite her excitement, she did not want to rush into anything. The man was a stranger. Remembering her editor's warning, she resolved to be cautious.

'Tell me who you are.'

'That's not important. All that matters is that I'm giving you the biggest news story of your life.'

They both knew she would not refuse him, despite her professed reservations. 'If it's such a good story, why are you giving it to me?'

'Someone put me onto you. That's all you need to know. They said you were looking for a story. Word gets around. I'm looking for a reporter who's hungry enough to take this on and you popped up, young and keen. Most journalists are too damn scared. They live in the shadows, keeping out of trouble. The ones with real guts and conviction get silenced and end up bleating, like all the rest. What I've got here is the biggest story you'll ever come across, and I don't think any of the old timers have got the nerve to touch it. They aren't after news that's going to shake things up around here. They spend their time covering their arses and being careful not to upset anyone for fear of reprisals.'

Her editor's warning echoed in Lucy's head again. She wondered if she was about to risk losing her job.

'So, what do you say? You want it or not? Only, if you accept it, you've got to give it so much publicity, no one will be able to hush it up. I can give it to you right now, but you've got to promise me you won't bottle it. Don't let on where it came from, and whatever you do, don't breathe a word about this to the police. You can't trust them. They'll bury the story, and you with it. Believe me, you won't be the first one to disappear without trace. Even the papers won't touch it if the police are involved. It'll be hushed up and more people will die. But once you've published it, no one will be able to stop it.' He paused for breath. 'Just get it out there and it'll go viral before you know it. Once enough people know about it, the authorities will be forced to do something.'

Glancing at the speaker's profile, Lucy saw him blinking nervously. Remembering his warning, she looked away. There was no denying her curiosity had been aroused. It could do no harm to take a look at his information. At least she could find out how much he wanted for it. If she chose not to pursue the story for whatever reason, she could forget about his information, or else pass it on to her editor to deal with. A promise made under these circumstances could not be binding, given that she had no idea what she was agreeing to.

'OK,' she said softly, talking into her phone. 'How much do you want for it?'

There was no response. She looked sideways, then turned her head round. The man had vanished. Scanning the crowds along the pavement in either direction, she could see no sign of him amongst the girls in summer dresses and young men in long shorts strolling past. With a sigh, she began to make her way back across the bridge. Somehow she had blown it. Perhaps he had sensed doubt in her momentary hesitation. His story was probably nowhere near as interesting as he had made out, and she was unlikely to have used it, but she was disappointed all the same. She could only speculate about what her mysterious informant had wanted to tell her.

'Hey, Lucy!'

One of the other young reporters from her office was walking towards her on the bridge.

'I'm meeting up with friends at Le Comptoir Général for a beer. Come and join us!'

Lucy was tempted. It had taken her a while to establish friendly relations with a few of her colleagues. Everyone seemed so busy at work and at the end of the day they all rushed off home. Here was an opportunity to socialise with Parisians her own age. She glanced at the time on her phone.

'I promised to meet a friend later,' she said, thinking of Nina, 'but I'm free for half an hour or so. Is it far?'

'It's just across the bridge, off the Quai de Jemmapes. Come on.'

As they walked, he told her about the bar. 'Le Comptoir Général's a very cool place. I'm surprised you've never been there. I mean, I thought everyone knew it.'

Lucy shook her head, and admitted that she had never even heard of it.

'The bar's on the site of what was originally a stable for horses towing boats up the canal. It's very different to the other bars and restaurants in Paris, but it's a great place to hang out, if we can get a seat. It gets very busy. There's a Caribbean bar, an African second-hand clothes stall, and all sorts of relics, and you can get really unusual cocktails there, although I usually stick to beers. It's owned by an eccentric philanthropist who employs a team of scavengers to bring him any strange objects they find, so you never know what you might find there.'

'Sounds interesting.'

Pleased that her outing had not turned out to be a complete waste of time after all, she followed her colleague along the crowded pavement beside the water. Before long, he led her through a gate in a green fence. They walked along a path that led them past high white walls with black beams painted on them and through a doorway into a long corridor where crimson walls and a matching strip of carpet were dimly illuminated by huge crystal chandeliers. Passing an eclectic collection of furniture, random light fittings and a curious stack of old typewriters, they entered a large room, warm despite its open ceiling rafters. The venue was packed with customers, mostly young, all chattering and drinking. Noise bounced off the faded black-and-white tiled floor so it was difficult to hear what her companion was saying. Lucy followed him to an unvarnished table where two girls were sitting on wooden chairs with metal frames that reminded Lucy of school furniture. Gazing around as she sat down, she noticed an old black-and-white television set which was showing a film in one corner of the room, beside a large bay packed with bizarre objects, under a sign *Le Centre des Objets Perdus*. Most of the items looked very old. She made out a couple of metal bowls, a rail of what appeared to be vintage clothes, a series of sepia photographs and a stuffed cockerel among the haphazard bric-a-brac. From a distance, she was not sure if it was a real bird that had been stuffed, or a life-sized model.

Someone put a large glass of red wine on the table in front of her. Muttering her thanks, she fished out her purse, but her colleague shook his head when she offered to pay for her drink.

'I can't stay long enough to buy a round,' she shouted to him across the table, above the noise.

He waved his hand, as though to bat her words away. 'Another time,' he called back.

'Cheers!'

The time passed quickly. Lucy was reluctant to leave, but she had promised to be back at the flat by nine.

'Why don't you tell your friend to join us?' the girl beside her asked.

'Well, she probably won't be able to find it, but I can give her a call.'

'You might need to go out in the corridor so you can hear her,' the other girl suggested. 'The signal in here's not great, even apart from all the racket.'

In the corridor, Lucy took out her phone and saw that Nina had left her a message.

'No need to hurry back. I'm going out.'

Lucy smiled. The Marais was an interesting area to explore. Besides, Nina had said she had no intention of leaving Paris before she had enjoyed a fling.

'You might have to wait a long time,' Lucy had answered. 'I've been here for months without even a hint of any romance.'

'Who mentioned romance?' Nina had replied, and they had both laughed.

Slipping her phone in her pocket, Lucy felt something else in there. Puzzled, she pulled out a key attached to a black fob. Her heart pounded as her fist closed around it. She had never seen it before. It could not be a coincidence that the key had appeared in her pocket just after her meeting with an anonymous informant. If he was a thief of some description, he might plausibly have slipped the key in her pocket without her noticing, in a kind of reverse pickpocketing move. Her colleague's words took on a strange significance: 'You never know what you might see there.' With a shrug, she dismissed the suspicion that her colleague might be in cahoots with her mysterious informant. The meeting with the stranger had unsettled her, making her paranoid. For all she knew, he would turn out to be a harmless crank. But it was possible that he had given her a lead to a huge scoop. The key might lead her to a hoard of stolen treasures: priceless paintings, fabulous diamonds and millions of euros. It was an unlikely scenario, but not impossible.

Shoving the key in her bag, she glanced around. The corridor was empty. Through an open doorway she could see the profile of a black guy standing behind what appeared to be a makeshift bar, but he was not looking in her direction. There were no security cameras in sight. In any case, the key was probably too small to show up on CCTV film. Trembling with excitement, she did not dare take it out of her bag again to examine it more closely in case she dropped it. Her first job was to decide what she was going to do about it. Apart from any other considerations, after a large glass of wine, she was not sure she was thinking clearly. In the meantime, no one knew about her meeting with her anonymous contact. She decided to sleep on it and work out what to do in the morning. There was a chance this could turn out to be something really important. She did not want to rush and end up regretting her decision.

3

UNDER NORMAL CIRCUMSTANCES, Lucy would happily have stayed for another glass of wine, but she was distracted by the presence of the key in her bag. She wondered how she was going to discover what it opened, and what might be revealed, locked away in a secret location. Her informant had talked of people's lives being at risk. She wondered who else knew about the key, and whether anyone had observed her meeting with her informant. All at once, Le Comptoir Général did not feel welcoming. Wherever she looked, strangers seemed to be staring at her. Abruptly she stood up.

'I have to go.'

Her companions merely smiled at her, nodding their goodbyes, oblivious to her stress. Their relaxed response to her announcement was reassuring, but outside on the dark street she felt nervous. The bridge was packed with people passing in both directions as she scurried to the station. Everything appeared more sinister at night. The roar of departing trains sounded savage and wherever she looked, she noticed shabby characters shuffling around like spies from a criminal underclass, and the graffiti, which had seemed vibrant and colourful during the day, now looked menacing. In the carriage, she was unnerved by a man staring at her. It was not the first time she had attracted unwelcome attention, but tonight, for the first time, she felt genuinely frightened by a stranger's gaze.

Arriving back in the Marais just after eleven, she walked past shops shut up for the night: jewellers, shoe shops and vintage clothes shops. Only the small restaurants, falafel cafés and bars were still busy with customers sitting at tables on the pavement. Reassured by the familiar cheerful bustle, Lucy made her way past a noisy queue of people waiting outside a comedy theatre, where an up-and-coming comedienne was performing that evening. As she turned into her own street, the pavement was less crowded. She passed a quirky boutique, a shop specialising in all different designs of flip-flops, a parfumerie, an estate agent, a chemist, a couple of small restaurants and various clothes shops. Tapping in the code, she opened her street door and entered a narrow covered passage-way that opened out into a paved courtyard. When she had first moved into the area, she had been surprised to learn how many of the street doors did not lead directly into buildings, but to peaceful inner courtyards, hidden from passers-by, surrounded by entrances to apartments.

Her relief at being home was short-lived. To her surprise, she saw the front door to her flat was ajar. Grumbling at Nina under her breath, she went in and closed it. Switching on the light she stared, aghast, at the utter devastation in the hall. Coats and jackets had been pulled off the coat stand and were strewn across the carpet amid splinters of glass from a mirror that had been taken off the wall and smashed. She went into the living room. The table had been upturned, as had the sofa which had been slashed with a sharp blade exposing the stuffing. The television had been ripped off its shelf and lay face down on the carpet. Books, magazines and CDs were scattered around the room, along with the few photographs and ornaments she had brought with her or purchased in Paris. A bunch of bananas had been knocked off the table and trodden into the carpet.

17

Shouting Nina's name, and with her heart pounding, Lucy ran into the kitchen. It had been similarly ransacked. A jar of jam lay smashed on the floor beside tins of tea and lentils and packets of biscuits that looked as though someone had stamped on them. A box of washing powder and a bag of rice had been emptied onto the floor, the grains sprinkled over shards of broken plates and mugs. It was impossible to walk in without treading on the detritus of food and crockery. Shaking, she opened the door to her bedroom and groaned. All her clothes had been pulled out of the wardrobe and lay in disarray around the room, covering the bed and most of the carpet. Her bedside cabinet had been tipped over and emptied. Her iPod, pills, a small bottle of perfume, a shell she had brought back from her last holiday, all lay in a shambles on the floor, smashed to pieces. Her pillow had been torn. Even her mattress had been ripped open.

She ran into the small spare room where Nina was staying. It had been trashed as thoroughly as the rest of the flat. The bed had been pulled apart. Sheets, pillows and clothes lay around in a jumble of ripped fabric. Shaking, Lucy stepped over a stray leather ankle boot. The walls seemed to be spinning around her. She was thankful neither she nor Nina had been at home when the flat had been broken into. It was past eleven o'clock, but Nina's text had not said what time she would be back. Impatient to tell her what had happened Lucy called her, but the phone went straight to voice mail.

'Where are you? Call me when you get this.'

Lucy wondered where Nina could be, and whether she had met a guy. She could really have done with her company right now. Returning to her own room, she cleared a space on the bed and sat down, her thoughts racing wildly. She was not the tidiest of people, but she usually knew where everything was. Now her room looked as though it had been in the path of a tornado. She struggled to control the tears that were welling up in her eyes. She had to sober up and think. She knew she had to report the break-in to the police, and in the morning she would inform the landlord. The intruders might have smashed their way in to search for the key she had been given earlier that evening. With everything that had happened, her head was spinning.

Taking a deep breath, she tried to think sensibly. On reflection, she decided she was being paranoid. The break-in was hardly likely to relate to her earlier meeting that evening.

Returning to the hall to check how the intruders had gained access, she frowned. Apart from all the mess, there was no sign of forced entry. Either the door had been expertly picked, or else Nina had gone out without shutting it properly. Before she reported everything to her landlord, Lucy needed to find out what had happened. Her father would know what to do, but her parents had gone on a cruise while her mother was recuperating from a recent illness. There was no one in France she could call so late at night; she had not been living here long enough to have made any real friends. Until Nina returned, she was on her own. Glancing at her phone, she saw that her hand was shaking.

In the meantime, she needed to call the police. Her informant had warned her not to tell them about their meeting, but this was an unrelated matter. Having made the phone call, she waited for nearly an hour until two uniformed officers arrived, a woman of about twenty-five and an older man. After a cursory glance around the apartment, they interrogated Lucy so sternly she was afraid they suspected her of trashing the place herself. Faced with a barrage of questions, she began to feel guilty, even though she had done nothing wrong.

'And you haven't seen your friend since you went out earlier?' the man demanded, challenging her account.

'That's right.'

'Did the two of you quarrel before she went out?' the young woman asked.

19

'No! Look, she sent me this text.' Lucy held out her phone.

'You've been drinking,' the female officer said. It was a statement, not a question. They could smell the alcohol on her breath.

Cursing herself for not having cleaned her teeth before the police arrived, Lucy gave a reluctant nod. 'I had a glass of wine with some friends earlier on, that's all.'

'Was anything taken?'

'I don't know. It's difficult to say with everything in such a mess.'

'Whoever did this certainly didn't hold back,' the policeman said.

The two officers left soon after, with assurances that they would look into the break-in. They did not appear at all concerned about Nina.

'She texted you to say she was going out,' the woman pointed out.

As they were leaving, they stopped to examine the lock on the front door. Telling herself that they only wanted to ensure she was safe, Lucy thanked them for coming. It was a relief to close the door behind them. Alone again, she sat on her bed, shaking. For all her posturing about being an independent woman, now she was in trouble she could feel herself crumbling. Taking the keyring out of her pocket, she studied the key, wondering what it opened. She slipped it underneath the lining of her small leather jewellery box. Her own cheap jewellery had been tipped out on the floor. Gathering it up, she returned her rings, beads and baubles to the box before snapping the lid shut and putting it away in the cabinet beside her bed. Lying down, she waited for Nina to come back from her night out, until, after a while, she drifted off to sleep.

4

WAKING WITH A HEADACHE on Monday morning, Lucy reached out to turn off her alarm. For a moment she thought she was suffering from a hangover, but as she sat up and saw the state of her bedroom, she remembered the events of the previous evening with a sickening jolt. A lot had happened after she had drunk a glass of wine at Le Comptoir Général, and she had not managed to sleep until three in the morning. It was no wonder her head was thumping and her eyes felt heavy.

'Nina!' she called out as she clambered out of bed, tripping over a pile of clothes. There was no answer. Even though she remembered the mess in her room, she was still shocked by the state of it. After checking the spare room and finding it empty, she sat on the bed and called Nina again. There was still no answer. Lucy tried not to panic. She was annoyed with Nina for staying out all night without telling her, but she was also becoming increasingly anxious at the prospect of her friend being alone and out of communication in a foreign city. She began picking up a few items of Nina's clothing and dumping them on the bed. As she did so, she noticed Nina's bag lying on the floor. Emptying it, she was dismayed to find Nina's purse and keys. Not only that, but her phone and her passport were lying on the floor. Lucy's stomach lurched. No girl would go out without her bag. It was beginning to look as though Nina might have been caught up in the attempted robbery. Lucy could not ignore the possibility that she might have fled from the apartment and been too frightened to return.

Lucy called the police who repeated that she could not file a report until the person had been missing for forty-eight hours.

'She left her bag here,' Lucy protested, but she was helpless against the official procedure concerning missing persons.

Too upset to go into work, Lucy phoned her boss to explain that her flat had been broken into the previous night. When she described the extent of the damage the editor suggested she take a few days off.

'Are you all right? I don't suppose they'll find out who did it,' he added glumly. 'Sadly it's all too common these days, although it does sound as though you had a particularly unpleasant experience. They were probably off their faces and didn't know what they were doing. Still, as long as you're all right.'

'I am, but—'

'But?'

'I had a friend staying with me,' she blurted out, his sympathy breaking down her reserve.

'A friend?' he repeated blankly.

'Yes, a girlfriend, over from England. Only she wasn't here when I got home last night, and I've no idea where she's gone.'

'What do you mean?'

'I don't know, but she wouldn't have gone off without telling me where she was going. She'd know I'd be worried.'

Her editor laughed. 'It's not unheard of for a young woman to go out for a night. Maybe she met someone?'

'I thought of that, but . . .' Lucy explained that Nina had left her bag behind along with her purse, phone and keys.

'I can see why you're concerned,' he replied, 'but there could be another explanation. She could have met a young man. But I tell you what,' he went on, more seriously, 'I've got the number of a private investigator I can give you, if you're really worried about her. Tracking down missing persons is his speciality. He's helped us once or twice in the past, although I haven't heard anything from him for a while. He didn't want his details recorded on our system, but I think I've got his card somewhere. Hang on, I'll see if I can find it.'

Lucy waited.

'Ah! Here it is,' he cried out at last, reading out the name, Alain Michel, and the mobile number.

'If that's still his number,' the editor said, 'and if he's still using that name. It might not be his real name. Anyway, you could give it a try. Let me know how you get on. Now, I really have to go. Take a few days off and get yourself sorted out. I'm sure there's a perfectly reasonable explanation for your friend staying out all night.'

With a final charge not to worry, the editor rang off. Reluctantly Lucy stood up and went into the kitchen. She could not put off the clearing up indefinitely. The kitchen was far worse than the bedrooms because she had to wipe up spilled food. It was disgusting. Soon it would start to smell. Stuck to the floor in a mess of honey she found a receipt from a café in Montmartre, Chez Catherine. She had never been there. Someone must have dropped it in her kitchen. The tiny scrap of paper nearly made her cry. Somehow it made the intruders seem more real. Miserably she carried on wiping and scrubbing. Before long she had exhausted her meagre supply of cleaning materials and went out to the local grocery store to stock up on scourers and the most powerful kitchen-cleaning products she could find.

As she stepped out into the street, the sun was shining and the drama of the break-in and her missing friend seemed to belong to a different world. Apart from the fact that her flat had been trashed, it could have been a normal day. The pavements around her flat were crowded with shoppers and tourists, all chattering cheerfully. The friendly manager of her local patisserie greeted her with a broad grin when Lucy stopped for an almond croissant. As she walked along the street, dropping flakes of pastry on the pavement, she could almost imagine that everything was normal. But her anxiety about Nina made the sweet pastry stick in her throat. After a few mouthfuls, she stopped even trying to eat it.

Usually on a sunny day she would wander along the Rue de Rivoli, perhaps turning left along the Rue du Temple, and then right down the Rue Sainte-Croix-de-la-Bretonnerie, left into the Rue Vieille du Temple and right into the Rue des Rosiers with its cafés and restaurants where she could wander around the labyrinth of narrow streets. Round the corner from her apartment, in the Rue Ferdinand Duval, she would linger outside the falafel bars and bakeries, sometimes stopping for a drink or something to eat, soaking up the smells and sounds of the place, foreign yet familiar. She loved the lively warm atmosphere of the Marais, teeming with people, its winding streets so different to the elegant but grandiose wide avenue where she worked. If she allowed her eyes to shift out of focus, she could almost imagine she had slipped back in time to the Middle Ages, except when an occasional car or moped went by, nudging its way between the pedestrians.

This afternoon she made her way straight back to her flat with her purchases. It was afternoon and Nina had been gone for over sixteen hours. Looking up the numbers of all the hospitals in Paris, Lucy started to call around in case Nina had been brought in during the night. She found herself hoping to hear that Nina had suffered a minor accident. The enquiries were time-consuming, involving long periods of waiting on the phone, but she persisted. No one was able to help her. Each time she was told that no one matching Nina's description had been admitted, she felt a flicker of relief and disappointment. She was still no closer to finding out what had happened to her friend. The calls took up most of the afternoon.

Eventually she called the police again. 'I'd like to report a missing person.'

Initially alert, the woman at the other end of the line lost interest when Lucy gave Nina's age and said how long she had been gone.

'Nina Wilson,' the policewoman repeated dully. 'And your name?'

'Jane Briggs,' Lucy replied promptly.

Her lie was not premeditated. Somehow it just slipped out. Her anonymous informant's words had rattled her more than she had realised.

'Your friend is twenty-three,' the woman at the police station said dismissively. 'And she has been missing for less than one day.'

Miserably Lucy repeated what she had told her editor. Nearly twenty-four hours had elapsed since Nina had disappeared. For a girl alone in a foreign city, that was a long time.

'What you are reporting is not a crime. Your friend went out without telling you where she was going.' A tutting sound was clearly audible over the phone.

'I know you deal with many major crimes here, and this doesn't sound very serious, but my friend doesn't know anyone in Paris and I'm worried about her,' Lucy insisted.

'You can complete a missing person's report if your friend is still missing after forty-eight hours.'

With that, the woman rang off. It did not sound as though Lucy's report was going to receive attention any time soon. There was nothing more she could do. Feeling hungry, she went out to buy some provisions. At least there would be something to eat in the flat for Nina when she returned. She hurried back along the Rue Ferdinand Duval, hoping to see her friend waiting outside on the pavement. There was no sign of her. Lucy did not know what more she could do so once she got back home and had had something to eat, she set to work again, scrubbing the kitchen. Eventually it was tolerably tidy, but she still had the rest of the flat to tackle. And all the time she listened out for Nina ringing the bell.

5

GAGGING AT THE STENCH OF ROTTEN MEAT, it took Nina a few moments to register that her eyes were open. With a shock she realised she had gone blind. The sound of voices shouting nearby reassured her that at least she could hear. It was common knowledge that losing one sense made the others sharper. Turning her head towards the noise, she was confused to see a sliver of light cutting across the darkness. If she blinked, it vanished. Opening her eyes, she saw it again. Its position never altered whichever direction she turned her head. Either her brain was playing tricks on her, or she could still see. As her panic subsided, she gathered that she was lying on her side, in a foetal position.

Attempting to sit up, she discovered her wrists and ankles were bound. It struck her that if she had been tied up there might also be a blindfold over her eyes. That would explain the near total blackness, broken only by one thin line of light at the bottom of her vision. She tried to establish whether her eyes were covered or not but she could not move her hands. The more she focused on the problem with her eyes, the more convinced she became that she could feel a tight narrow band around the back of her head. If she was right, it could be holding a blindfold in place, but she was not sure.

Trying to ignore her fears over her eyesight, and the putrid smell, she turned her attention to her surroundings. She was lying on a cold, hard surface. Pressing her cheek down, she thought she could feel a concrete floor. After a while she became aware that she was terribly thirsty. At the same time, she realised that she needed the toilet. Physical needs overcame her terror and she called out in panic, hoping she had not been abandoned. If no one came to her assistance soon, she would wet herself.

'Hello. Is anyone there? Can someone help me, please?'

Rough hands pulled her hair sharply as her blindfold was ripped off. Her momentary pain was forgotten as she blinked, dazzled, relieved to discover that she had not gone blind. Accustomed to darkness, it was a while before her eyes adjusted to the light and she was able to look around. She was lying on a concrete floor. Two large, dirty white trainers stood inches away from her face. From their size, she guessed they belonged to a man. Stocky legs in greasy-looking dark-blue jeans towered above the shoes. Looking up, she could see a grey sweatshirt and stubble growing underneath the man's pimply chin. Twisting her head round the other way, she could see a filthy white wall. Overhead a single, naked light bulb hung from the rafters of a high ceiling.

She knew she ought to feel angry, but she was too tired to protest about being tied up. All she wanted to do was have a drink and go to the toilet. Unable to think beyond her immediate needs, she asked for some water. If she did not have a drink soon, she was afraid she would be ill. Already her head was pounding and she felt sick. Dehydration was a far more worrying prospect than wetting her trousers.

'I'm really thirsty,' she called up to the man. 'I need a drink.'

She did not understand his gabbling, but he sounded angry.

'I need a drink,' she said in French.

The man muttered to himself in a hoarse voice and the trainers moved away.

'Water! I'm dying of thirst!' she screeched at his retreating figure.

The man shouted at her suddenly in heavily accented English, 'You put your sock in it!'

She heard his footsteps receding, and a door slammed shut. Closing her eyes, she gave way to a fit of sobbing. She did not want to die alone in an unfamiliar place. Even a hostile stranger was company of a sort. She knew she ought to be conserving her energy, but she could not stop crying. She was only dimly aware of the man returning. Without warning, icy water splashed on her face, making her gasp. The man held a bottle to her lips. Out of the corner of her eye she could see black hairs sprouting on the backs of thick fingers, nails bitten to the quick. The frayed edge of his sleeve had shifted up his arm, revealing the edge of a tattoo on the back of his brawny wrist. Not knowing when she might be offered another drink, she gulped greedily, coughing and retching as some water went down the wrong way.

'No,' the man bawled at her in English. 'You drink it slow. You know nothing. Not even how to drink. It is like the baby. They teach you nothing in England?'

'I'm sorry,' she mumbled. 'Pardon. *Pardonnez-moi.*'

She regretted her grovelling apology at once. She had just texted Lucy to tell her not to hurry back as she was going for a walk, when she had heard the doorbell. Assuming Lucy had forgotten her key, Nina had opened the front door. The men had seized her and blindfolded her before she had seen them clearly. Her memories of what happened next were a blur, all she remembered was being carried out and thrown in the back of a van, but after that, she could remember nothing until she had woken up, bound and blindfolded. She had no idea where she was, or how long she had been unconscious, or why she had been brought to this foul-smelling place.

'I don't know what the hell possessed me to apologise to a shit like you,' she muttered.

Her bravado was a lie. She knew very well what had prompted her apology. It was fear.

6

HAVING CONTACTED EVERY HOSPITAL she could track down without learning what had happened to Nina, and attempting to report her disappearance to the police, Lucy settled down with her iPad to scan through the local news for the past twenty-four hours, searching for anything about an accident involving a blonde English girl. All at once she started and opened up a story. She read it through several times with growing unease. The body of a man identified as Jérôme Meunier had been fished out of the canal in the early hours of Monday morning. According to the report, he had been involved in a fight shortly before he committed suicide. Such deaths were not uncommon, but there was something familiar about the victim's face. Deeply troubled, she enlarged the image and stared at a jagged scar on the dead man's chin. She was almost certain she had just discovered the identity of her anonymous informant.

It was beginning to look as though someone was desperate to retrieve the key that was now in Lucy's possession – desperate enough to kill. If the dead man really was her informant, he must have been murdered very shortly after he had given her the key. Perhaps he had been killed as a warning to whoever now had it that they would be next unless the key was returned. She had no idea who wanted it back. With a sick feeling, she realised that might be why her flat had been broken into and searched so thoroughly. Someone had come there looking for it.

If that was true, then her informant must have divulged that Lucy had the key. She might be the next victim. She could hardly bear to think what might have happened to Nina if she had been in the flat when the intruders had arrived. She might have opened the door to them. Lucy's informant had promised her the biggest story of her life. She was beginning to believe he was right. But whatever story lay behind the key she had been given would have to wait. Her priority was to find Nina.

Nina had been gone for around twenty-four hours. Frantic with worry, Lucy called the number her boss had given her. It was growing late, but she did not know who else to turn to for help.

'This is Alain Michel. Thank you for calling. Please leave a message and I'll get back to you as soon as possible.'

'My name is Lucy Hall. My editor at Current Affairs International gave me your number. My friend has gone missing. It might not be connected, but she disappeared the same evening that someone broke into my flat searching for something a man called Jérôme Meunier gave me.' She hesitated to give out her address. 'Can you call me?'

Unless the private investigator returned her call, she decided to visit the police station in the morning and insist they instigate a search. By then thirty-six hours would have elapsed since Nina had gone missing and they would have to start taking the situation seriously. Nina was a foreigner who knew no one in Paris apart from Lucy. They could not wait forty-eight hours to start looking for her. After that, Lucy would check the hospitals again. If she still could not find out where Nina was, it would be time to start fearing the worst.

After tidying the living room, she went to the kitchen to put the kettle on. Once she had made a mug of tea, she decided not to wait until the next morning, but to set about calling all the hospitals again straight away. If the answer remained the same, she would put out a message online. But before she did that, she would have to contact Nina's family. She did not want them to learn about Nina's disappearance by reading about it online. She hated the thought of calling Nina's mother, but this was not something Lucy could keep hidden. Besides, one of her friends might know of a contact Nina had in Paris, apart from Lucy. Someone must know where she was. Once she knew Nina was safe, Lucy would set about fulfilling her promise to Jérôme Meunier. It was not solely about the story. She had given him her word. Somehow she had to discover what the key was for, and expose his killer. There had to be a way.

The kettle had just boiled when there was a knock at her front door. She leapt to her feet and ran to open it.

She was almost crying with relief. 'Nina, where the hell have you been?'

She broke off at the sight of a man standing on her doorstep.

Before he could move, she slammed the door in his face. Presumably he had come back to have another hunt for the key. But since she was there, he might dispose of her once she had handed over what he wanted. Terror galvanised her. She was not going to give up her life without a fight. She ran to the living room and took her phone out of her bag. Across the narrow hall she heard the front door rattle. The man was trying to get in. By the time the police arrived she might already be dead. With a spasm of anger, she knew she was not ready to hand over the key without even finding out what it opened.

Swallowing hard, she felt a rush of determination forged in despair. She refused to be terrorised in her own home. If her life was in danger, she would step up and deal with the threat herself. Her flat had already been turned over while she was out. This time she was home and ready to defend herself. There had been no sound of

7

NINA CLOSED HER EYES. Very little light reached the cellar, apart from the one electric bulb overhead now swinging like a brilliant pendulum in the slight gust of air from the open door. After her being so long in darkness, the moving light made her feel dizzy. Cautiously she opened her eyes a slit and peered around. A stocky man was standing in front of her. His arms hung loosely by his sides, his head was lowered. Despite his lax posture, he gave the impression of brutish force. She did not think she had seen him before, but she had only a hazy recollection of the men who had burst into Lucy's apartment. Behind the man, she could see dirty white walls. The floor was hard and pitted with tiny irregularities. In one corner, a large drain was clogged with a morass of glistening filth that emitted a foul stench.

'Follow me,' a loud voice shouted.

The man took a step towards her. Instinctively she crawled backwards, until her back was pressed against the wall. With her eyes firmly shut, she felt someone slashing through the cords that bound her ankles. She wriggled her feet and her legs were seized with agonising cramp. A large hand grabbed her under one arm and hoisted her to her feet. She shuddered at how easily he was able to lift her. Even if she had wanted to resist him, she was powerless against his strength. She trembled, unable to conceal her fear. She had no idea what was happening to her, or why she had been brought there. She could only assume it was all a terrible mistake.

Ignoring her muttering, the man shouted at her again. Too scared to question him, she followed him along dank corridors, up several narrow flights of stairs and across a wide hallway. Entering a room, the first thing she noticed was how warm it was thanks to a fire flickering and crackling in the hearth. The blood-red sofa and armchairs looked inviting, and the carpet felt soft beneath her feet. After lying on a concrete floor with her wrists and ankles bound, she could have wept with relief at this luxury. A man was sprawling on the red sofa. His broad face creased in a smile when she entered the room and he sat up.

'Welcome,' he greeted her in English, smiling at her as though this was a normal social visit. 'I hope you are finding your stay here comfortable.'

Nina stared at him, wondering if he knew how cruelly she had been treated. 'Are you aware that I've been tied up in your cellar?' she blurted out.

'How quickly you are released is up to you.'

'I want to be released right now.'

'Of course you do,' he answered, still smiling. 'And I'm as keen as you are to see you safely on your way.'

Trembling, Nina held up her hands, which were still tied together.

'All in good time,' the man said. 'First, you must return to me what is mine.'

'What do you mean? I haven't got anything of yours. I don't even know who you are.'

'Oh, come now, we both know that's not true. Tell me what you've done with it.'

'I don't know what you're talking about.'

The man's expression grew sullen. 'Stop trying to play games with me, Lucy. You know what I want, and I'm going to get it, one way or another.'

With a shock, Nina realised that he had mistaken her for Lucy. About to deny it, she stopped herself just in time. Somehow she understood that once he learned of his blunder, he would go after Lucy. Nina would never be instrumental in letting that happen. Besides, if Lucy were locked up as well, they would never escape. As long as she remained free, Lucy would go to the police to report Nina missing, and she would be rescued.

The man was speaking again. He sounded calm, but there was a rigidity in his face that looked as though it might crack at any moment.

'You know what I want,' he repeated softly through clenched teeth.

'I don't know. I don't know.'

'Come on, Lucy. I don't want to hurt you,' he went on, his expression amiable again.

Nina trembled, knowing she must not give the slightest hint that she was not Lucy. 'Let me go then,' she stammered.

'I told you, I don't want to keep you here. I'd be happy to let you go home.'

Nina blinked, trying not to think about going home. England seemed very far away. In spite of her determination to remain aloof, she felt tears slide down her cheeks.

Without warning the man sprang to his feet. His face loomed large above her, flushed red. 'Take her away,' he yelled.

'What shall I do with her, boss?'

'Do nothing. Leave her down there. She'll soon change her mind.'

Unnerved by his sudden fury, Nina completely lost her self-control. 'No, no, please don't take me back there,' she pleaded, breaking down in tears.

He smiled at her, as though he had never raised his voice. 'Don't be obstinate then. You know you can't hold out for long.'

'I don't know what you want. I don't know what you want.'

'But you and I both know that's not true, don't we? Well, if you insist on enjoying my hospitality for a little longer . . .' A large diamond sparkled on his finger as he waved his hand in the air, dismissing her.

Nina moaned as the hefty guard grabbed her by the arm and propelled her from the room.

8

Standing behind the door, broken glass in hand, Lucy tried to sound menacing, but her voice was shaky.

'Who's there? What do you want?'

There was no point in waiting for the door to be smashed in. He knew she was there. She undid the latch. Slowly the door swung back on its hinges, creaking softly.

'Lucy? Lucy Hall?' a man's voice called out.

Expecting a vicious thug to burst his way into the flat, Lucy was surprised to see a slim, grey-haired man in a brown leather jacket hanging back with an anxious smile, as though uncertain whether he ought to come in. He had a square face and strong chin that contrasted with the hesitant expression in his blue eyes. With his lined face and iron-grey hair that was turning white at his temples, she guessed he was somewhere between forty and fifty. With her arm raised, poised to strike, she hesitated.

'Shall I come in?' he asked.

Catching sight of the glass in her hand, his eyes widened in surprise.

He leaned forward and spoke quietly. 'You're right to be scared and it's necessary to be cautious, but you're in no danger, at least not from me. Shall I come in so we can talk? There's a possibility your situation could be a lot more dangerous than you realise.'

Still clutching the broken glass, Lucy asked who he was.

'Who am I?' For the first time he looked worried. 'You are Lucy Hall, aren't you?'

There was no point in denying it.

'I thought maybe I'd made a mistake.' His face creased in a puzzled smile. 'You contacted me about your missing friend.'

The penny dropped. 'You're Alain Michel, the private investigator. Please, come in.' She held out her hand.

He hesitated before inclining his head, with a slight smile. 'Yes, you can call me Alain. I'm pleased to meet you.' He must have seen her relieved expression as he took her hand in his firm warm grasp. 'Were you expecting someone else?' He glanced pointedly at the broken glass she was holding.

Lucy apologised. 'I thought you might be one of the gang who searched my flat, coming back to have another look.'

'Yet you opened the door?'

'Well, to begin with I thought you were my friend. She's the reason I called you. I'm afraid something's happened to her. But I don't understand. How did you find me? You don't know anything about me.'

'I know more than you think,' he replied as they crossed the hall and went into her living room. 'You told me you work for Current Affairs International, and your voice told me you're English and quite young. It wasn't difficult to find you, Lucy. But you mentioned a gang came here?'

Briefly she described how her flat had been trashed and her friend had vanished.

Alain's expression darkened as he listened. 'If they turned the place over so thoroughly, it looks as though they were searching for something.' He stared intently at her. 'And if they didn't find what they were looking for the first time, they might return. I suggest we leave here and go somewhere we can talk without any fear of interruption.'

Lucy hesitated to tell him what she thought the intruders had been looking for. As far as she knew, he could be a member of the criminal gang, sent to wheedle information out of her, or he might be working alone, trying to get his hands on the key. If it opened up a store of stolen treasure, that could be enough to tempt anyone.

Alain frowned. 'Have you reported all this to the police?'

Lucy described the response she had received when she had told the police. 'They as good as accused me of trashing the place myself!'

'And there's no chance your friend could have been responsible?' he asked. 'You didn't have a quarrel?'

She shook her head. 'Absolutely not. Apart from the fact that we didn't argue, I've known Nina for years and she never loses her temper. Look,' she held out her phone, 'this is the text she sent me while I was out. And before you ask, I've never known her drink more than a glass or two of wine, not often anyway,' she added truthfully, 'and she doesn't take drugs. Neither of us does. But she disappeared last night, the same evening the flat was broken into, and I haven't heard anything from her since. She's been gone twenty-four hours. It's not like Nina to just go off like that. She'd know I'd be worried.'

'And she's not answering her phone?'

'That's partly why I'm so concerned. She left her phone and her purse and keys here. I'm afraid she's had an accident. I phoned all the hospitals in Paris.'

'Well, let's not jump to any conclusions about what they were looking for until we know who we're dealing with. I'll ask around—'

Before he could say any more, there was a loud crash. Lucy's front door was being battered. It would not stand up to such an assault for long.

'I see they're taking the subtle approach,' Alain muttered.

41

'Follow me,' Lucy whispered urgently. 'There's another way out.'

She led him into the kitchen. Clearing a pile of plates off the draining board, she clambered up beside the sink. Leaning forward to open the window, she froze. A man was standing outside the window. With his broad back to her she could not see his face, but there was something unnerving about his immobility.

Quietly Alain climbed up next to her. 'Leave this to me,' he whispered.

He shuffled over and she shifted out of the way. Slowly he reached forward to open the window. Lucy held her breath while he fiddled with the latch. There was a knack to opening it, and he frowned as it refused to budge.

'Here, let me,' she whispered. 'I know how it works.'

Behind her, she heard a crash. In a panic, she elbowed Alain out of the way, seized the handle and jerked the window. It flew open with a sudden lurch, whacking the man outside on the back of his head. With a yell, he fell forwards, disappearing from view. Quickly, Alain pushed past her, straddled the windowsill, and leapt to the ground. Squirming backwards on her stomach, Lucy wriggled out through the window and landed on the path beside Alain with an awkward jolt.

'Do you think he's OK?' she asked, staring at the stranger who was lying face down on the ground without moving.

'Don't worry about him. He's just stunned. Now come on, there's no time to hang around. We need to get going. Give me your phone.'

Lucy handed it over. Before she could stop him, Alain removed the SIM card and ground it into the dirt with the heel of his shoe.

'No!' she cried out as he dropped the phone and stamped on it.

'They could be tracking your phone. Come on, we need to get away from here.'

There was no time to protest. In any case, the damage was done. In just a few moments Lucy had been cut off from her home and everyone she knew. She had never been off the radar like this before.

'Come on,' Alain urged her again.

She hoped he really was Alain Michel, private investigator, because she had no choice but to follow him along the narrow alley, back to the street. After dashing along to the Rue des Rosiers, they turned left at the end, and then right into a maze of little streets. Slipping round corners and scurrying past sauntering pedestrians, Alain darted through a door into a dimly lit bar. Without exchanging a word, they crossed the small seating area and left by a side exit that took them into a narrow lane. A moment later they turned at right-angles around the back wall of the bar into a deserted alley. Without slackening his pace, Alain led her through a back door into another bar, illuminated with soft amber lamps that shed a gentle light. There were a few young people sitting at tables drinking cocktails. No one took any notice of them as they made their way over to a table in the corner where it was relatively dark. Although they were not sitting right beside a speaker, the music was loud. No one would be able to eavesdrop on their conversation.

'Here,' Alain said, putting a cheap phone on the table. 'I usually carry a few spares. You'd be surprised how often they can be useful. I'm afraid it's not a smartphone, but it's best to stay offline when you don't want to be found. Just hit one on speed dial if you need to contact me. Now, suppose you tell me what this is all about. Who's interested enough in your flat to search it like that?'

Lucy shrugged. 'What are we going to do about Nina?'

'All in good time. What we need to do first is examine what we know for certain. Now, these people who searched your flat, what were they looking for?'

'I don't know.'

She wanted to ask Alain if he thought the stranger outside her kitchen window had been seriously injured, and then focus on finding Nina, but he was speaking again.

'I can't help you if you don't tell me what's going on. And keep your voice down.'

There was no point in Lucy continuing to pretend she did not know what the intruders were after. Briefly she described how an anonymous informant had slipped a key in her pocket. 'It's quite small. It could be a car key, because it's on a black fob. I know it sounds unlikely, but that's what happened.'

'Assuming you're right, and it *is* a car key, the fob could be for a garage or a car park,' Alain suggested. 'But I wonder why he gave it to you without telling you what it was for.'

'He told me he'd heard I'd been asking around, looking for stories, and he wanted someone new on the scene to take it on. He said anyone who'd been around for a while wouldn't want to run the story. I don't know why.'

Alain scowled, muttering that it did not sound good.

'Whatever the key's for, it must be pretty important to the person who wants it back. The man who gave it to me has been murdered, my flat's been trashed hunting for it, and now my friend's gone missing. Nina doesn't know anything about Paris,' she added, her voice slightly unsteady. 'You don't think she's come to any harm, do you? Do you think she was there when they came to search the flat?'

Alain leaned forward and lowered his voice. 'What do you mean, they killed the man who gave it to you? What makes you think that?'

'I read about his death in the news and thought I recognised him. His name was Jérôme Meunier, although I didn't know that until I saw the report. He was pulled out of the canal last night, just hours after I met him, the same night my flat was trashed.'

Alain stared at her for a moment. 'How do you know it was the same man?' he asked at last. 'How could you be sure from seeing his photo in the paper, when you'd only met him briefly, once?'

'I can't be sure, but I think I recognised a scar on his chin.'

'Even if it was the same man, what makes you think he was murdered?'

'Only that he was terrified. He said he was being watched. And now he's dead.'

9

A WHITE-HAIRED MAN APPROACHED and took their order. They sat in silence until he brought over their coffees. Although not a word passed between them, Lucy had the impression that the old man knew Alain. They could not sit for long, knowing that someone might be out on the streets looking for Lucy.

'The manager of the club is a friend of mine,' Alain said as they left. 'He won't tell anyone we were here.'

'How do you know you can trust him?' Lucy asked.

She was wondering the same herself about Alain Michel.

'I helped him out once and saved his life. He assured me he would die rather than betray me.'

'Let's hope his loyalty is never put to the test.'

They left the club and Alain took her along a quiet back street down to the river. Aware she might be walking into a trap, Lucy reasoned that Alain had given her no cause to suspect him of double-crossing her. Recommended by her boss, he had only come to see her in response to her call. Anyone would feel paranoid in her present situation, but she had to trust someone. Having been in Paris for only three months, she had no established friendships yet, and her current problems were hard to handle all by herself. Besides, it was unlikely that Alain and her editor were both acting on instructions from the leader of a criminal gang. She had to get a grip on herself and control her suspicions. All the same, she resolved to be cautious and tell no one where the key was hidden.

It was growing dark by the time they approached a vast brick building overlooking the river. Above an imposing entrance Lucy read an engraved sign, *Institut Médico-Légal*. She followed Alain up the stone stairs and through an arched doorway.

'Where are we?' she whispered as they entered a long hallway.

'We're at the morgue,' he muttered.

'What?'

'We're here to try and establish whether Jérôme Meunier was your anonymous informant.'

'How are we going do that?'

Alain stopped in his tracks and turned to look at her. 'I know someone here who can get us in to see the body. Are you ready to see if you recognise him?'

Lucy nodded without speaking. If the victim turned out to be her informant, it was possible she had been the last person to speak to him before his death.

Even with the intervention of Alain's contact, they had to wait for quite a while before they were taken to view the cadaver. The door to the metal cabinet swung open. As the tray slid out, Lucy pressed her lips together to suppress a cry. The dead man's face was mutilated with multiple lacerations, yet it was not the crude pattern of bloodless wounds that made her stare in horror, but a small crooked scar on his chin. There was no longer any doubt in her mind. She was looking at the corpse of the man she had met by the Canal Saint-Martin. She nodded at Alain.

'Looks like he was involved in some sort of knife fight before he died,' the technician said. 'He didn't put up much resistance,' he added, pointing to weals around the dead man's wrists.

'Was he tied up?' she asked.

The technician raised his eyebrows but did not reply. The answer was self-evident.

'What did he die of?' Alain asked.

'Coronary failure, no doubt brought on by shock and blood loss.'

Lucy frowned. 'He didn't drown then?'

'No. He was dead before he hit the water.'

'And those cuts on his face?'

'All the injuries were inflicted before he died.'

'Thank you,' Lucy whispered.

'You were lucky to catch him,' the technician said.

'What do you mean?'

'He's due for cremation tomorrow morning.'

When Lucy protested that the death needed further investigation, the technician explained there was no family to object, and the police were not interested in pursuing the matter.

'But he was murdered. You said so yourself.'

The technician looked agitated. 'I never said anything of the sort.' He covered the body up and pushed the tray back out of sight.

'You told us he was dead before he was thrown in the canal. And anyway, how could he have been in a fight if he was tied up? He was murdered. The killer can't be allowed to get away with it. Once he's cremated, there'll be no evidence to show how he died.'

The technician exchanged a glance with Alain. 'There's no point in complaining to me. It's not my decision. I'm sorry, Miss, I know it's upsetting seeing a friend like this, but there's nothing you or I can do about it. He's going to be cremated, and that will be the end of it.'

When Lucy tried to insist the police should be notified, he told her the police had ordered the cremation. It seemed they were not interested in investigating a gang murder. Lucy had given her word to her informant that she would not suppress whatever story he was giving her. Besides, the circumstances of Jérôme Meunier's death indicated that the story was far more serious than she had realised when he had spoken to her. She had to investigate his murder and uncover the truth. As well as honouring her promise to a dead man, this could be a once-in-a-lifetime opportunity for her. Noticing Alain was frowning at her, she thanked the technician, and resolved to keep her concerns to herself.

Leaving the morgue, they took the Metro to the Gare du Nord. It was not as pleasant an area as the Marais, but Alain suggested they would be safer there. The population was transient, and with thousands of travellers passing through each day, it would be relatively easy to hide among the throngs of pedestrians on the pavement outside. Leaving the crowded station, they crossed the busy main road and took a side turning close to the station.

'We can check in here without any questions asked,' Alain said, opening the door.

'Are they past clients of yours too?'

'No,' he smiled. 'They don't know me here. But this is one of the hotels where we can't be traced, as they're lax about asking to see identification on check-in.'

'I thought that was illegal?'

Alain did not answer and she followed him inside. She hoped he was right that no one could trace her there. Whoever had killed her informant must be looking for her.

10

THE HOTEL FOYER WAS POKY, its poor lighting not helped by dull brown decor. A small group of men were hanging around. They were dark-skinned and talking in a language Lucy did not recognise; their djellabas suggested foreign origin. One of them returned her curious glance with a hostile glare and she looked away quickly. Behind the reception desk, an old woman was talking on the phone. She hung up as Alain stepped forward to book a room.

'Do you have a room overlooking the street?'

'Yes. How long are you staying?'

He shrugged. 'We're not sure.'

'You need to give twenty-four hours' notice before you leave.'

'That won't be a problem.'

The receptionist gave them a key and pointed to a narrow staircase. 'Room thirty-nine, third floor. The lift is round the corner.'

They found their room, where Lucy was relieved to see two single beds. Alain double-locked the door and went over to the window. Pressing himself flat against the wall beside it he peered down, explaining they needed a room with a view of the street so they would know if they were being watched.

'Now, tell me everything that happened in as much detail as you can,' he said at last, turning away from the window. 'There's no hurry. We've got all night.'

Lucy sat on one of the beds and recounted recent events. It was hard to believe she had only met Jérôme Meunier the previous evening. So much had happened since then.

'Tell me exactly what you told the police.'

'I called them after the break-in and a couple of officers came round eventually, but they weren't that interested. And then I phoned again the next day to report Nina was missing, but once they found out she was an adult, they didn't take much notice. They told me to report it if she hadn't come back after forty-eight hours. And that was it, really.'

'But did you tell them you had spoken to the man who was fished out of the canal?'

Lucy paused, trying to recall events in the right sequence. 'I didn't find out my informant was dead until after I'd spoken to them. The first I knew about his body being pulled out of the canal was when I read about it in the news. He'd warned me in no un-certain terms not to go to the police. So I haven't said anything about my meeting with him to anyone, apart from you. I was afraid of getting too involved.'

Alain looked thoughtful. 'You already were involved. As soon as Meunier gave you the key, you were in it up to your neck.'

Lucy noticed that he was not pressing her to tell him where the key was hidden. She wondered if he was deliberately keeping her away from the flat so that his accomplices could search it, but that did not really make sense. They would have been far more likely to want to keep her there, in the flat, so they could persuade her to hand over the key. She was not sure she would be able to withstand torture. In any case, they would only have to convince her that they might kill her, and she would hand over the key without hesitation. In the meantime, her priority was to find Nina. She had only contacted Alain because she wanted him to find her friend, but he did not seem any more interested in looking for her than the police had been.

'And you're sure you haven't told anyone else about this?' Alain asked.

Lucy shook her head. 'I told my editor about the break-in, and about Nina going missing, but that's all. I didn't mention my meeting with Meunier.' She hesitated. 'I wanted to wait and see if it was a genuine lead before I said anything. If it was genuine, I didn't want my editor handing it over to a more experienced reporter.'

Alain nodded. 'In his position he must hear a great deal about what goes on in criminal circles. But you can't contact your workplace at the moment, not without risking giving away your location. Don't forget, violent criminals are searching for you. They went to your flat once, and they came back again this evening. Whatever you do, and wherever you go, you need to cover your tracks. Don't look so worried. I can help you. That's what I'm trained to do. But you need to keep your wits about you and don't do anything careless.'

Lucy stared at Alain. It was all well and good him telling her not to worry, but he was not the one whose life was in danger.

'We have to go to the police,' she said. 'They didn't listen to me because I wasn't able to back up my story. It was all so vague, and in any case they thought I was just a silly hysterical girl. But you know exactly what's going on. They'll listen to you. You have to persuade them to take a look at Jérôme Meunier's body before it's cremated. As soon as they see what's happened, they'll start a murder investigation, and then we can look for Nina.'

'You can't come out in the open to look for her yet,' Alain replied, 'and you can't rely on the police to protect you. Remember, they ordered the cremation.'

Lucy was horrified. 'Do you think the police are part of all this?'

Alain shrugged. 'Who knows? All I can say is that these are very murky goings-on. In any case, even if the police are on the level, by the time they trace your informant's killer, it will be too late to save you.'

'But—'

'I'm not disagreeing with you. All I'm saying is, we need to plan what we're going to do very carefully and not give anyone a chance to discover where we are until we know more. Let me do some research before we reach any decisions. You have no idea what you might be getting into. Before we do anything, we need to establish who was behind Jérôme Meunier's murder. We could be up against a very formidable enemy. If he's behind the ransacking of your flat—' He broke off with a sombre expression.

'Do you think he's taken Nina?'

'I sincerely hope not.'

'Who is he?'

'I'm not sure. So far it's just a suspicion. I need to ask a few more questions before I can be certain. I'll call a few of my contacts tonight, and tomorrow I'll go out and ask around. If I'm right, believe me when I say your life could be in danger. Give me a day. I'll spend tomorrow asking around, and see if I can find out for certain who was behind the break-in at your flat. And then we need to decide what to do with the key you were given.'

'First we need to find Nina.'

'Yes, of course, we'll come to that. Now I suggest you let me get on. We'll find your friend more quickly this way, believe me.'

Lucy took a shower. When she came back, Alain was talking quietly on his phone. He rang off when he saw her.

'I've asked around, as far as I can from here. It's not looking good. We need to keep you safe. Have you got the key on you?' he asked her as she sat down, towelling her wet hair.

'No. It's not here. I still think we should go to the police.'

53

'After what happened to Meunier, you can't dismiss anything he said as an idle threat. He warned you not to, and I think he might have been right. You don't want to make matters worse than they already are. They might have killed Meunier as a warning, so you'd take the threat to your life seriously.'

'That occurred to me. It's a terrible thought, a man being killed just to send me a message.'

Alain shook his head. 'They would have killed him anyway.'

'What do you mean? Who would have killed him?'

He leaned further forward. 'He was afraid, wasn't he?'

'Terrified.'

'Exactly. He knew the risk he was taking. But he went ahead regardless. Why? What was he up to? We need to take a look at that key. Where is it?'

Lucy stared at the floor, wondering whether she was right to trust Alain. For all she knew, he could be intent on gaining her confidence. Once she told him what the killer wanted to know, her life might be of no further use to them. In the meantime, the key was still in her flat, hidden beneath plastic beads and baubles.

'What did you mean when you said I'm in grave danger?' she asked, avoiding answering his question.

'A man has already been killed,' he replied. 'You could be next.'

Lucy was not sure if that was a threat or a warning.

11

His eyes narrowed, always a dangerous sign. As he leaned back against the wall, the men around him inched closer together, as though seeking reassurance from each other's company. Ignoring their nervous shuffling, he stared down at his shoes. Expensive polished leather shone faintly back up at him in the dim light of the cellar. For a few moments no one spoke. No one stirred. Without warning a loud clattering shattered the silence as one of the men dropped a knife on the concrete floor. Glancing anxiously around, he swooped down to retrieve it. The other man flinched, but Patrice appeared oblivious to the disturbance. At last he raised his head, turning it slowly to glare at each of them in turn. He continued leaning against the wall with studied nonchalance, but the energy in his voice commanded attention.

'What exactly are you talking about?'

The young man jolted at every accentuated word, as though he was dodging missiles. Wiping his sweaty forehead on a grubby sleeve, he stammered a reply. 'It's only what I heard. I thought you'd want to know.'

'What? Speak up. I can't hear a word with you mumbling like that. What's wrong with you? Talk like a man, for fuck's sake.'

On either side of the young man there was a barely perceptible movement, as though his nearest companions wanted to edge away from him without attracting attention.

'It's just what I heard,' the young man resumed, his voice shrill with the effort to speak loudly. 'Someone wants to know what happened to Jérôme. Someone is asking around.'

While he was speaking, several of the other men began muttering. At the mention of their former companion's name, they fell silent. Patrice straightened up and took a step forward out of the shadows, until the light shone directly on his wide forehead. His thinning hair glistened ginger in the beam of light.

'Who wants to know?' he asked quietly.

'I don't know who's been asking, but Céline and Gigi both told me they heard someone's been going round asking questions about Jérôme. That's all I know. It started this evening and I got back to you straight away, soon as I heard. Céline and Gigi are good girls. They keep their ears to the ground. You can trust what they say. They don't bullshit,' the young man answered, garrulous now he had started talking. 'It might not mean nothing, but I thought you'd want to know right away.'

'Too right I want to know.' All eyes were fixed on Patrice. 'I want to know everything that goes on in this city.' He snapped his fingers and the large diamond on his finger sparkled with the movement. 'I don't want anything going on that I don't know about, not a breath, not a whisper. Got it? No one moves in this city without my knowledge. No one breathes without my say-so.'

There was a mumble of acquiescence.

'As long as I keep an eye on things, we're all comfortable. You know that as well as I do. Now,' he went on, turning back to the young man, 'what did your girls say about this individual who's been poking his nose in where it doesn't belong?'

'They both said he was a private investigator. That's all they heard. But if they said it, you can believe it. Those girls know what's going on.'

'Don't tell me who knows what,' Patrice snapped. 'You just tell me what you heard. Leave the thinking to people who've got brains. They said it was a private investigator, did they? Are you sure those were the words they used?'

The young man glanced helplessly at his companions. No one came to his aid.

'That's what the girls said. They said he was a private investigator, and that's all they knew.'

'Well, he's not much of an investigator, and what he does isn't that private.' Patrice's broad face broke into a grin. 'Fuck me if I don't know who it is.'

A huge man stepped forward, fists clenched, his massive head swaying slightly from side to side as though it was too heavy for his body. 'I'll get him for you, boss,' he growled. 'Just let me at him. Who is it?'

Ignoring the interruption, Patrice carried on speaking. 'Yes, unless I've lost my touch, I know exactly who it is. And what's more, he's been making a nuisance of himself for far too long. It's time I did something about that busybody. I should've got rid of him years ago.'

'Let me at him, boss,' the big man repeated, waving his fist in the air. 'I'll stamp him out for you. I'll smash his fucking head in. Just tell me who it is.'

Patrice shook his head. The atmosphere in the cellar lightened as the other men saw that he was smiling, his good humour restored.

'No need to go wasting your energy on scum like him,' he said amiably. 'I have other plans for our friend the private investigator. And don't you worry, I'll take care of it. He won't be bothering us again.'

12

ALAIN SAT GAZING OUT OF THE WINDOW, sitting to one side of it so he could not be seen from outside. Worn out, Lucy lay on the bed and closed her eyes for a moment. When she opened them again she realised she had dozed off. Alain was looking at his phone.

'Oh, you're awake,' he said, seeing her watching him. 'I'm just nipping out. I'll be back in ten minutes.'

She heaved herself up on one elbow, instantly alert. 'Where are you going?'

He shook his head and muttered vaguely about needing a breath of fresh air. Lucy did not remonstrate. Although she realised he was going out in response to a text he had received, she was pleased he was leaving her on her own. His excursion gave her a chance to try and rest. But, tired though she was, she could not sleep. An hour passed, and still Alain did not return. As midnight came and went, she began to worry. He had told her he would only be away for a few minutes, but it was more than an hour since he had gone out. Everyone around her seemed to disappear. She was wondering what to do, and whether to try and call him, when her phone buzzed with a text.

'Le Cheval Rouge. Hurry. A.'

Worried, she tried his number, but he did not answer. Although it was after midnight, she had no choice but to answer the summons. Alain had asked her to hurry. Either it was a trap, or he needed help. Resolving to be cautious, she pulled on her hooded jacket and slipped out of the hotel. No one saw her leave. The Gare du Nord felt unsafe at night, so she walked quickly along the street. Unsure where she was going, she hailed a taxi that was cruising past the station.

'Le Cheval Rouge,' she said.

'In Rue Vieille du Temple?'

'I think so.'

The driver dropped her at the end of the road. Pulling up her hood, Lucy made her way along the pavement, not far from her own flat. It was a mild evening and the Marais was busy, even at one o'clock in the morning. Several cafés still had tables on the pavement, many of them occupied. She found Le Cheval Rouge easily, situated on a corner. She had walked past it a dozen times without stopping. Several people were sitting outside, chatting quietly, drinking and smoking. Inside, a circular bar had been constructed around a wall of optics glinting in red lights strung across the ceiling. Above the optics, a carved wooden horse pranced on the wall. She looked around. Alain was not there. Cursing under her breath, she went up to the bar. Alain's message had not been a cry for help after all. She must have misunderstood his text and rushed out on a needless mission. In the meantime, she decided she might as well have a drink before she left. There was no point in having a completely wasted trip.

'Not seen you here before,' the girl behind the bar said.

'No, I was looking for a friend.'

'Who's that then?'

Lucy handed over her money. 'He's about forty, with grey hair and blue eyes, wearing a brown leather jacket.'

'Oh, yes. There was a bloke like that in here just a few minutes ago. He was with a blonde woman in a red dress. They were sitting over there in the corner, only now they've disappeared. Funny that, because they didn't go past the bar. They must have gone out the back. There's a fire exit that takes you to the bins. No one goes out there at night, except to throw up.' She pulled a face. 'Stinks out there sometimes. One of them must've been feeling ill.' She shrugged and gave Lucy her change.

Setting her drink down on a table near the fire exit, Lucy glanced over her shoulder. No one was watching her as she sidled over to the fire door and slipped outside. It was dark in the alley. She looked up and down, calling out Alain's name softly. In the light coming through the back window of the bar she could just about make out the figure of a woman scurrying off through the shadows, high heels clattering as she ran. About to turn and go back inside, Lucy noticed a pair of legs on the cobblestones, naked down to the ankles. She rushed forward. Alain was lying propped up against the wall, his eyes closed, his face deadly pale. He was not moving. She knelt down to check if he was still breathing.

'Alain, Alain, open your eyes. Say something,' she urged him, shaking him gently by the shoulders.

He let out a feeble groan. The sound of retreating footsteps was now very faint. Lucy looked up. Apart from herself and Alain, the alley was deserted. After running to the corner of the building, the woman had vanished. Abandoning any thought of sprinting after her, Lucy turned her attention back to Alain. Fighting to control her panic, Lucy dashed back to the bar for a glass of water.

'Is your friend all right?'

Lucy hesitated, but she did not know who she could trust in this place. 'I think so.'

The barmaid's eyes slid away, uninterested. She was clearly used to people drinking more than they could handle. As long as Alain did not return to the bar, his state was of no concern to her. Lucy hurried outside and forced Alain to drink some water. His eyes flickered open as he gagged and spluttered, and she heaved a sigh of relief.

'Are you all right?'

He nodded gingerly, his eyes struggling to focus on her. 'I will be. Where are we? What happened?' Looking down he noticed his bare legs and his eyes widened in shock. 'Oh, Jesus, what have I done?'

'As far as I can tell, you haven't done anything. You met a woman in the bar, a blonde woman in a red dress. Do you remember her?'

His eyes closed again.

'Alain! Don't go to sleep! You need to wake up.'

She dipped the corner of her shirt in the glass of water and dabbed his forehead with cold water. His eyes flickered, but did not open.

'Alain, wake up!'

She held the glass to his lips. Forcing his mouth open, she poured water between his lips. Most of it spilt down his chin. Coughing and choking, he opened his eyes.

All of a sudden his eyes widened in panic. 'Going to be sick. Can't move.'

Just in time, Lucy managed to shove his head over to one side so that he vomited on the ground.

'That woman,' he muttered, without looking at Lucy. 'Yes, she was blonde. I remember . . . very blonde . . .'

He leaned back against the wall and his eyes closed again.

'I'm going to get you some strong coffee, and then we need to make you throw up again.'

It was a while before Alain was able to keep his eyes open and answer her questions. Together they tugged at his trousers until he was more or less fully dressed. The movement, as much as the coffee, seemed to revive him.

'You should start to feel better now you've been sick,' Lucy said, as cheerfully as she could.

'No,' he muttered feebly, 'this is not alcohol.'

'What do you mean?'

He struggled to explain what had happened. Through his rambling speech, Lucy gathered that he had received a summons to meet someone at the bar. He showed her his phone. The text was brief but compelling. 'Le Cheval Rouge. Information about JM.'

'Jérôme Meunier?'

He nodded. 'That's what I thought. I'd started asking around, just making a few calls, while you were in the shower at the hotel.' He paused, and took a few deep breaths. When he had arrived at the bar, a blonde woman in a red dress had approached him. Assuming she was a tart, he had offered her a drink. 'Women like that, around on the streets at night, they meet people, they hear things, they know what's going on, more than you think.'

When Alain had mentioned Jérôme Meunier to the blonde woman, she told him she had some information he would find interesting.

'Why do you want to know?' she had asked him. 'You're not a copper, are you?'

'No, he was a friend of mine. I just want to know what happened to him. Someone was after him.'

The woman had laughed a lot, he said, his eyes glazing over. Lucy shook his arm and he winced.

'Don't fall asleep, Alain. We need to get you up and moving. Come on.'

With difficulty she hauled him to his feet. Throwing one of his arms around her neck and clinging to his hand, she dragged him towards the door to the bar. Her beer was still on the table where she had left it. She manoeuvred Alain onto the seat, aware that the

girl behind the bar was watching them suspiciously. Satisfied that
Alain was not going to throw up, she lost interest.

'My head feels muzzy but I'm not going to be sick again.'

'You've had too much to drink.'

'No, no. This is not alcohol,' he insisted, shaking his head and
groaning. 'This is more than the effect of a few drinks. That woman
put something in my glass,' he said, nodding gingerly and looking
around the room. 'I remember now. She laughed when I said he
was a friend of mine. We were sitting right here when she insisted
on getting me a drink. I thought it had a strange taste, but she kept
on talking at me and, God help me, I didn't want to insult her by
refusing to drink it.' He gave an embarrassed laugh. 'I can't believe
I was so stupid. I've never been caught out like that before. Even
teenagers know better than to let a stranger buy them a drink. Not
long after that I started to feel peculiar, and that's when I texted
you under the table. I realised something was wrong. She asked
me again if I was a policeman, and then she took me outside.' He
frowned. 'She must have pulled my trousers down after I passed
out, because I don't remember . . .'

'If I hadn't come along and scared her off . . .'

Lucy did not finish her thought aloud. Neither of them spoke
for a moment. The blonde woman could have left Alain there to die,
if she had not finished him off herself. Either way, by the time his
body was discovered it would have been too late to resuscitate him.
The police would have assumed he had drunk himself to death, and
that would have been the end of it.

'How do you feel now?' she asked at last.

'It's just like a god-awful hangover. It was that drink. What the
hell did she put in it?'

The bar was closing at two. Lucy called for a taxi to pick them
up. With the assistance of another customer, she managed to drag
Alain outside, but when he saw her companion, the driver refused

to take them, convinced that Alain would throw up once they got moving.

'Would I be able to talk to you like this if I was drunk?' he asked, in a reasonably clear voice.

'Why can't you walk then?'

'It's his arthritis,' Lucy complained. 'The stupid idiot only went and lost his crutches and he's impossibly unstable without them. I told you to be more careful,' she added crossly, looking at Alain. 'It's not the first time,' she added, turning back to the driver.

'OK, get in then.'

It was two o'clock by the time she dragged Alain to the lift, with the help of the taxi driver.

'That's great, thank you. I can manage from here,' she said, giving him a generous tip.

At last they were back in their room, and after a visit to the bathroom, Lucy settled Alain on his bed in the recovery position, then collapsed onto her own bed, shattered and aching. But her thoughts kept returning to Nina. Despite her exhaustion, she couldn't sleep for worrying that the people who had tried to kill Alain were the same ones who had abducted Nina from the apartment.

13

'I'M STARVING,' Lucy said, sitting up.

Alain mumbled incoherently.

'How are you feeling? Did you sleep?'

'Yes. I think I slept it off, whatever it was.' He grimaced. 'If I ever see that bitch again—'

'Would you recognise her?'

'Oh, yes.' His expression hardened for a second. 'But we've got bigger fish to fry. She was only a puppet. We need to deal with whoever was pulling the strings. Someone sent that woman to kill me, and I've got a shrewd idea who it was.' He paused. 'Before that woman knocked me out, I'd spoken to a few other contacts of mine, and the same name kept coming up. What happened at Le Cheval Rouge clinches it. I'm sure I know who's behind all this.' He shook his head. 'I remember what happened before I met that blonde, but after that it's all just a blur. Shit, I'm so confused.'

Alain refused to tell her any more until they had eaten something. He said he was afraid he might not have the energy to tell her everything, and he did not want to stop halfway through his account. He was clearly genuinely weak after his experience, so Lucy offered to go round the corner to the McDonald's opposite the Gare du Nord and bring back a takeaway breakfast. She hurried to the bathroom to get washed and dressed. When she returned to the bedroom, Alain had managed to haul himself off the bed and was staggering over to the chair beside the tiny table by the window. Although he assured her he was fine, he was blatantly suffering from the after-effects of his near fatal encounter.

'Get plenty. I'm starving,' he called after her as she left the room.

Relieved to hear that he had a healthy appetite, she called back that she would bring as much as she could carry. Trotting down the stairs, she thought about what he had said. He claimed to remember what had happened before he was drugged, but was confused about everything that had followed. Reminding herself that she had not rescued him to earn gratitude or admiration, she could not help hoping he knew that her prompt intervention had saved his life. And she needed his help in return, to save Nina. It was seeming more and more likely that her friend was in the clutches of Jérôme's murderer.

Across the street from the Gare du Nord, the pavement was crowded. Making her way through the throng, Lucy spotted the yellow McDonald's logo about a block away. Before going in, she nipped into a chemist for some toiletries. Spotting a shelf of hair dye, she bought a packet. With her purchases in her bag, she went to McDonald's and joined the queue. Smelling fresh coffee, surrounded by chattering young people, Lucy felt as though she existed in a bubble, cut off from normal life. Years seemed to have passed since she had gone to meet a stranger by the Canal Saint-Martin. If only she could turn the clock back, she would spend Sunday evening with Nina instead of going out to meet an anonymous informant. Once this was all over, she was going to be more careful about the kind of news stories she pursued. With luck, she might manage to hang onto her job once the story broke, but worrying about her job was not high on her list of priorities. All that really mattered was saving herself and finding Nina. Alain had indicated that he knew who was behind recent events. After breakfast, she was going to insist he tell her everything he knew. She had to find out what was going on.

Reaching the front of the queue, she turned her attention to ordering breakfast then hurried back to Alain.

'I went for the biggest of everything,' she announced with a grin, putting down two enormous cups of coffee.

'Just as well you've got a big bag,' Alain smiled back, watching her unpack two large breakfasts.

With the curtains open and the net curtains closed, they sat by the window, the small table between them.

'McDonald's is actually not that bad,' Lucy said. 'At least you get a proper cup of coffee there.'

Alain shrugged. 'I'm going to have to stay here for a few hours until I can walk,' he said, as they finished eating. 'My legs are very wobbly and every time I stand up I feel dizzy. It might be best if we keep a low profile anyway. So it looks like we're going to be stuck here for the rest of the day. After that, I'll see about getting you safely back to England. There's no reason for you to be mixed up in all this. It's too dangerous.'

Lucy frowned. 'This isn't just about you, Alain. I have to find out what's going on. Until I know whether all of this has got anything to do with Nina, I'm not giving up. Now please, tell me everything you know.'

Alain nodded. 'I was asking around, calling in a few favours, and finally getting some answers, when I received the text to go to Le Cheval Rouge. I walked straight into the trap. Before that woman knocked me out, she talked about Jérôme Meunier. It's all a bit of a blur, but she definitely told me Meunier had something that belonged to someone else. Then she asked me about my interest in him.'

'You didn't mention me?'

'Of course not. Your name never came up. She told me Meunier had stolen something from a friend of hers and that her friend wanted it back. I pretended not to know what she was talking about. To begin with, I told her Meunier was a friend of mine and I wanted to know the circumstances of his death, and that was all there was to it. But then she wormed out of me that I didn't actually know him. I wasn't feeling very sharp, to be honest. It was the drugs talking. Anyway, I told her I was working for a friend but I never mentioned who. I wasn't that far gone. At the time I thought she believed me, but with hindsight it's clear they'd got wind of my interest and had sent her to get rid of me. It was lucky I managed to text you without her seeing before I blacked out. But you can't stay here holed up in a hotel room forever. Won't people be worrying about you? Family? Boyfriend?'

Lucy explained that her editor would assume she was sorting out her flat, her family in England would be oblivious to the fact that she had disappeared since her parents were on a cruise, and there was no boyfriend. When Alain expressed surprise, she felt herself blush, even though she knew he was just being polite.

'There was someone once, but the fact is I was a gullible idiot and he was a rat. You know how it goes.'

'He didn't deserve you.'

'That's easy to say. You don't know anything about me.'

'I know that you're resourceful, intelligent, quick-thinking, courageous, kind-hearted, and you appreciate a proper cup of coffee. I'd say I know you pretty well.'

She laughed. 'What about you?'

'What about me?'

'Won't anyone miss you?' She broke off, seeing a sour expression on his face. 'What's up? Are you going to be sick?'

'It's not that. It's just . . .' He shook his head. 'Lucy, you seem like a nice girl. More than that, you saved my life.'

Lucy felt herself blush at the acknowledgement, and looked down. 'It's time for me to return the favour,' Alain went on. 'You shouldn't be here. I know where you can get hold of false papers, and it won't cost the earth.'

She started to protest that it was out of the question for her to leave Paris without knowing what had happened to Nina, but he spoke over her, determined to finish what he had to say.

'Just hear me out, please. You can leave everything to me. I'll cover the expense. It's the least I can do. You saved my life. I can't sit back and watch you get yourself mixed up in this. Let me send you home. This is no place for a decent girl like you. You came to me for help and, believe me, that's what I'm giving you. Take my advice and go home to England before things turn nasty.'

Lucy stared at him. 'My informant's been tortured and killed, my best friend's disappeared, you were nearly murdered last night, and my flat was almost destroyed. I'd say things have turned pretty nasty already. And in any case I can't leave Paris while Nina's still missing. Don't you get it? I already *am* mixed up in it. Nina could be in trouble. I have to get shot of whoever's after me so I can be free to find her, wherever she is. You said you know who was behind the attack on you last night. If you know who it was, you have to tell me. You have to.'

Alain sighed. 'I can't,' he said at last. 'It's too dangerous for you to get involved in.'

'It's too late for you to try and warn me off, because I already am involved.' She stood up. 'I'm going to find Nina, with or without your help. Now, are you going to tell me what you know or do I need to go out there and investigate this on my own and risk being caught by whoever killed Meunier?'

'All right, sit down and I'll tell you what I know.'

It took a while. Halfway through his account, Alain closed his eyes. Lucy felt callous shaking him to prevent him falling asleep, but

Nina had been missing for nearly two days. The situation was growing desperate. Lucy had to be free to go to the police.

Alain was almost certain the woman who had tried to kill him was working for a man called Patrice Durand, a criminal with a reputation for being involved in all kinds of depravity. The powerful leader of a gang of violent thieves and murderers, he had been questioned in connection with several suspicious deaths, but as yet the police had not managed to pin anything on him. He never did his own dirty work, and was never seen anywhere near a crime scene. As far as Alain was aware, Patrice never used an alias. He had become something of an urban legend. In fact, many of Alain's contacts did not believe Patrice was just one man. They thought there must be a team of hired killers adept at evading capture, all operating under the name Patrice Durand.

'I suspect Patrice exploits this image to enhance his status,' Alain added. 'No other gang leader in Paris dares to challenge him. They're all scared of him, criminals and law enforcers alike. What else can I tell you about him? He's a sadistic psychopath who's cobbled together a gang of the most reprehensible characters in the country. He attracts deviants and psychopaths like a magnet. He has no respect for the law, he doesn't respect any code of ethics, he exploits his wealth to corrupt the authorities, and he has no respect for human life. If they ever manage to arrest Patrice Durand, I hope they lock him up and throw away the key.'

'Has he never been implicated in any crime?'

'Patrice is like Teflon. The police don't seem able to make anything stick. Or they choose not to.'

'And you think he's responsible for Meunier's murder, and for trashing my flat and trying to get you killed as well?'

'We can't be sure, but that would be my guess.'

'So what am I going to do about Nina?'

'It's possible she's perfectly safe. Most missing persons turn up. She's probably wondering where you are right now.'

Lucy nodded. Alain had a point. She could be worrying unnecessarily about Nina, who could be trying to get in touch with her while she was hiding in a dingy hotel room with a stranger. But Alain's opinion that Nina was probably safe did little to reassure Lucy. She wondered whether he was pursuing an agenda of his own, an agenda that did not include looking for Nina.

'Your informant, Jérôme Meunier, was a long-term member of Patrice's gang, one of his right-hand men,' Alain continued, 'and I can only assume that the woman who tried to kill me was an intimate associate of Patrice. I thought I'd be able to wheedle some information out of her. Turns out she was one step ahead of me the whole time. You're not to mention any of this to anyone. If he finds out I've been talking about him, neither of us will live long enough to regret my indiscretion.'

14

ACCORDING TO ALAIN, the circumstances of Patrice's early life were obscure. Records indicated he was the illegitimate son of a sex worker who had moved to Paris from Eastern Europe and died of an overdose when Patrice was still very young. Following his mother's death, he had lived in a succession of children's homes until he was sent to a juvenile detention centre as a teenager. After that, there had been no official record of his whereabouts until he had emerged again, years later, the wealthy leader of a criminal gang. What he had done in the interim, and how he had made his fortune, was shrouded in mystery. All that was known for certain was that he was living in Paris, in possession of a vast fortune. Alain mentioned drugs and people trafficking, theft and extortion, but reiterated that nothing had actually been pinned on Patrice. So far his dreadful rackets were nothing more than rumour and speculation. Many of his associates had been in and out of jail, but since his spell in the detention centre, Patrice had not even been questioned by the police. They seemed to give him a wide berth.

Lucy felt a flicker of suspicion. 'You seem to know an awful lot about this Patrice Durand character.'

Alain nodded. After a moment's hesitation, he continued. 'I made it my business to find out everything I could about him. I had a particular reason to be interested in him.' He paused, frowning, as though he was trying to make up his mind. 'My name isn't really Alain Michel,' he said at last. 'Oh, there is a private investigator who goes by that name. We've worked together on several cases. He passed your enquiry onto me, when you left a message on his phone. He didn't want to touch it, but he thought I might want to follow it up. He knew about my interest in Patrice.'

'But I don't understand. I only called about Nina.'

'You mentioned Jérôme Meunier. He's been suspected of being involved with Patrice.' He shrugged. 'It was interesting enough for me to want to meet you, and you know what happened after that.'

'So who are you? I've just got used to calling you Alain.'

'You might as well carry on calling me Alain then. It's as good a name as any.'

'But why are you so interested in Patrice?'

'You could say it's personal. I had three sisters and a brother. I was the oldest, and my brother was the youngest, the baby of the family. There were nearly ten years between us. Although he was a bit wild, he was a good kid, and he was smart. The trouble was, my mother spoiled him. He was just a kid of eleven when our father died. As his older brother it fell to me to look after him, but I was preoccupied with my career. I was so busy investigating problems for strangers, I neglected to take care of what was happening in my own family. Eventually one of my sisters told me how worried they all were about the kid, only by then it was too late. I tried to look out for him, put him straight.' He shook his head. 'I could see where he was heading.' He paused again, a distant look in his eyes. 'Anyway,' he went on at last, 'he went off the rails. Before he was even twenty, he got involved with—'

'Patrice,' Lucy interrupted to finish the sentence.

'I was going to say he got involved with drugs. But, yes, you're right. Patrice drew him in and got him addicted, deliberately I don't doubt. God only knows what atrocities my kid brother had to perform as part of his initiation into that gang. He refused to give me details, but—' He shuddered. 'A few years after he disappeared, my kid brother came to see me. He was sick of the depravity and wanted out. He was desperate. Some of the things he told me turned my stomach, and I've seen more horrors in my life than you can imagine, even in your worst nightmares. The men who'd got hold of him were a bunch of perverts, and the most vicious of them all was Patrice Durand. My brother begged me to help him escape, and I promised to get him away.'

'What happened?'

'Patrice got to him first.'

'What do you mean?'

'I was making enquiries, getting the ball rolling to set my brother up with a false identity and spirit him away into rehab overseas, somewhere he would be safe from that monster, but Patrice got wind of it. Not much goes on that he doesn't know about. He has sources everywhere. Two days after my brother came to see me, his body was fished out of the canal.'

'I'm so sorry about your brother,' Lucy stammered. 'What a sad way to lose him. But you can't be certain it was Patrice. I mean, your brother was a drug addict. Surely his death could have been an accident?'

'I wish I could believe that, but he'd been cut.'

'Cut?'

'Mutilated. It's one of Patrice's trademarks.'

'Trademarks?' Lucy repeated, remembering the bloodless lacerations on Jérôme Meunier's face.

'Yes. My brother was by no means Patrice's only victim. The more I delved, the more victims I learned about who'd been tortured to death before they were thrown in the river. Some of them were as young as thirteen. The deaths were attributed to drug addiction and rarely investigated thoroughly. Who takes any notice when a drug addict or a prostitute is fished out of the river? But I knew who was behind them. There were others, of course. Wealthy businessmen and even politicians, but the murders were hushed up or reported as suicides. I became obsessed with preventing Patrice from destroying any more lives, and I was determined to avenge my brother.' His voice trembled with suppressed emotion. As he turned away, Lucy saw his face twisted in anguish. 'I wanted to put a bullet in Patrice's brain, but I couldn't get near him. Anyway, after a while I calmed down enough to realise that if I did that, I'd be no better than him, a cold-blooded murderer. So I decided to gather enough evidence to get him convicted, but it's impossible to pin anything on him. I've been after him for years, on and off. And then, out of the blue, you turned up.'

'If everything you've told me is true, Nina could be in danger. I need to find out what's happened to her, and if he's taken her, I need to return Patrice Durand's key to him as soon as possible. Where does he live?'

Alain shook his head. 'Don't be naive. You can't just knock on his door and ask to see him. This is no ordinary man we're talking about. He's one of the most influential men in Paris right now. He's bribed and blackmailed his way to immense wealth and power. He surrounds himself with an army of contract killers. I hate to imagine what he might do to a pretty young woman like you if you turned up on his doorstep asking to see him.' He shook his head. 'No, I'm afraid it's not that simple. There needs to be evidence before we can make an arrest, and it has to be as watertight as possible if we're to make it stick. We need to get hold of the evidence Jérôme Meunier gave you. Listen, Lucy, we have a chance to stop his atrocities once and for all. We have to get that key and find out why it's so important to him to get it back.'

'But you must have something to prove he was behind your brother's murder?'

75

'Believe me, there have been many victims of Patrice's depravity. But I can't prove it.'

'There must be some reason why you think he's behind these deaths?'

'All hearsay and rumour. Nothing that would stand up in court. But I believe my sources. And I believed my brother when he told me what he had become involved in, and what went on under Patrice's roof.' He sighed. 'There are so many voices whispering against Patrice, but no one's prepared to speak out.'

'So what happens now?'

Alain frowned. 'Our only chance of stopping him is if we retrieve that key and work out what it's for. There might be more than enough stolen valuables hidden away to get him locked up, if we can only find out where they are.'

'Surely it can't do any harm for me to speak to him? Alain, I understand we want to stop him if we possibly can, but we can't allow Nina to suffer while we're trying to nail this criminal. I need to talk to him. If he's got Nina, he can have his key back on condition that's the end of it.'

'Take it from me, you don't deal with a dangerous psychopath by throwing yourself at him. He'll take his key back and kill you anyway.'

'I won't take the key with me. I'll tell him only I know where it is.'

'If you don't have the key he's after, he'll swat you like a fly. No, there's nothing to be gained from going to see him.'

'Do you know where Patrice lives?' Lucy repeated firmly.

'My information is a bit out of date,' Alain admitted, not answering her question directly.

Lucy suspected he was fobbing her off, but she persisted. 'Tell me what information you have, and I'll take it from there.'

Alain shuffled over to his bed. He was recovering well and able to move his legs freely, but he was still weak. Lying down, he closed his eyes and sighed heavily.

'I need to find him. Where does he hang out?'

'He used to frequent the cafés in Montmartre, so I think that might be a good place to start,' Alain muttered without opening his eyes.

Lucy suspected Alain was giving her the runaround. There were many cafés around Montmartre. She could spend weeks questioning people who worked there without discovering anything useful. She dithered, but there was no point in pestering Alain for any more information while he was so sleepy. The mention of Montmartre reminded her of the receipt she had found in her flat from a café in the Place du Tertre, right in the heart of Montmartre, near Sacré-Coeur.

'Why don't I go there and ask around and see if I can find out where he lives?'

Alain opened his eyes and sat up. 'Do you really expect it to be that easy? Think about it. Even if you somehow managed to get hold of his address, what then? Do you imagine you're going to simply march up to his house and demand that he speaks to you, just like that? Why? Because you ask him? No, in any case, whatever happens, we want to face him in a public place. Once we go to his house, who knows what might happen to us? We might simply vanish, and no one would ever find out what happened to us.' He glared at her. 'Don't even think about going out without me.'

Lucy thought about Nina and shivered, even though the room was warm. Sitting down obediently on one of the chairs, she watched Alain fall back on the bed and close his eyes. Just sitting up seemed to sap his energy. She decided to wait for him to fall asleep before proceeding with her plan. He was soon snoring.

It did not take her long to dye her hair, it was so short. With her appearance altered, she would be able to return to her flat to collect the key Meunier had given her. Armed with the precious key, she would set off for Montmartre and see what she could discover. As soon as she found Patrice, she would use his key to persuade him to leave her alone. If he had kidnapped Nina, she would insist he release her too. If not, at least Lucy would be free to start a search for her. Everything hinged on her returning the key to Patrice.

When she walked out of the bathroom, Alain was awake. He looked surprised to see her with dark hair. She suspected he had not recognised her immediately.

'What are you doing? Where are you going?'

'I just thought I'd pop out for a bit,' she replied, turning to him as she reached the door.

'Stay here,' Alain mumbled, his eyes closing again. 'It's not safe to go poking around, asking questions—'

'I'm not going to poke around, but I might go for a walk around Montmartre, and keep my eyes and ears open. No one knows who I am or what I look like. If they've seen any photos of me, they won't recognise me with dark hair. If anyone notices me, they'll think I'm a tourist. Don't look so worried, I'll be back soon. In the meantime, you have a rest.'

He groaned. 'I'm afraid I'm not feeling that great. Why don't we start later? I'm sure I'll be fine by then. This evening we'll work out how to retrieve the key Meunier gave you, and then we'll decide what to do with it. In the meantime, stay here.'

'I'm just popping out,' she repeated.

'I suppose you can't stay cooped up in here all day. Go to the Louvre or take a trip to Versailles. But whatever you do, keep out of sight. Don't start asking questions on your own. Asking about Patrice was how I ended up like this, and I'd be dead now if you hadn't come along and rescued me. Patrice will be scouring Paris right now, searching for you. You mustn't let him find you.'

'All right, I won't speak to anyone,' Lucy lied. 'I'm only going to have a look around.'

There could be no harm in asking a few questions, as long as she was discreet.

15

ANGELINE WAS DOING HER BEST to return his gaze but Patrice could see she was frightened. He could always tell. These days it was rare for people not to tremble in his presence, knowing he could kill with a twitch of his eyebrow. He had earned the right to exercise such power. He had only to nod at Marcel or Sacha and Angeline's life would be over. It was that easy. No wonder she did what she was told. But sometimes even that was not enough. He gazed around the cellar. Marcel and Sacha had hosed it down until just a trace of blood glistened in a pool in the corner where the floor dipped. Only the stench lingered. He nodded to himself before turning his attention back to Angeline. A good-looking woman, she had outlived her usefulness.

'You failed,' he said quietly.

Her expression did not alter, but her blonde hair quivered around her painted face. His mouth relaxed into a smile. Her lips trembled then, because she could not tell whether he had forgiven her. Nervously she smoothed her bright red dress over her hips. He walked over to her and stroked her fair hair, admiring the way his diamond ring sparkled under the electric light. In her heels she was nearly as tall as him.

At this sign of forgiveness she became animated and began to babble. 'I didn't do nothing wrong. I followed him into Le Cheval Rouge just like you told me. I didn't even need to get him in the toilet where someone could've seen us. I had him in the alley behind the bar, unconscious, with his trousers round his ankles. By rights he shouldn't have lasted much longer. I could've finished him off easy, only then some little tart turned up. It wasn't my fault. Usually there's no one around out there at that time of night. It was just bad luck that we was disturbed.'

'It wasn't bad luck for him,' Patrice growled. 'Were you spotted?'

'No.' She shook her head vigorously and her curly hair bounced. 'I was careful. You know I'm always careful. He didn't know nothing about it. He wasn't looking when I spiked his drink, and before that he was too drunk to notice anything what was going on. I promise you, he won't remember nothing about it. He wouldn't even recognise me if he saw me again.'

'What about when you were outside with him? You said someone came along and found him.'

'Yes, but they didn't see me. I made sure I kept out of sight. No one saw me. No one. I was careful.' Her voice rose in panic. 'It wasn't my fault.'

Patrice scowled. 'Don't shout. I didn't come here to listen to you screeching at me.'

She ducked her head, wringing her hands. 'I was careful. It wasn't my fault. I did what you told me, just like I always do.'

'We're going to have to do something about you,' he said grimly, and then smiled. 'I can still use you.'

'I know you're always good to me. And I'm good to you too, aren't I?' Her voice softened, coaxing him to like her again. 'You know who your friends are, don't you? Who was it told you about that film? That was me, wasn't it? I didn't have to tell you, did I? If it wasn't for me, you wouldn't have known about it. What if I'd said nothing? Soon as Jérôme come boasting to me, saying how he was going to see you finished, I come straight to you to make sure you knew all there was to know. You can rely on me.'

Patrice scowled at her. 'He was stupid to tell you his little plan. But you'd have been even more stupid not to tell me once you knew about it. No one keeps secrets from me and gets away with it. No one.'

'You know there's nothing I wouldn't do for you, nothing at all. I won't never let you down. You can trust me, I promise. You can always trust me. There's plenty of men would give anything to have me be good to them, but you're the only one I want to please, I promise.'

'You're always full of promises, aren't you? Promising this, promising that. But even you can't get this next job wrong.'

Encouraged, she spoke up. 'I always do my best. It wasn't my fault someone came along and found him before the job was done.'

Ignoring her protest, he turned to Marcel. 'Bring the English whore over here.'

The thickset bodyguard stomped across to the far corner of the cellar where Nina was crouching, her face hidden in her arms. Angeline stood with her head lowered, waiting, while Sacha leaned against the wall, picking at his fingers, his eyes darting from Patrice to Angeline and back again. Marcel yanked Nina to her feet. Shoved roughly from behind, Nina stumbled, blinking. For hours she had been locked in the dark cellar by herself. Now she squinted in the bright light of the one naked light bulb suspended from the ceiling.

'You know what I want, you stupid whore,' Patrice growled at her.

Nina stared at him, eyes wide with fear, her pale face streaked with filth. He knew she understood him, but she shook her head.

'Please let me go. Stop all this. I've no idea what you want from me. Let me go home. Please. You have to believe me. This is all one big mistake.'

'Another mistake.' Patrice's blue eyes glittered. 'Everyone is making mistakes, it seems. Only this time you're the one making the mistake, if you think you can stop me getting what I want. Watch carefully, Lucy Hall.'

He walked over to Angeline and put the tip of his index finger under her chin to force her head up. 'Look at me.'

She lifted tearful eyes to meet his gaze. 'I told you about Jérôme's film, didn't I?' she whispered. 'You can always rely on me.'

Patrice leaned forward and kissed her softly on the lips. She shivered at his touch. 'I need you to do one more job for me.' He turned to Nina. 'Your obstinacy won't get you anywhere. I'll find what he gave you and destroy it, with or without your help. Now you'll see what happens to people who are stupid enough to refuse me.'

Patrice nodded at Sacha. Understanding dawned on Angeline. She backed away from Patrice, pressing herself against the wall, whimpering. 'No, no, it was a mistake. It wasn't my fault. No, no!'

Sacha lunged forward, seized Angeline by the throat and twisted her head, just once. There was a muffled scream, followed by a startlingly loud crack. Angeline's dress swung loosely from Sacha's huge hand, a bright splash of scarlet in the still room.

Nina's voice burst into the silence. 'How could you do that to her?' she shouted, wild with fear. 'You're an animal!'

Patrice turned to her. Behind his smile, his eyes were cold. 'That's what you can expect, unless you tell me where it is.'

'I don't know what you want to know. I don't understand what's happening. You're making a mistake. I don't know anything. I'm English. I haven't been in Paris long.'

'Long enough to meddle in things that don't concern you.'

'I don't know anything. I don't know what you're talking about. You're making a mistake.'

'I don't make mistakes. Now where the fuck is it?'

'Where's what?'

'Don't play the fool with me.' He stepped forward and raised his hand, then thought better of it and let his arm drop. 'You won't hold out on me for long. I have many ways to make you speak. You can spare yourself a lot of pain, if you tell me now.'

Sobbing uncontrollably, Nina insisted she had no idea what he was talking about. 'You can threaten me all you like, starve me, beat me, kill me, I can't tell you what I don't know.'

'What if she really doesn't know, boss?' Marcel asked.

'Shut your mouth and don't try to think. She knows what I want. Now get a move on for fuck's sake. There's work to be done.' Patrice looked at Sacha. 'Take the body down to the river. After that make yourself scarce, and be quick about it.' Next he nodded at Marcel. 'Take the English whore and fetch what Jérôme gave her. She knows where it is. She'll take you to it, now she understands what's going to happen to her if I don't get what I want.' He glared at Nina. 'No one refuses to give me what I ask for. No one. Not here in Paris. This is my city.'

Nina shook her head, trembling. 'I don't know what you're talking about,' she whispered.

Marcel seized Nina's arms and shoved her towards the stairs as Sacha went over to a large metal filing cabinet in the corner of the room. Nina watched in horror as he picked up a pair of thick plastic gloves. Pulling them on, he flexed his fingers before opening a drawer and taking out a black body bag. Patrice grunted with satisfaction before turning on his heel and following Marcel up the steps and out of the cellar. In one of the garages behind the villa, he watched Marcel cram the English girl into the boot of a car. When she tried to climb out, Marcel waved his huge fist at her until she cowered away. A moment later he slammed the boot shut.

Sitting behind the wheel of his latest Bugatti, Patrice spoke into his carphone. 'Olivier? It's Patrice. There's been another suicide. A blonde whore threw herself in the river. Why do people do it?

Anyway, see to it no one starts asking questions when the body comes to light. No point in raking up muck.'

He rang off without waiting for an answer, and put his foot down. Driving out through the high gates, he roared down the long lane and swung out onto the road, cutting up a passing taxi. The cab driver hooted loudly.

'Oh, fuck off,' Patrice grumbled, picking up his phone again. 'Olivier? I forgot to say, you remember the private investigator who tried to cause trouble a few years ago, the brother of one of the boys? He's started snooping around again, asking questions. Dispose of him for me. And don't hang about. I want him dealt with today.'

16

THE BUS CARRIED LUCY towards the Georges Pompidou Centre, which was not far from her apartment. Not until she reached the Rue Ferdinand Duval and was fishing around in her bag, did she realise that she had left her front door key in her bedroom, along with the key Jérôme had given her. Grabbing her bag before she had clambered out through the kitchen window, there had been no time to run to her bedroom and get either of the keys. She had not really thought about it at the time. Cursing under her breath, she considered her options. There was no point returning to her flat if she could not get inside. The only person who had a spare key was the landlord. The trouble was, if she contacted him he might want to come over. He had only to step over the threshold to see what a state the place was in. If she told him that the apartment had been ransacked, he was bound to be furious that she had not told him about it straight away. Once he discovered the extent of the damage, he would probably throw her out.

Unable to get hold of Patrice's key, she decided to leave it where it was for the time being. At least it would be safe in her flat. Having already searched the place so thoroughly, it seemed unlikely that Patrice's men would return for another look. She decided instead to try and track him down. The only clues she had to his whereabouts were Alain's mention of Montmartre, and the receipt from one of the restaurants there that someone had dropped in her flat. Glancing up, she noticed a thin man in a black jacket watching her from across the street. As she looked at him, he turned away. Wherever she went, someone seemed to be staring at her. Dismissing her fears as needless paranoia, she strode quickly away.

The sun was shining as she walked along the Boulevard de Magenta, past cheap clothes shops with *Soldes* signs painted on their windows in large letters. Her eye was caught by a number of stores displaying extravagantly decorated frocks, but she could not stop to look at them. They flashed past in a colourful blur of ruffles and lace. Reaching a railway bridge across the road she turned left and crossed the Boulevard de Rochechouart. On the far side of the wide, tree-lined avenue, tall elegant apartment blocks with delicately wrought metal railings on their balconies formed a stark contrast with the ugly graffiti scrawled between shop windows on her side of the street. She took a side road off the main thoroughfare and walked up the hill to the Place des Abbesses.

Reaching a small square she sat down on a bench to decide where to go next. After checking her map, she sat back and gazed at a church in front of her. Decorated in a juxtaposition of Moorish and Art Deco styles, the unlikely combination created a surreal beauty. She had not discovered this particular square before and sat for a moment, studying the artwork in front of her. Not many cars drove by, but the pavements were packed with pedestrians. Somehow she felt safer among the crowds of people. An old man stopped to play his accordion. After only one tune, he walked around the people seated in the cafés nearby, begging for money. Although he had done so little to earn it, Lucy dropped a euro in his hat as he passed by her bench and he gave her a toothless grin.

The day was warm and bright and she wished she had not left her sunglasses in her flat. Starting up the hill again, she stopped at a small shop where she bought two pairs. Slipping one pair into her bag, she put the others on. Feeling as though she was in a spy film, she gazed out at the world through pink lenses and walked around the corner to joined the queue for the funicular to Sacré-Coeur at the top of the hill. The line of people shuffled forwards and a few moments later she was through the turnstile and waiting to ascend. She had walked up the steps, but had never been up to Sacré-Coeur in the funicular before. Above her she could see the domed roof of the famous church before the car carried her swiftly to the top. Remembering how she had toiled up the steep steps, she was amazed at how quickly they arrived at the top, and was glad she had taken the lift.

She wondered what her friends might say if they knew she was in Paris hiding the key of a notorious hitman. But she was an investigative reporter, and with any luck this would be the first of many such adventures. Despite her anxiety over what had happened to Nina, she was excited. With luck she might solve the mystery of the key and have Patrice arrested.

Disembarking, she walked along the cobbled street around Sacré-Coeur. Far below she could see the Eiffel Tower, dwarfed by the distance. She followed the road round to the Place du Tertre. The central covered seating area was bordered by artwork, in turn surrounded by cafés with coloured awnings. Above the lively scene on the road she gazed at a row of shutters, still elegant despite their faded paintwork. She walked slowly round the square, rejecting the advances of an artist who offered to paint her, and peering into all the cafés. There was no sign of Nina. It was not surprising. She had hardly expected to find her friend sitting there having a drink, as though nothing had happened. Having walked all the way round the square, she sat down at a small round table on the pavement outside Chez Catherine and waited to order a cold drink. The comfortable wicker chairs were protected from the sun by a red canvas awning. Despite the circumstances that had brought her here, she could not help relaxing.

Many of the passers-by looked as though they were in a fashion show. Concealed behind her sunglasses and dark hair, she watched a succession of chic, expensively dressed women with stylish hair walk past. Above them, the trees swayed gracefully in the breeze. A group of frazzled tourists stopped on a corner nearby. Noticing their guide was talking in English, Lucy struggled to hear what he was shouting. All she managed to distinguish was something about the shops, and, 'You have five minutes. Five minutes.' The crowd of people dispersed as a large car nudged its way along the cobbled street. 'Be back here in five minutes,' the guide called out again. Lucy wondered who would want to come to the Place du Tertre in the centre of Montmartre for just five minutes.

Swept up in the romance of the setting, all at once she felt painfully alone. The feeling hit her without warning. Everywhere she looked she saw couples, many of them young, all smiling. Catching herself wishing her ex was there with her, she pulled herself up short. It was not enough simply to cope with being single. She had to learn to enjoy her own company. One day she hoped to meet a partner, but as long as she was unhappy on her own, she risked sinking into another relationship where emotional insecurity drove her to surrender her independence to the wrong person. Meanwhile, she had more pressing matters to concern her than regret over the absence of romance in her life. A young waiter put her orange juice down in front of her. Taking a deep breath, she asked him if he knew a man called Patrice Durand.

'I am not familiar with the name,' he replied, glancing around to see which other tables were waiting to place an order.

'You don't know where I can find him?'

He shook his head and walked away. An older waiter passed her table. She beckoned to him and asked him the same question. This time there was no doubt the name meant something to the man. With a startled frown, he shook his head too vigorously for someone who had just heard a name he did not recognise.

'Do you know where I can find him?' she continued. 'He's my uncle. My family lost contact with him many years ago, and now my mother wants to see him again. Can you tell me where he lives, please? I'd be very grateful.'

The waiter hurried away without answering, but not before Lucy had seen a frightened expression on his face. Unnerved, she left Chez Catherine and went to sit in the next café along the square. After half an hour, she tried again. She had resolved to spend the afternoon asking the staff in one café after another if they knew where she could find Patrice Durand. Apart from the old waiter in Chez Catherine, no one recognised the name. Long before dusk began to gather over the city, she returned to the hotel where Alain was waiting for her. Sitting up by the window, he appeared a lot livelier than he had been earlier.

'My guess is Patrice is around there somewhere,' Alain said when she told him where she had spent the afternoon. 'He'll get the message that someone's looking for him soon enough, once we start asking questions. But we need to plan how we're going to proceed, before we do anything. If we go rushing in headlong, before we're fully prepared, we'll get ourselves killed.'

Lucy did not admit that she had been asking around, and that one of the waiters at Chez Catherine had recognised Patrice Durand's name. She and Alain clearly had different ideas about how to conduct their investigation.

'We need to make contact with Patrice as soon as possible,' she said, trying to impress on Alain the urgency of the situation. 'The sooner I get his key back to him, the sooner I can get on with looking for Nina, whether she's with him or not. Wherever she is, I've got to find her.'

'What about Patrice's key? Isn't that more important?'

'More important than Nina's safety?'

Alain frowned. 'Nina's probably fine. She's an adult and I'm sure she's capable of taking care of herself. You're not her nanny.'

'But she doesn't know Paris—'

'You talk about her as though she's mentally challenged. She's not a child. Now, let's get back to the serious business. Where's Patrice's key?'

'Right now it's in my flat and I can't get in. Plus, I'm afraid he could be watching out for me there.' She hesitated, embarrassed to confess that she had thought she had seen someone spying on her flat. 'If I go back to the flat, he could take the key off me before I have a chance to find him and talk to him.'

'It won't be a case of *us* finding *him*,' Alain replied. 'When he finds us, you need to leave the talking to me, or we might not be asking anyone about anything ever again.'

'If he's really as dangerous as you say he is, I think we should go to the police.'

'If they'd be willing to help us. They weren't exactly cooperative once before when I tried to share my suspicions with them. And I can assure you, I'm not the only one who's tried. I wouldn't be surprised if your editor at Current Affairs International had a go, and got his fingers burned. Accusations against Patrice always seem to be batted away, because no one can ever provide any proof of his guilt. You know, he's never so much as picked up a parking fine. I told you, he's a slippery bastard. Somehow he always manages to get away. If anyone takes the rap for his crimes, you can be sure it won't be him. No, we need to go to them with proof against him that even the cleverest lawyer won't be able to deflect. Otherwise . . .' He sighed. 'You know, maybe I should just put a bullet in his head, knowing all the terrible things he's done. The world would be a better place without him. Oh, I know I'd be signing my own death warrant, but at least my life would have served some purpose.'

'You can't take the law into your own hands, Alain, however difficult it is to pin Patrice down.'

He turned and stared at her for a moment. At last he turned away, muttering. 'What's the law worth if it protects the wrong people?'

17

EVERY TIME NINA CLOSED HER EYES she could see a red dress swinging gently around a woman's dangling legs. It was hard to believe the other witnesses had accepted her death so nonchalantly. The worst of it was that Patrice had apparently only killed the woman in order to convince Nina herself to take his threats seriously. But there was nothing he could do to force her to talk. She could not tell him what she did not know. All she knew was that Patrice had mistaken her for Lucy. And whatever he wanted with Lucy, Nina was not going to do anything to help him discover his mistake.

If she had not known she was in the boot of a car, a sensation of acceleration accompanied by the vibration and roar of an engine would have told her. They seemed to drive for hours, stopping and starting, swerving round corners, until she felt sick. At last the car drew to a halt. She waited to be let out. Nothing happened. She lay curled in a tight ball, her muscles stiffening with cramp, her head throbbing. If she was in a deserted car park, no one would hear her calling for help. On the other hand, people might be passing by all the time, inches away from her, oblivious to her plight. She strained to listen. Silence. She yelled, hoping the boot was not soundproofed. Wriggling around, she managed to get her feet in a position to kick the door while she screamed and shouted at the top of her voice.

'Help! Help! Help! I'm in the boot! Help!'

Her throat felt as though it was being rubbed with sandpaper. No one answered. It was hot in the boot but she was shivering. She would probably die there in that dark space, not much smaller than a coffin. As she succumbed to despair, she heard voices. If she could hear them, it was logical to suppose that they would be able to hear her. She began screaming and shouting again, banging on the lid of the boot as hard as she could. For a moment there was no response, then a voice called back. It sounded very close to her.

'Where are you?' a woman's voice shouted.

'I'm in the boot of the car!'

'Over here! There's someone stuck in the boot of the car!' a man's voice took up the cry.

Someone rattled the lid but it did not open. The car shook.

'Hang on!' another voice shouted. 'Wait there, we're getting help.'

As though she could do anything but wait. Nina heard a lot more jabbering in French. Now that rescue seemed imminent, she became unbearably impatient. Her skin itched and she had excruciating cramp in her legs. Finally, a siren rang out over the noise of voices. After more talking and fiddling with the lock, the boot burst open. Blinking in the evening light, she was hoisted out of her coffin. Two uniformed policemen supported her as she hobbled to a police car. Her legs were so stiff with cramp, one of them asked if she needed an ambulance.

'No, I'm fine,' she lied. 'I want to talk to the police. Please, can you take me to a police officer who speaks English?'

She was too stressed to try and explain what had happened in French. Apart from the fact that it was all too complicated, she could not risk being misunderstood. It was vital the police believed her story, and it would be difficult enough to convince them in English.

The policeman looked at her. 'You are hurt?'

'I don't know. But before I see a doctor, or anyone else, I need to talk to a policeman who speaks English. Please, can you take me to the police station straight away. There must be someone there who speaks English.'

After nodding to show he understood, the policeman began talking rapidly on his phone. Finally, he turned to his colleague and gabbled something Nina did not understand before he turned back to her.

'We will take you to see an inspector who speaks English. He is eager to speak with you.'

Nina smiled up at him weakly. 'Thank you. Thank you very much.'

As the police car sped through the city, its siren wailing, Nina leaned back in the seat and closed her eyes. She could hardly believe her ordeal was over. In the space of a couple of days she had changed from a relatively sane and cheerful person to a suicidal wreck. Now she could begin to return to normality. A wave of fury shook her as she recalled the man who had all but destroyed her will to live. He had lost his physical power over her, but she wondered if she would ever completely recover from the experience. Patrice had exposed her to the fragility of her own sanity. She would never forgive him for that.

She sighed. Lucy must be wondering why she had disappeared without a word. She was not sure how long she had been gone, but it felt like months. As soon as she had reported her captors to the police, she would ask them to contact Lucy and tell her what had happened. She must be going out of her mind with worry. Opening her eyes as they slowed down, she saw they were stopping outside a large grey building. The presence of other police vehicles and officers in uniform reassured her. The memory of Patrice would fade and she would return to her life in England. But first she had to make sure he was arrested and charged with murder. Nina had watched the woman in the red dress die, and she was determined that her death would not be dismissed as an accident.

'It is here we look at the big crimes,' the policeman told her. 'You go out now from the car.'

The memory of the woman in the red dress made Nina feel momentarily weighed down by the responsibility of bringing her killers to justice. She felt as though she could not move. Glancing down at her filthy hands, she wondered what her face must look like. She put her hand up and tried to smooth down her short hair. It felt matted and dry.

'Come with me,' the policeman said.

Clambering down from the car, she shuffled stiffly after him. A woman seated behind a desk in the entrance hall nodded at her escort as he led her through a swing door and along a corridor to a small interview room. The woman had barely glanced up. As far as she knew, Nina was a homeless tramp brought in for questioning.

'You can wait here for the inspector.'

'Does he speak English?'

'Yes. Inspector Joubert is here soon. He speaks English.'

A female constable brought her a cup of black coffee. She drank it gratefully, wincing as she saw the ugly weals on her wrist when she reached for the cup. After a few minutes, the door opened to admit a tall, lean figure dressed in black. Moving with swift elegance, he sat opposite her. Although his hair was grey, his face was unlined. She judged him to be in his forties.

'Good afternoon,' he greeted her in English. 'I am Inspector Joubert. Please tell me, why were you in the – how do you say it? – the back of the car? I am eager to hear your story. My ears are all yours.'

Taking a small black notebook from his pocket, he jotted down notes in silence while she told him what had happened.

'And these men took you from your apartment?'

'Yes. I was there on my own when they forced their way in. I don't know what they want with me. They must have taken anything worth taking while they were in the flat, but they say they want something from me.'

'Who are they?'

She shrugged. 'The man in charge is called Patrice. There's a man called Marcel, and there are others, but I don't know their names.'

'What is it they want?'

'I don't know.'

The inspector put his notebook away.

'Have no fear,' he said. 'You will be taken care of, I promise you that. Now,' he leaned forward, 'who have you spoken to about this?'

'No one. I was locked up the whole time. I haven't been able to contact anyone. I need to phone my friend. She'll be really worried about me. I've been gone for – oh God, what day is it today?'

'Today is Tuesday. It is understandable that you have lost track of the days.'

'Oh, my God, I've been gone since Sunday night. She'll be going out of her mind with worry. I must call her straight away.'

The inspector's eyes glittered as he scrutinised her then he stood up abruptly. 'Please do not alarm yourself. Everything that is necessary will be done. Wait here. I will return.'

As the door closed behind him, Nina wished she had asked to use the toilet. When he had not returned after what felt like a long time, she shuffled to the door. It was locked. Vexed, she went and sat down again. There was nothing she could do until he came back. Finally, the door opened and the inspector entered.

'At last,' she burst out. 'I'm sorry, I don't mean to be rude, it's just that I'm desperate for the toilet. I should have said something earlier but—'

She broke off in alarm as a second man stepped into the room. Her legs gave way and she collapsed onto the chair with a cry of terror. The newcomer closed the door gently and turned to smile at the inspector standing beside him. Slender and debonair, Joubert was taller than his stocky companion, yet somehow Patrice seemed to tower over him, his presence dominating the room. Golden highlights shimmered in his hair, while a receding hairline made his broad forehead look huge, in keeping with his square shoulders and massive hands. Coming from such a powerfully built man, his voice was incongruously soft.

'Yes, that's her. What I don't understand is how she managed to get herself out of the boot of the car. Where was that moron, Marcel?'

'Marcel stopped to get some cigarettes,' the inspector replied. 'He told me he was not gone more than a few minutes but while he was away from the car, someone heard her shouting for help. Luckily Marcel returned to the car in time to see what was happening. He had the wit to call me, and I made sure she was brought straight here. No one else is involved. You needn't worry. It's all been taken care of.'

'Thank you, Olivier. You've saved me a lot of bother.'

'It's my pleasure,' the inspector replied politely. 'Now, what do you want me to do with this girl? If she stays here, we'll need to charge her with something.'

'Don't concern yourself with her.' Patrice smiled at Joubert. 'She's coming with me.'

'No, no.' Panicking, Nina appealed to the police inspector. 'I won't go with him. I won't! Please! He frightens me. He killed a woman for no reason. I'm not making it up. I saw it happen. He's keeping me against my will. Please, help me. He's going to kill me.'

Patrice shrugged. 'You see what I have to put up with.' He shook the inspector's hand. 'Thank you again, my friend.'

The inspector inclined his head to Patrice. 'I am at your service.'

Passing through high electric gates, they approached the entrance to Patrice's villa. As they drew to a halt, a pair of huge Rottweilers bounded over to them, yelping frantically. Marcel opened Patrice's door and the dogs cowered away from him as he stepped out of the car. When Marcel opened Nina's door and beckoned to her, the dogs snarled and leapt forward. She could see no way of escaping Patrice's security. If she was not shot, and the dogs did not tear her to shreds, the high metal railings around the perimeter of his property would confound any attempt to get away. But if escape was impossible, staying there meant certain death. Once she was no longer useful to Patrice, she would suffer the same fate as the woman in the red dress.

Laughing at her terror, Marcel dragged her from the car. Slinging her across his shoulder, he strode towards the house, while the dogs growled and snapped at his legs. Every time one of them came too close, he swore loudly. At the sound of his voice, Patrice turned round and the dog retreated, whining, its tail between its legs. Through a fog of fear, Nina wondered what Patrice had done to inspire such terror in the savage beasts.

18

As soon as it was dark they made their way to Chez Catherine together. Alain was subdued, but Lucy felt optimistic. Returning to Montmartre, she was confident they would find Patrice. It made sense to confront him in a public place, and the few clues they had gathered about his whereabouts all pointed to Chez Catherine. Lucy followed Alain into the dimly lit café filled with square tables and chairs upholstered in red velvet. Above a white and gold bar, rows of wine bottles were stacked on shelves. The walls were hung with paintings in ornate gilt frames. The central light was supported by a huge plaster statue of a woman, naked above the waist, her lower body draped in carved swathes of material. The ambience of fake classical elegance combined with opulence was attractive. Were it not for the circumstances that had brought her there, Lucy would have been enjoying herself.

The waiter who had served her earlier was not around. A young waitress came over and Alain asked for a jug of water. When the girl brought it, he glanced up from the menu and casually enquired about Patrice Durand. The waitress shook her head. She had never heard of him.

As they finished their food, Alain leaned forward. 'Lucy, you're not going to like this, but it's time for you to go back to the hotel.'

'What?'

'This is no place for you. There's nothing you can do, and it could be dangerous—'

'I'm not giving up now,' she said quietly. 'I'm going to confront Patrice, with or without you. If you refuse to come with me, I'll find him and see him by myself. But one way or another, I'm going to speak to him. Whatever it takes, I have to find out what's happened to Nina.'

'Are you determined to get yourself killed?'

'What do you mean?'

'I don't want to see you getting hurt, that's all. You might think you have it all planned out, what you want to say to him, but you don't know the first thing about him. Believe me, he's not the sort of man you can talk to. I feel responsible for your safety—'

'Well, you're not responsible for me.'

'Of course, whatever you decide to do is up to you, but I can't help feeling responsible for what happens to you. You came to me for help.'

'It was my idea to come here and try to find Patrice. You never asked me to come. In fact, you did your best to stop me.'

'Lucy, I'm warning you as a professional—'

'I'm not sure what that means and, in any case, other than warning me at every possible opportunity that this is dangerous, all you've actually done is nearly got yourself killed.' She struggled to suppress her frustration, aware that alienating Alain would not help her to find Patrice. 'Look, I don't want to argue with you, and I don't really want to do this on my own if I don't have to. Surely the two of us together stand a better chance of finding him and making him see reason than I would on my own?'

'And what then? Do you expect to have a civilised conversation with him? He's a psychopath.'

'If Patrice is so insane that we can't even talk to him, we should go to the police.'

'Trust me. That's been tried.'

'So you keep saying, but they've got to listen sooner or later, haven't they?'

Lucy looked up and saw that the old waiter she had spoken to earlier had appeared. He was watching her. She dropped her gaze and told Alain about her earlier visit.

'It's all right,' she added quickly, seeing Alain's expression of alarm. 'He has no idea who we are. I gave him some cock and bull story about Patrice being my uncle. But if Patrice hears about it, he's bound to be curious. He'll come and find us and then we'll be able to find Nina.'

'We can't stay here like sitting ducks waiting for him to come for us.'

'He's not going to recognise me now I've dyed my hair.'

'But he knows who I am. I don't want you to be seen with me.' Alain put some cash on the table and stood up. 'Don't look round. We're going.'

'I thought we came here to find him.'

'But not for him to find us.'

Lucy frowned. What Alain was saying did not really make sense. His paranoia was beginning to seem insane.

'What difference does it make if we find him or he finds us?'

'If he learns we're here, we'll be in trouble. Come on. We have to leave. Now.'

Lucy's suspicion that Alain was delusional was reinforced as he kept glancing over his shoulder when they hurried away along the shadowy streets. He refused to use the funicular. Instead they ran, panting, down the long staircase back to the foot of Montmartre. Neither of them spoke until they were back in their hotel room.

'We mustn't show our hand,' Alain said as he shut their door, his eyes bright with fanatical determination. 'Remember, all we have on our side is the element of surprise. Now, let's get some sleep. First thing in the morning we're going shopping.'

'Shopping? Are you kidding?'

'I've never been more serious. Come and sit down and I'll explain my thinking. If we want to stand any chance of finishing this finally with Patrice, we need to get into his house without being seen.'

Lucy was not sure she was happy for Alain to seize the initiative, especially as she was beginning to suspect he was unhinged, but she sat down to listen. Having accepted that she was not going to give up, he said their first step was to study Patrice's house and work out how they could enter unobserved.

'But we don't know where he lives.'

'I managed to do some hunting around the other evening, before that woman drugged me, and he's almost certainly still at the address I have for him. There seems to have been a lot of activity around there recently.'

'What sort of activity?'

Expecting Alain to talk about reports of shootings or fights, she was surprised when he mentioned deliveries of expensive cuts of meat, wine, beer and prostitutes. Reckoning Alain had known Patrice's address all along, Lucy kept her distrust to herself. Once she had Patrice's address, she would be free to part company with Alain. She was beginning to think she might be safer looking for Nina on her own. Alain said he was prepared to help her, but all he seemed to care about was finding evidence against Patrice.

Over breakfast the next morning, they agreed to make an initial reconnoitre under cover of darkness. Lucy went out and bought them black sweatshirts and black jogging pants. Alain's hair was naturally dark, and Lucy had dyed hers, so they were able to dispense with hats. To complete their camouflage, she looked for black-face make-up, but it proved impossible to find. Having tried cosmetic departments in large stores and several pharmacies, she settled on cheap black plastic face masks from a fancy dress shop.

At last the sun set over the city and they were ready. Packing their masks in a new dark rucksack, they set off. No one gave them a second glance as they hurried along the streets of Paris, following the map Alain had brought with them – they had no smartphone, to ensure their location could not be tracked. Taking an indirect route, it was a long walk down to the Seine where Alain hailed a taxi to take them the rest of the way. Lucy took care to memorise the address he gave, which was across the river.

By the time they approached Patrice's house, it was nearly midnight. Alain led her along a main road. Rounding a corner, he left the pavement to cut across a grassy wooded area. There was no moon. Pulling on their masks, they stole forward through the trees and turned off sharply into a poorly lit lane. They walked for a while in silence. Suddenly they froze, dazzled by security lights triggered by their approach. Their black-clad figures would be clearly visible in the beam of bright light. Before the lights went off they had time to see the way ahead barred by large metal gates. On either side of the gates, high metal railings protected the property. There was no way in. As if that was not enough of a deterrent, from the other side of the gate they heard the sound of dogs barking. Alain reached for Lucy's arm, pulling her back. As the darkness of the lane shielded them once more, they stopped to confer.

'What do we do now?' Lucy whispered.

'We get the hell out of here. Come on! Those guard dogs sound vicious. Let's hope no one lets them out.'

'Why can't we ring the bell and ask to speak to him?'

Through the darkness she saw Alain staring at her.

'He'd kill me.'

With a sickening feeling, Lucy realised that she really had no choice. She would have to approach Patrice alone. Either Alain was right in thinking Patrice would shoot him on sight, or he was crazy. Either way, she could not hope to have a civil conversation with Patrice while Alain was with her. There was too much history between them. She did not want to believe Patrice was incapable of listening to reason. Alain's opinion was warped by what had happened to his brother who had, after all, been a heroin addict, hardly a reliable witness. When she met Patrice, she would make up her own mind about him.

They hurried back the way they had come, only stopping to remove their masks when they were back in the shelter of the trees. Struggling to keep up with him, Lucy felt more certain than ever that Alain was unhinged.

'Well, that was a complete waste of time,' he grumbled. 'There's no way we can break in there.'

Lucy agreed there was no point in trying to effect an entry secretly in the dark. The guard dogs put paid to that idea. But she was not ready to give up yet. If she could not break in by stealth, she would come up with a plan to march in right under Patrice's nose.

'Don't forget, we still have the element of surprise,' she said, repeating what Alain had said. 'He's not expecting us to turn up, so he won't be on his guard.'

They made their way back towards the river and finally found a taxi to drop them a few streets away from their hotel. Checking that no one was following them, they returned to their room. Lucy knew she had been naive to hope they might creep into his villa and confront Patrice that night. Nevertheless, she was bitterly disappointed. After all the effort they had put into their expedition, they had achieved nothing.

'Let's talk in the morning,' she said, as she fell on her bed, exhausted.

She closed her eyes and pretended to fall asleep straight away. She wanted to be alone with her thoughts. Somehow, she would come up with a foolproof plan, with or without Alain's help. She drifted into a dream where a pair of massive black dogs burst into the room and began systematically tearing her to shreds. Paralysed, Lucy watched as one of the beasts tore great lumps of flesh from her leg. Strangely, she felt no pain. She watched as the animal tore her heart from her chest. As she tried to cry out, she woke up, sweating and trembling.

19

LUCY HAD NOT KNOWN ALAIN LONG, and for most of that time he had been in the hotel, recuperating from the attack at Le Cheval Rouge. She had been happy to go out by herself, fetching their breakfast and scouting around. Now that Alain had fully recovered from being drugged, he was completely different. Pacing up and down the small room he said he would go stir crazy if he spent another day cooped up in the hotel.

'I feel like a vampire,' he complained. 'I daren't go out on the streets until the sun sets.'

Lucy realised he had been passive only because he had been feeling groggy. Nevertheless, he stayed indoors while Lucy scurried out to buy breakfast.

'This may not be glamorous, but it's discreet,' Alain muttered, as they ate.

'The important thing is, we can be pretty sure Patrice still lives there,' he said quietly. 'Who else would have that insane level of security? First off we have to get back to your flat, fetch that key and work out what it opens. Once we know exactly what we've got on him, we can decide what to do about it.'

'I haven't got the key to get into my flat,' she reminded him.

'You know the code for the keypad to get us in off the street. Leave the front door to me. It's only a lock.'

As she sipped her coffee, Lucy wondered about Alain's change of mood. After her disturbed night she felt drowsy and confused, while Alain was buzzing with energy. She realised she had been naive to think she could get away from him any time she chose. Now he was fit he had taken control of their situation, as though authority came naturally to him. She wished she had never joined forces with him, but she could not leave him just yet. Without his help, she might never retrieve Patrice's key. Once she had it, she would go and see Patrice and get him off her back, even if it meant relinquishing the all-important key. She no longer cared about that. It was not worth dying for. Once she'd dealt with Patrice, she would be able to focus on finding Nina, if she was not with Patrice.

'I need to get this over with so I can find Nina,' she said.

Alain gave an impatient nod. 'Of course we want to find Nina, but we mustn't let that distract us from the possibility that this could be an opportunity to get Patrice locked up once and for all.'

'Nina's the reason we want to see Patrice.'

'Yes, yes. We've agreed we need to speak to Patrice so we can find Nina.'

Alain's dismissive tone suggested he had a different agenda. In the meantime, every day that went by was another day not knowing what had happened to Nina.

'The place is impenetrable,' Lucy said. 'Don't you think it's time we went to the police?'

'What would we say? Do you think Patrice keeps the victims of his sadism on display for everyone to see? If we go to the police he'll fob them off, and we'll be thrown out, having shown our hand. He'll have us tailed back to the hotel and murdered in our beds, most likely.'

After his experience at Le Cheval Rouge, Lucy could understand Alain feeling nervous about giving away his whereabouts. She imagined her parents and friends learning that her dead body had been found in a hotel bedroom with a strange man. Patrice would probably leave them both naked to put the police off the scent, as had clearly been the intention when Alain had been attacked and left with his trousers around his ankles. Her editor would probably run a story, 'English journalist slaughtered in love triangle', or some such nonsense.

'What we need to do is think up a plan for getting in there without being recognised,' she said.

'And how do you suggest we do that?'

'We'll have to think up a scam of some sort to get us inside the house.'

Alain looked sceptical. 'He'd recognise me as soon as he clapped eyes on me. So that's not going to work.'

Lucy nodded. Alain might not be able to sneak into Patrice's house undetected, but she could.

'We'll think of something,' she said quietly.

Alain would never agree with acceding to Patrice's demands, but if Lucy refused to give Patrice what he wanted, she was genuinely afraid that he would kill her. Meunier had been tortured and killed. An attempt had been made on Alain's life. Nothing was worth that sacrifice. One way or another, she had to speak to Patrice and re-assure him that she was willing to return his property, and persuade him to let her and Nina go. She was not interested in Patrice's criminal activities. She just needed to find out if he was responsible for Nina's disappearance.

'Are you really sure we wouldn't be better off going there with the police?' she asked, remembering the baying dogs they had heard at Patrice's house.

'Lucy, you don't know the French police. They don't move quickly, particularly if an English woman is accusing a Frenchman of committing a crime.'

'You're not an English woman.'

'No, but I'm a private investigator, not the kind of guy the police rush to work with. The problem is, there's no evidence to back up what we have to say. Another investigator tried to persuade them to build a case against Patrice. I knew that investigator. He was a decent guy. He jumped through all sorts of hoops to get an arrest, but he was batted back at every stage. It didn't go anywhere. Lucy, the police aren't going to believe us if we turn up with a load of unsubstantiated allegations against Patrice. And we've still no idea what that key is for.'

'Why don't we get in touch with the man you mentioned, the other investigator, the one who tried to build a case against Patrice? If we work together, surely between us we could get somewhere?'

'We can't get in touch with him.'

'Why not?'

Alain shrugged. 'He ended up under a train.'

'You mean he killed himself?'

'That was how it was reported.'

'Do you think he was pushed?'

'There's no proof, but yes, that's what I think happened. Look, even if we convince the French police to turn up at Patrice's house to take a look around, they aren't going to find anything. All that's likely to happen is that Patrice will put a bullet in my head after they've gone, and yours too. I'm sorry, but that's the reality.'

'So you're saying we're on our own with this.'

Alain looked solemn. 'I'll think of something. And if I don't, I'll arrange for you to go back to England and change your name—'

'I'm not going to change my name!'

'I'm only thinking of your safety. But if we could just get inside somehow, I can have him up against the wall with a gun to his head before he realises what's going on. Then he'll have to tell us what the key is for, in spite of his army of accomplices.'

Lucy wondered how that would help her, but she kept silent. She had her own plan. She would turn up pretending to be a Hollywood scout looking for a location for a new film. Patrice's house was bound to be large, with grounds for his dogs to run around in. There was no reason why he should see through her ploy. And once she was inside, she would be able to talk to him. It had to be worth a try.

'We'll think of something,' she repeated.

Fed up with being stuck inside the same four walls, Alain was keen to be out in the fresh air, so they agreed to go out and find somewhere discreet to discuss their plans. They walked south towards the river, following a circuitous route along narrow side streets. All at once, Alain grabbed her by the elbow and shoved her through a shop doorway.

'Ow! What are you doing?'

Without answering, he spun round and stood at the door, peering out. After a moment he turned back to her, mumbling an apology.

'What was that all about?'

'I thought we were being followed.'

With a troubled frown, he led her back out of the shop and along the street. From time to time he looked over his shoulder.

'Well?' she asked him at last. 'Are we being followed?'

'It's difficult to say. I think so. Probably.' He glanced round. 'Oh, yes, there he is again. Don't look now but there's a skinny guy in a black jacket who's been tailing us for about twenty minutes.'

They turned a corner and Alain half turned to gaze along the pavement behind them. 'Yes, here he comes. Same ugly mug. Wait a minute and then look back. Your life might depend on your recognising him if he turns up again. He's wearing a loose black jacket, that's to hide his weapon. Don't let him see you staring at him, but make sure you get a clear view of his face.'

Lucy waited a few minutes and then stopped and pretended to search for something in her bag. Deliberately dropping her purse, she turned and crouched down to pick it up. Glancing back along the pavement as she straightened up, she spotted a scrawny man in a loose black jacket. He had a gaunt face, with hollow cheeks and thin lips. She turned away quickly.

'Did you see him clearly?'

'Yes. He's not much to look at.'

'He'll be a darn sight uglier by the time I finish with him.'

Alain's threat did not make Lucy feel any safer.

'Are you positive he's following us?'

'I can't be sure, but we need to watch out for him, just in case. It could be coincidence, but he's been behind us for a long time. Stay alert, and keep your wits about you, and if he gets too close, run.'

Lucy was not sure how close might be considered too close, especially if their stalker was armed. It was possible Patrice had sent him with a view to recovering the key. They walked on, the man in the black jacket tagging along behind them, until they reached the river. Entering the Tuileries Gardens, they lost sight of their stalker. In a way that was worse, because he could be anywhere, concealed in the shrubbery. Alain was not comfortable sitting still so they kept on walking down to the river and along the Quai des Tuileries. At least they were out in the open there and able to see if the man who had been tailing them reappeared. Passing a platform from where river trips departed, they saw people boarding a boat. Alain looked around. The riverbank was busy, but there was no sign of the man in the black jacket.

'I think we've shaken him off,' he said, 'but keep your eyes peeled in case. And whatever you do, don't let him get you on your own.'

20

'WHY DON'T WE TAKE A BOAT TRIP?' Lucy suggested. 'Once we're on board, we'll be able to discuss our options without fear of being followed or overheard.'

Alain agreed and they hurried over to the ticket booth. Instead of joining the zigzagging queue, they hung back until the rest of the passengers were on board. As the crew were about to cast off, Alain grabbed Lucy's arm and pulled her forwards. They dodged beneath the barriers and raced along the ramp and onto the boat.

'Here,' Alain said, thrusting their tickets at the crew member who had been collecting them.

Ignoring the man's protest, Alain pushed Lucy ahead of him onto the deck.

'He's trying to tell us we've missed the boat,' Alain quipped. 'But here we are, and we're not getting off, not without getting more than our feet wet. I hope you don't get seasick.'

'Not on a river.'

'Come on, then, we're paid-up passengers. Let's find somewhere we can talk.'

Most of the deck was covered by a dirty glass roof. They made their way past rows of orange plastic seats, which were mostly occupied, to the back of the boat. No one else had left the limited shelter of the cabin. The ceiling was so dirty, it provided some protection from the sun, which was beginning to beat down with fierce heat. There were a few empty chairs outside and Alain led her past them, right to the end of the boat, behind the last row of seats.

'Are we allowed to stand out here?' Lucy shouted above the noise of the engine and the wind that carried her words away.

'We've paid, we can go where we like.'

They leaned back against the waist-high metal barrier. No one could approach them without being seen. Lucy only managed to hear Alain because she was standing very close to him. As the boat glided away from the quay, a gust of wind blew a fine spray over them.

'Sorry,' he yelled. 'This wasn't such a good idea. Do you want to go inside?'

'This is fine!' she shouted back. 'I'm fine!'

The spray was a welcome relief from the heat.

'We're getting wet.'

'It's cooling us down. I don't mind, if you don't.'

They passed under several bridges. Lucy admired the beautiful architecture, and the lovely trees bordering the river. She envied the other passengers on the boat who were laughing and joking, enjoying themselves looking at the view. Ignoring the guide talking through a crackly PA system, Alain talked about how they might gain access to Patrice's house without being seen. Lucy kept her own plan to herself.

'The dogs are a problem,' Alain said.

Joining in his discussion to avoid arousing his suspicions, Lucy suggested taking some meat doused in sedatives, but they were not sure how to get hold of drugs strong enough to knock out the massive animals. They had no idea how many of them there were. From the racket they made, Alain thought there were quite a few of them.

Lucy agreed. But before tackling the dogs, they had to get past the gates. Alain suspected the fence might be electrified.

'That's all we need,' Lucy said. She was not sure whether Alain heard her, in all the noise from the wind and the engine, but it made no difference.

'Let's say we get through the gate—' he began.

She interrupted him. 'How?'

Alain shouted about the mechanism being electronic. That meant there had to be a scanner that read number plates. If they could alter that to recognise a different registration number, the gates might open to admit them. Driving in would protect them from the dogs, he added.

'But how are we supposed to get it to recognise a different number?' he went on. 'I've got contacts who can tamper with such mechanisms easily enough, but they'd need access to the control system. And to do that, we'd probably need to get inside . . .'

'And in any case, we haven't got a car.'

'Getting hold of a car isn't a problem.'

'But what if the gate's not automatic? For all we know, there's a security guard watching a screen, checking cars and only letting in the ones on his list.'

'Yes,' Alain agreed, 'we're more likely to be able to climb over the fence than fix some complex electronic system or get past a guard. We'll have to take a ladder with us, or a rope that we could hook over one of the railings. I don't suppose you're any good at throwing lassos?'

Lucy shook her head.

'It's hopeless, isn't it?' he said at last, when he had run out of ideas. 'But whatever happens, and however I get in, I can't let you come with me. If we're caught breaking in, we're unlikely to leave there alive. Don't worry. If your friend is there, I'll get her out if I can. I'm sorry, but I have to do this alone.'

Lucy looked down at the river, her throat sore from shouting. 'You and me both,' she thought.

She still was not sure how much she could trust Alain. This was personal for him too. Alain straightened up, yelling that he needed the toilet.

'I'll wait here,' she replied, happy to be out in the fresh air, in spite of the noise from the engine.

'I won't be long. Stay here and don't talk to anyone.'

Lucy twisted round and leaned her forearms on the rail. Peering over the side of the boat, she watched the water churned up by the engine. A brisk breeze ruffled her hair. It was exhilarating. Listening to Alain talking about the possibility that they might not leave Patrice's house alive had given her goosebumps. But if he was prepared to take the risk, she was not going to bottle it when Nina might still be alive and in danger. In any case, she was not sure whether to believe Alain's claim that their lives were at risk. Not for the first time, she wondered why she was going along with his crazy claims without questioning his motivation, or even his sanity. She did not really know anything about him.

She wished she had simply reported the situation to the police, and left it to them. But then again, Alain did not think the French police were likely to take her allegations seriously, and she was inclined to agree with him, plus, she remembered Jérôme's warning only too well. Without Alain bellowing in her ear, she became aware of the guide talking about an elaborate bridge they were approaching, and learned that the Pont Alexandre III had taken three years to complete. She gathered that it had been built in the nineteenth century but, with the PA system competing against the wind, she missed the exact date of its construction. Named after Tsar Alexander III, with the first stone laid by his son Tsar Nicholas II, it was an elegant structure, with ornate lamps and sculptures and large gilded statues. As she stood gazing back at the beautiful bridge, she felt a hand on her shoulder. Expecting to see Alain, she turned round and let out a strangled scream.

There was no mistaking the haggard cheeks and thin lips of the man who had been following her and Alain. For the first time she was able to see the man's eyes, dark and devoid of expression; a man with a job to do. Glaring at her, he lunged forward and seized her by the throat. Holding her in a powerful grip, he lifted her off her feet. Choking, she lashed out, punching wildly. He caught both her fists in his free hand, and held them tightly. She winced as his bony fist crushed her fingers. It was difficult to kick him with both of her legs dangling off the floor. When she tried to move, her assailant tightened his grip. She was afraid he was going to break her neck.

This was how her life was going to end, strangled on a boat on the Seine. There would be a short news item on the Internet about an English woman killed on a river boat in Paris. No doubt it would be reported as an accidental drowning. She could imagine the Current Affairs International headline: 'Tragic Death of British Journalist in Paris'. Her parents would struggle to believe their daughter's body had been pulled out of the Seine. She was surprised that she felt no fear, only bitter anger that her life was to end like this, anonymously, among strangers in a foreign country.

21

BEHIND HER, LUCY COULD HEAR the engine whirring and whining. The sound of her strangled screams was carried away by the wind. The man in the black jacket leaned towards her until his mouth was almost touching her ear.

'You got something that don't belong to you,' he said.

She stared over his shoulder, praying that Alain would return and save her.

'You can squirm all you like, but Jérôme spilled the beans. He told someone all about how you met him down by the Canal Saint-Martin, and she told me. He was an idiot. He should have kept his mouth shut. He got what was coming to him. But never mind all that. Jérôme knew the risk he was taking. He's history. It don't matter no more.' He turned his head and spat on the deck. 'He give you something, didn't he? There's no point in lying. Jérôme told us what he'd taken. He tried to hold out, but Patrice knows how to make a man talk. Now you hand it over, nice and easy, and you don't get hurt. Listen, you been lucky so far, because my boss thinks he's got his hands on you. That's the only reason he's not been out looking for you. But I knew he had the wrong girl. I seen her passport in your flat, and I saw it was her face. I knew it wasn't you we took back with us from your flat, only I never said nothing. I figured I could do us both a favour if I got to you first. So it's best for both of us if you don't make no fuss.'

'What do you mean, he's got the wrong girl?' Lucy gasped.

But she knew exactly what he meant. He had confirmed her worst fears. Patrice had kidnapped Nina. Meanwhile, a maniac was threatening her life. A wild hope crossed her mind that he was going to throw her over the side of the boat. If she managed to avoid being sliced to pieces by the engine, she could swim to safety. The water must be cold, and was probably horribly polluted, but at least she would have a chance of escaping with her life. As long as she kept moving in the water, it would not take her long to reach the bank. The sides looked steep, and she might have to swim further along before she could climb out, but the water would be less dangerous than the man who had his filthy hand at her throat.

'You're choking me,' she gasped as loudly as she could, with her windpipe being crushed.

He loosened his grip on her throat without letting go of her wrists.

'Are you going to chuck me in the water to drown?' she asked, trying to sound as though she was against the idea.

The man leaned forward again, clearly agitated. He spoke rapidly. 'We don't have much time. I come here to warn you. Patrice isn't what you might call a patient man. He wants what's his. It's only fair. Now you just let me have it, nice and easy, and we're both safe.'

'I've no idea what you're talking about.'

'You don't know nothing about who you're dealing with. But I do.'

'I know who he is.'

'Then you don't need me to tell you he's a dangerous man. You should be more careful who you mess with.'

'I'm always careful,' she snapped. 'I'm not an idiot. And I understand perfectly well what's going on. But you can tell Patrice I'm not going to give him what he wants until he lets my friend go. I know what he's after. I've got it hidden away where he'll never find it. I've got a friend as well, and we look out for each other, and he can be dangerous too. He must be on his way back by now, so you do yourself a favour and get lost. If he catches you here, he'll kill you.'

'Don't you mess me about. Time's running out. So just hand it over and no one gets hurt.'

'You don't really think I'm walking around with it in my pocket, do you? I'm not that stupid. I've hidden it, somewhere you'll never find it. But,' she added with a flash of inspiration, 'you can tell Patrice, if anything happens to me or my friend, I've left instructions about what to do with it, and then the whole world will know all about it.'

Leaning forward until their faces were almost touching, the man spoke again, his eyes darting around, his lips twitching. Close up, Lucy could see an anguished expression in his eyes, and hear his voice shaking. He was terrified.

'You need to give me what I want or we're both dead. You're looking at a desperate man. You got to believe me.' He took a step back. In the bright sunshine, his face shone like a skull. 'I need this.' His voice broke with emotion. 'You don't understand. It won't be long before he starts looking for you. It was lucky for both of us I found you first. I was watching your flat. I saw you in the street outside and I been following you ever since. You was clever, changing your hair colour, but not clever enough. I recognised your face.'

Lucy recalled noticing a figure standing motionless across the street when she had last gone back to the Rue Ferdinand Duval.

'I need to get hold of what he wants,' he continued in an urgent whisper. 'It's the only way to save my skin, and yours too.

119

If I don't I'm a dead man, and you'll be done for too, because he'll find you. No one walks away from Patrice. You won't never be safe. There's no hiding from him. This is my last chance, and it's a chance for you too. You don't get it, do you? You don't know what he's capable of.'

'Why don't you shoot Patrice if you're so scared of him?' she asked, trying to humour him until Alain returned, but also genuinely curious.

The man's face twisted with derision. 'I thought you said you knew who you were dealing with? You think a bloke can just walk up to Patrice and shoot him?'

'That shouldn't be a problem for a man with a gun in his hand. By the time he realised what was happening, he'd be dead.'

'Patrice knows what's going on. He always knows. Now, give it me. I won't – I can't – leave here without it. He'll get it from you, if I don't. You got to tell me where it is, or you and your friend'll both end up like Jérôme. If you don't hand it over right now, I'm going straight back to tell Patrice he got the wrong girl and he'll be after you like a shot. He'll find you, just like I did. There ain't nowhere in Paris you can hide from Patrice. You got to believe me. Now, where is it?'

Lucy stared around frantically but the man was blocking her escape. In desperation she took a step away from him, pressing herself against the railings until they dug into her back. He was about to say something else, when over his shoulder she saw Alain dashing along the aisle. Seeing her expression change, the man looked round and spotted Alain belting towards them. He stepped away from her, swearing under his breath. Alain was about ten yards away when a member of the boat's crew stepped in front of him, blocking his way.

'No running,' the crewman barked. 'Return to your seat, please. We're about to dock.'

As he was speaking, a voice over the tannoy announced the end of the trip, and began issuing instructions. The man in the black jacket darted away from her. Pushing his way past the seats, he disappeared in the queue of passengers who were lining up to disembark.

22

FOLLOWING THE REST OF THE PASSENGERS off the boat, they walked quickly away from the small crowd dispersing on the bank. Alain appeared calm, but his face was pale. Shocked at receiving confirmation that Patrice was keeping Nina prisoner, Lucy tried to control her alarm and focus on getting away from Alain. She could not afford to be distracted from her plan. Nina was in danger. After what Lucy had heard on the boat, she was more convinced than ever that she needed to speak to Patrice alone, and she needed to do it urgently. One of Patrice's associates knew her true identity. If the man told Patrice he had the wrong girl, she would be hunted down before she could explain herself.

As they walked away from the river, she thought about her plan to ring Patrice's bell posing as an American film scout. The more she thought about it, the more effective the idea seemed in principle. Genuine Americans might notice inconsistencies in her accent, but she was sure she could pull it off in front of someone for whom English was a foreign language. She would just have to hope that no one there recognised her. It would give her a perfect excuse to explore the property. She could claim to want to survey the grounds, and insist the guard dogs were locked away. Without the dogs patrolling the grounds, it would be relatively easy for her and Nina to make a run for it. Once they were away from Patrice, Alain would take it from there, going to the police with Nina as a witness.

With her plan clear in her mind, she was keen to go ahead with it as soon as possible. The longer she waited, the longer Nina would remain in danger. But before she could do anything, she had to get away from Alain. It was essential Patrice believed her cover story. She would have to wait until the following morning to make her approach.

'How did you know he was following us?' she asked Alain, as they walked back into the Tuileries Gardens.

Alain shrugged. 'I recognised him. He was tailing us for hours. I don't know how he slipped on board without my noticing. I'm sorry. I should have been more vigilant. I should never have left you on your own like that. I thought you'd be safe on the boat. He would have killed you if I hadn't come back when I did.'

'You don't know what he intended to do,' she protested, remembering the terror in the other man's eyes. 'He wasn't trying to kill me. He was frightened of Patrice and wanted to get the key for him.'

'Those men are all ruthless psychopaths. Once he'd got his hands on Patrice's key he'd have wrung your neck, and if you didn't give him what he wanted, he'd have killed you for refusing him. Either way, he was out to kill you. Lucy, I know all about these people. You came to me for help, and I'm not going to let anyone hurt you. I mean it. Whatever happens, I'll protect you.'

'You don't know he was going to kill me,' she insisted. 'You might think he was, but you don't know. He said he was giving me a chance.'

Alain shook his head. 'He wasn't the slightest bit interested in giving you a chance. A chance for what? These people, they're not like us, Lucy. When they're not unconscious they're high, users and alcoholics. Most of the time they wouldn't know the truth if it came up and hit them in the face. People like that are violent and unpredictable. They use other people and throw them away when they no longer have any use for them.'

He took her by the elbow and led her to a bench. They sat side by side, gazing at the shrubbery.

'I knew he was following us,' Alain muttered at last. 'I thought I recognised him as soon as I saw him behind us on the street.'

'Who was he?'

'I've only seen him once before.'

'What's his name?'

'I don't know his name. They call him Ferret. Shall I tell you why?'

'I think I can guess.'

'When ferrets bite they never let go.'

A young girl jogged by, her ponytail swinging behind her. An old man shuffled past, head down. Lucy wished she was living a humdrum existence like the other people in the park. She must have been mad to ever long for some excitement in her life. She would have given anything to be back at her desk, or sitting in a bar in the Marais, gossiping and giggling with Nina.

'Are you hungry?' Alain asked suddenly. 'It's getting late and I'm ravenous. Why don't we go and get something to eat? Come on.'

Lucy stood up. Until Alain had mentioned eating, she had not realised she was starving. 'Where are we going?'

'Come on, I'll take you to a little place not far from here.'

'What if he's still following us?'

'At least we'll be out in public. Better if he catches up with us in a crowded place where other people will see what happens and might call the police, rather than him finding you holed up in a hotel room. Come on,' he said. 'The chances are no one will see us, so let's just forget about him for a while. It might be our last chance to go out for a good meal,' he added, suddenly solemn.

They walked in silence along the riverbank, turning off along a quiet side street where Alain took her to a dimly lit bistro. He laughed when Lucy asked him if the patron was a friend of his.

'I don't know everyone in Paris,' he protested.

The restaurant was surprisingly busy. No one took any notice of them as they sat down in a corner. The service was slow, and while they waited, Lucy asked Alain what Patrice looked like.

'It's difficult to say, really,' Alain told her. 'His hair's sort of dark gingery and he's clean-shaven, or he was when I saw him. He's got a receding hairline that makes his forehead look very large, and he's well built. Not fat, but he looks strong, hefty almost. He's very distinctive. Once you've seen him, you never forget him. That's not a very helpful description really, is it?'

'No. And he doesn't sound very distinctive.'

'It's more about his presence than anything else. He's got an air of confidence, a kind of charisma, I suppose, as though nothing can touch him.'

'Arrogant?'

'Yes, but it's more than that. He exudes an aura of power. You can't miss it.'

'You sound as though you admire him.'

Alain looked taken aback. As he began to remonstrate the food arrived, and they were both distracted. Relaxing over dessert, he asked her about her ex-boyfriend.

'What do you want to know?'

'I'm just wondering why a girl like you is single.'

'A girl like me?'

'Stop fishing for compliments.'

'When I told you there was someone, I meant it. But it's over.' She shrugged. 'It was a long time ago.'

Alain burst out laughing. 'It can't be that long ago. You're only twenty-four.'

'I mean, it feels like a long time ago,' she explained, momentarily flustered by his amusement. 'I suppose I may meet someone else one day, but I'm not in any hurry. What about you?'

'What about me?'

'Is there a wife or a girlfriend waiting for you at home?'

This time his laughter was not so hearty. 'Can you seriously imagine any girl putting up with me?' He hesitated. 'There was someone once . . .' He broke off, a distant look in his eyes, before he snapped back to his customary briskness. 'But that was all a long time ago. A very long time ago.'

Lucy was surprised. Alain seemed so self-contained. Even when she had rescued him after the attack at Le Cheval Rouge, he had spoken only about his physical aches and exhaustion, not about his feelings. For the first time, she sensed an air of vulnerability about him that seemed at odds with his tough image.

'Do you have any children?'

'No. But if things had worked out differently, I like to think I might have had a daughter like you.'

'Like me?'

'Gutsy and intelligent.'

Lucy refused to be distracted by compliments. 'So what happened? Why did it end? If you don't mind my asking,' she added, afraid she was being intrusive.

'Oh, you know,' he shrugged. 'Boy meets girl. Boy loses girl. And that's it. There's nothing more to say. We were together for ten years. She met someone else. She's probably been happily married to him for ten years. That's how long it is since we split up,' he added, brushing it off with a smile.

'But—'

'She told me I cared more about my brother than about her.' He stared at her, his expression suddenly troubled. 'Maybe I did. You know, I've never spoken about her since the day we split up.'

'I'm sorry.'

'Don't be. It doesn't matter any more.'

But after ten years, it seemed he still found his failed love affair too painful to talk about. Curiosity overcame her pity.

'Was there no one you could talk to?' she asked, as gently as she could.

'What?'

'Why haven't you told anyone about it?'

'No one has ever asked me before.' He smiled at her and raised his glass. 'You know, you're the first woman to save my life. She wasn't the only one to do her best to ruin it, but no other woman has ever saved my life.'

Glass raised, he waited for her to respond. Although she was not persuaded he really had saved her life on the boat, he clearly believed she had been in mortal danger. Besides, his disclosure about his past life convinced her that she could trust him.

'We look out for each other,' she replied. 'I know you want to keep me safe, and I do appreciate it.'

As his face relaxed into a smile, she realised she would not have been able to evade Patrice without his help. His concern for her welfare was evidently genuine. She felt fleetingly sad to think that once this was over, they would probably never see one another again.

He smiled at her again. 'This is very pleasant, isn't it? I haven't been out for dinner with an attractive young woman for a long time. Not since I was a young man, in fact, and that's going back more years than I care to remember.'

Now that they seemed to have reached an understanding, Lucy felt guilty about keeping her plans secret. The trouble was, if she confided in Alain, he would insist on accompanying her for her own protection. He was bound to be recognised when they introduced themselves as Hollywood scouts. She decided it was best to keep her idea to herself. And she was determined to visit Patrice as soon as she could. The longer she delayed, the longer Nina could be in danger.

As she returned Alain's smile, she wondered if she would end up like him when her hair was turning grey, her only love affair an engagement that had ended when she was little more than twenty.

23

Patrice picked up his glass, turning it so the dark red liquid revolved slowly. Just as he was raising it to his lips, the door opened and Marcel stepped into the room.

'Sorry to interrupt you, boss.'

Patrice scowled. 'What do you want?'

'Ferret's here.'

Patrice put his glass down with an impatient growl. 'So what? Can't you see I'm having my dinner? Tell him he'll have to wait.'

'I told him, but he said he needs to see you straight away. He seems a bit het up.'

'Ferret's always het up. What's so important that it can't wait?'

Marcel shook his head. 'I don't know. He wouldn't say. He just insisted he had to see you. I think he's losing it.'

Patrice nodded. 'Oh, very well. You've interrupted me now. You might as well bring him in. But this had better be worth it.'

A few moments later, Ferret appeared and stood fidgeting in the doorway. Short and scrawny, he looked absurdly small beside Marcel.

'Well?' Patrice barked. 'Come in then. This had better be important.'

While Patrice grumbled about his dinner being interrupted, Ferret took a few steps forward into the room and ducked his head, muttering that it was extremely important. 'I got information for you.'

Patrice leaned back in his chair and stared at his visitor, his eyes cold. 'Everyone's got information.'

Ferret nodded his head rapidly.

'Stop doing that. You're making me dizzy. Well?' Patrice's voice rose in irritation. 'Are you going to tell me why you're here, or are you just going to stand there, grinning like a cretin, while my dinner gets cold?'

Ferret shuffled his feet and cleared his throat nervously. 'It's about the English girl,' he blurted out. 'There's something you got to know. You got the wrong one.'

'What are you talking about?' Patrice turned to Marcel. 'What the fuck's he talking about?'

Marcel shrugged his broad shoulders. 'How should I know? Shall I throw him out, boss? I told you, he's lost it.'

Patrice picked up his knife and fork and began cutting up his meat.

'That girl you got downstairs, the English girl. You got the wrong one,' Ferret stammered.

Patrice scowled at him and put down his cutlery. His voice was very quiet. 'What the hell are you talking about?'

Ferret took a step forward, clasping his hands together in a gesture of supplication. His face was horribly pale and he blinked as sweat dripped into his eyes.

'Oh, get out.' Patrice slapped his fist on the table. 'I don't want to look at you. It's enough to put me off my dinner.'

As Marcel took a step forwards, Ferret shouted out in a panic. 'You got to listen to me. The girl you got isn't Lucy Hall!'

Patrice raised a hand to warn Marcel to wait. The big man obediently stood still.

'What are you talking about?' Patrice asked. 'You told me you found her in her apartment.'

Ferret edged away from Marcel. 'Because that's where she was,' he said earnestly. 'That's why we brought her to you. But turns out she's not Lucy Hall after all.'

'I don't believe you.' Patrice narrowed his eyes. 'What game are you playing, Ferret? If I find you've been trying to double-cross me, I'll feed your balls to the dogs.'

'It's true, what I'm telling you. Her name's Nina Wilson. Look.' Ferret held up his phone. 'I took this photo when we were searching the apartment.'

Beckoning him to come closer, Patrice snatched the phone from him. Screwing up his eyes, he studied the image for a few seconds. At last he put the phone down on the table and raised his head.

'Who is this Nina Wilson?'

'I don't know, but you seen the picture. It's her, isn't it? The girl downstairs. She's not Lucy Hall, she's called Nina Wilson.'

Patrice swore. Pushing his plate away, he rose to his feet. Ferret retreated a few paces and glanced over his shoulder, as though contemplating flight. Marcel was standing in the doorway, staring contemptuously at him.

'I come here to tell you, because I'm loyal to you, boss,' Ferret stammered. 'You should thank me. I didn't have to come here. I didn't have to say nothing. I could've—'

'You took this picture on Sunday night!' Patrice roared suddenly, red-faced. 'You've known about this for days. How come you waited so long to tell me?'

Reaching his visitor in one stride, Patrice seized his throat in one large hand and squeezed. Ferret gagged, his eyes wide with alarm. He began to choke, and Patrice flung him away. As Ferret lost his footing, his arms flailed wildly. He staggered backwards, and Marcel caught him in a headlock.

'Shall I take him downstairs, boss? We could have some fun with him?'

Patrice shrugged. 'Why not? And now, perhaps, I can finish my dinner in peace.'

'No! Wait!' Ferret gasped, white with terror. 'You can't do this to me. I come here to give you information. You can't do this to me!'

'Why did you wait so long to tell me you brought me the wrong girl? Let him go, Marcel.'

Shaking himself free of Marcel's hold, Ferret felt his neck gingerly. 'I wanted to be sure Lucy Hall was still in Paris before I come to you. I only want to make myself useful. No point in having information if you can't do anything about it, is there?'

Patrice gave him a long hard stare. 'Where is Lucy Hall?'

'She's in Paris,' Ferret said, attempting an ingratiating grin. 'No one but me could've found her.' He glanced at Marcel before turning back to Patrice. 'And I come straight to you.' He took a step forward. 'I seen her today, by the river.'

'Shame she wasn't in the river,' Marcel said.

Patrice rounded on him. 'Shut up!' He turned back to Ferret, who was wiping his sweaty forehead on his sleeve.

'If you want to have any hope of saving your miserable skin, you bring me Lucy Hall,' he said. 'If you screw up again, next time you won't leave this house alive. I'll carve you up. I'll throw you to the dogs. Now get out.'

24

The following morning Lucy had intended to set off very early to find her way to Patrice's house by herself before Alain was awake. But since he was up and dressed before her, insisting on going out for breakfast, she was forced to put her plan on hold. Sitting at a small table in a dingy café around the corner from the Gare du Nord, Lucy rehearsed her American accent in her head while Alain tucked into a pastry. As he ate, his eyes flicked around the room, constantly checking if any other customers had come in. The place was empty apart from one elderly man reading a newspaper. Lucy felt on edge. She wondered if Ferret had told Patrice about his mistake yet. Time was running out. She needed to make her move soon.

'This is a quiet place,' Alain said, 'and easy to find. And there's a back exit. If we have to split up, we'll make this our meeting place. Will you remember the way here?'

She nodded, and they sat in silence for a few minutes. Worried Alain might notice she was distracted, Lucy made an effort to engage him in conversation. Racking her brains for something to talk about, she asked if he had always wanted to be a private investigator.

'Pretty much, yes. Since I was a teenager and saw *The Big Sleep*, you know, with Humphrey Bogart. Not that my work's been very exciting for the most part. The most I've got in common with Philip Marlowe is our struggle to make ends meet. It's a hand-to-mouth existence. If I hadn't inherited my share of my parents' meagre estate, there's no way I'd have been able to stay in Paris on what I make.'

'I envy you, knowing what you wanted to do when you were that young.'

He gave a little grunt. 'When I was your age, I was working for a firm of investigators, learning the ropes you might say. I didn't set up on my own until I was in my thirties.'

'Was that a good move, going on your own?'

'I suppose so. It was what I'd always wanted to do.'

'I had no idea what I wanted to do when I was a teenager. I only recently decided to become a journalist.'

'And was that the right decision?'

'I don't know yet. I've been working at the Paris office for three months, and it's my first post as a reporter.'

'What did you do before that? I suppose you went to university?'

'Yes.'

'What did you study?'

'English and French. Not particularly useful subjects, really.'

'It got you here, didn't it? Although maybe that doesn't seem like such a good idea right now.'

She smiled. 'I can speak French, and I can quote from Shakespeare, but apart from that, there's not much to show for—' She broke off as Alain let out an exclamation of dismay. 'What is it? What's wrong?'

Following the line of his gaze, she saw the elderly man rustling the pages of his newspaper. He looked about eighty, hardly a cause for alarm. There was no one else in the café, apart from a bored-looking waitress behind the counter.

'Wait here.' Without another word, Alain jumped up and ran out of the café.

This was a perfect opportunity to give Alain the slip and go to see Patrice. Suddenly feeling shaky, Lucy was fishing in her purse for some change when Alain reappeared, clutching a newspaper.

'Look!' he hissed, sitting down and leaning across the table.

'What is it?' she answered sharply, annoyed with herself for having missed an opportunity to get away from him.

'Look at this.' He put the paper down and pointed at a photograph of a woman. 'Read it and don't say anything.'

Lucy scanned the short report and frowned. 'How terrible.'

'Yes, yes, it's very sad, of course, but that's hardly the point. "A woman was pulled out of the river yesterday,"' he read aloud, under his breath. '"Angeline Colbert, 32, had been drinking heavily before she fell in the river. The inspector in charge of the case, Olivier Joubert, called it a tragic accident."' Alain glanced around before he went on. '"The inspector added that such drownings are rare."' He raised his eyebrows with a sceptical grunt and continued reading. '"The police are urging members of the public to take care when out drinking."'

'That sounds like sensible advice. But I don't know why you're showing me this. I'm not planning to get drunk and fall in the river.'

Alain interrupted her in an urgent whisper. 'That's the woman who spiked my drink in Le Cheval Rouge, the woman who tried to kill me.'

'Are you sure?'

'Yes.' He looked around. Satisfied there was no one sitting close enough to overhear their conversation, he continued slowly, struggling to recall the exact sequence of events. 'She was sitting right beside me so I had a good look at her, close up. I don't forget faces. I know it's not a very clear photo, but it's definitely the same woman.' He paused. 'She told me her name was Angeline. She wasn't there in Le Cheval

Rouge by chance. It all adds up. This woman, Angeline Colbert, was working for Patrice. He found out I was asking questions about him, and he sent her to kill me. And now he's got rid of her.'

'The police seem to think it was an accident.'

'That's how it was made to look, but he threw her in the river. If we could get a look at her post-mortem report, I dare say it would tell us she didn't drown. I'd bet you any money she was dead before she reached the water. But any records about the circumstances of her death have probably been destroyed by now.'

'Can they do that?'

Remembering what had happened to Jérôme Meunier, Lucy knew it was possible.

'Patrice's influence extends into all sorts of areas,' Alain said. 'He has police officers and pathologists on his payroll. And if anything does come out, nothing's going to lead back to him.'

'You don't know that.'

'No, but I'd put money on it that I'm right.'

Lucy considered the newspaper report. It was reasonable to assume that Patrice had sent someone to kill Alain, to stop him asking questions. Had death been the punishment for Angeline Colbert's failure?

'If this woman really *was* killed just because she didn't kill you . . .' she paused, struck by the full horror of what Alain was saying. 'That poor woman. How terrible.'

'That poor woman tried to kill me.'

Lucy sighed. It was hard to believe there were people living in a civilised city like Paris who had so little regard for human life. But she had already seen what had happened to her hapless informant, Jérôme Meunier.

Pulling herself together, she continued. 'This could be our chance to convince the police to get involved. If we can get them to investigate her death, maybe they'll come up with something incriminating.'

Alain hesitated then nodded, as though he had made up his mind. 'That could work. It's worth a try anyway. Go to the police. Ask for the inspector in charge of this case, Inspector Olivier Joubert. Tell him Angeline Colbert was working for Patrice Durand. I don't suppose this inspector will listen to you but at least we've got his name. It's a contact of sorts. Don't mention me, just say she drugged a friend of yours.'

Reluctant to go to the police on her own, Lucy insisted it would take two of them to convince the police to take their story seriously.

In spite of her efforts to persuade him otherwise, Alain refused to accompany her. 'My own name is well known to the police, and I can't let you cause problems for the real Alain Michel. The police already think I interfere in matters that don't concern me. Last time I was drawn into a criminal investigation, I was told in no uncertain terms to stick to searching for missing dogs and supplying evidence in divorce cases. The police regard private investigators as meddling amateurs, at best, and to make matters worse, they think I've got a grudge against Patrice. I have a reputation for causing trouble where he's concerned. It'll be best if you leave my name out of it altogether, otherwise they'll never take you seriously. They'll dismiss anything you tell them without listening to a word you say. Just say that a friend of yours was attacked by Angeline Colbert.'

Lucy finally agreed to go to the police by herself. Apart from anything else, it would give her a chance to get away from Alain. If the police were not prepared to help, as soon as she finished at the police station she would carry out her plan to go and speak to Patrice herself. As a last resort, she would throw herself on his mercy and beg him to release Nina. Having agreed to meet back at the hotel, they left the café together. Alain walked with her as far as the end of the road where the police station was located before he turned and vanished. Alone, she approached the impersonal grey police station and climbed the steps.

25

A UNIFORMED POLICE OFFICER with a machine gun barred Lucy's way at the top of the stairs.

'I need to speak to Inspector Joubert. Is he here?'

'Why do you want to see him?'

Lucy was surprised that a member of the public could not simply walk into a police station. Only when she mentioned the name Angeline Colbert did the heavily armed officer step aside and allow her to pass. A dour-faced woman was seated behind a desk opposite the entrance, her expression nearly as intimidating as the machine gun her colleague was holding.

'Excuse me.' Lucy faltered, slightly unnerved by the reception. 'Can you help me?'

'What do you want?'

'I would like to speak to Olivier Joubert.'

The woman scowled. 'You want to speak with Inspector Joubert?' she repeated.

Lucy nodded, wondering what she was getting herself into.

'Has the inspector asked to see you?'

'Well, no, not exactly. But I have some very important information for him.'

'What is this information concerning?'

'It's to do with the death of Angeline Colbert. Angeline Colbert,' she repeated carefully. 'You must know about her? She's the woman who allegedly drowned in the Seine. Angeline Colbert.'

'Yes, yes, Angeline Colbert. I understand what you're saying,' the woman responded more gently. 'Were you a friend of the woman who drowned?'

'No, no, I'm not her friend. I never met her. I don't know her. But I need to speak to Inspector Joubert. Please. It's very, very important.'

Looking puzzled, the woman acknowledged her request. With a nod she picked up her phone and began gabbling very fast. Lucy tried to listen, but was unable to follow a word the woman was saying. She was almost ready to give up and leave when the woman hung up.

'The inspector is busy,' the woman said. 'Who do you work for, and what do you wish to know about Madame Colbert?'

'No, no. I don't want to know anything. I don't work for anyone. I mean, I do, but I haven't come here to ask questions. I have some information for the inspector.'

The woman inclined her head, to indicate she was listening. 'What information do you have?'

Lucy sighed. 'It's complicated. I really would like to talk to Inspector Joubert about the investigation into the circumstances surrounding the death of Angeline Colbert.'

The woman picked up her phone and spoke again. After a moment a uniformed police officer appeared and muttered to the woman. Lucy could not hear what they were saying. After listening to him, the woman turned to Lucy.

'There is no investigation into the death of Angeline Colbert,' she announced. 'This woman's death was a tragic accident. She had been drinking.'

'OK, thank you,' Lucy said.

She did not feel inclined to argue with the woman. Her visit to the police station had been intimidating and pointless. As she was speaking, the phone on the desk rang. Answering it, the woman raised her hand to detain Lucy.

'Just a moment,' she said. 'You're English, aren't you?'

'Yes, but—'

'Wait here.'

The woman muttered into her phone.

A few seconds later, the uniformed officer returned. He beckoned to her. 'Inspector Joubert will speak with you now. Come this way, please.'

Lucy followed the officer along a corridor to an interview room where two chairs were positioned one on either side of a table. She felt unaccountably nervous, but there was no going back now. The officer who had escorted her there disappeared. All she could do was sit down and wait. After a few moments, the door opened to admit a tall slender man dressed all in grey.

'Good morning. I am Inspector Joubert.' He spoke with an almost perfect English accent. 'I was told you wish to see me?'

'Yes, thank you. We – that is, I – saw your name in the paper in connection with Angeline Colbert.'

'Ah, yes, the woman who fell in the river. It is a very sad case.' He sat down facing her. 'Did you know this woman?'

'No. We – that is, I – I don't think her death was an accident.'

'Indeed, it's hard to believe anyone could fall in the river by accident, but it does happen. You're not from Paris, are you?'

'No. I'm English. From London.'

The inspector's eyes flickered. 'Sadly this woman, Angeline Colbert, was very drunk, too drunk to know what she was doing.'

'The point is,' Lucy went on, 'we think she was murdered.'

The inspector raised his fine eyebrows. For a few seconds he did not say anything.

'Please,' he said at last, 'tell me everything you know about the poor lady who suffered this fatal accident.'

'I want to talk to you about Patrice Durand. We think he may be involved in Angeline Colbert's death.'

The inspector listened in silence as Lucy explained that Angeline Colbert had attempted to kill her friend, acting on instructions from a criminal called Patrice Durand.

'My friend met Angeline Colbert on Monday evening,' she explained, taking care not to mention Alain's name. 'She drugged his drink and tried to kill him. Luckily I got there in time to scare her off and save his life.'

She was afraid the inspector would not believe her, but he sat forward with sudden interest, speaking so quietly she could barely distinguish the words.

'Tell me your name.'

'Lucy Hall.'

'Ah.' He leaned back in his chair. His expression did not alter, but his eyes seemed to stare with renewed intensity. 'Your name is Lucy Hall?'

'Yes.'

'And this incident between your friend and Angeline Colbert, have you mentioned this to anyone else?'

'No. No one else knows about it, apart from my friend.'

'And do you have any proof of this attempted murder?'

'Well, no, not exactly. But we think if you investigate Angeline Colbert's death, you'll find it wasn't an accident. Have you examined the post-mortem report?'

'In this instance a post-mortem is merely a formality. The doctor at the scene confirmed this was an accident and the family were satisfied, as indeed were we. There was no reason to look into this any further as the woman had clearly drowned while under the influence of alcohol.'

'We don't think that's true. We think she was killed before her body entered the water.'

The inspector inclined his head. 'So you say. Very well. We will look into this matter and I will let you know what we find. Tell me, where are you staying?'

Lucy gave him the name of the hotel. He made a note of it.

'Good,' he said. 'Please rest assured that if we find Angeline Colbert was in Le Cheval Rouge on Monday evening, we will look into her death very carefully.'

Lucy thanked him, relieved that he had listened to her and was taking her accusation seriously.

The inspector rose to his feet. 'I take it you are returning to your hotel now to rejoin your friend?'

She nodded.

'Come.' He gestured to her to accompany him.

Lucy stood up and followed him out of the room. He escorted her along the corridor to the entrance hall. She left the police station and set off in what she thought was the right direction along the main road. As she walked, she went over the interview in her mind, rehearsing what she was going to tell Alain. Suddenly she felt her heart pounding. She had not mentioned where Alain had met Angeline Colbert, yet the inspector had known the encounter had taken place at Le Cheval Rouge. Short of being a mind reader, there was no way he could have known this. Alain had told her Patrice was like Teflon as far as the police were concerned, as though someone was protecting him. It had to be Joubert. What was worse, she had told the inspector where they were staying. Frantically she pulled out her phone, hoping she was not too late to warn Alain not to go back to the hotel.

'Alain, oh, thank goodness.'

He sounded half asleep. 'Who did you expect it to be?'

'Listen. Whatever you do, don't go back to the hotel.'

'What?'

'Don't go back to the hotel.'

'What are you talking about? I'm already here. Where did you think I'd be? And where are you?'

'Oh, no. You've got to get out of there now.'

'What's wrong?'

'There isn't time to explain. Just get out of the hotel before they get there.'

'Who?'

'The police. Joubert's working for Patrice.'

'Shit. I thought someone was protecting him.'

Lucy was nearly in tears. 'Joubert must have told Patrice about us by now. Listen Alain, before I realised what he was up to, I told Joubert where we're staying. He's probably on his way there now to arrest us both. You've got to get out of there before they arrive.'

In the background she heard banging and a muffled voice shouting. 'Open up! Police! Open the door!'

Her warning had come too late.

26

SEEING A TAXI CRUISING PAST, Lucy hailed it and jumped in, calling
out the name of the hotel.

'Hurry!' she yelled as they moved out into the slow-moving
traffic. 'I need to get there as quickly as possible!'

Grinning at her in the mirror, the driver gabbled in French
about women and patience. He gave her a toothy grin and looked
away from her as the car revved and shot forward. Hooting wildly, he overtook the car in front of them, narrowly missing a car
speeding towards them on the other side of the road. All Lucy
could do was lean back with her eyes closed and pray that Alain
would escape, as the taxi raced along through the morning rush-
hour traffic. She felt sick. She had no idea what she was going
to do once she reached the hotel, but at least she might have a
chance of rescuing Alain once she was there. She would come up
with something, if he had not already been carted away to a police
cell. Looking out of the window, she did not recognise anything
outside her window. In a panic she shouted out the name of the
hotel. The taxi driver ignored her. She closed her eyes again, fighting not to give in to despair. If Alain was locked up by the police,
it would be her fault.

With a squeal of brakes, the taxi jolted to a halt. She opened her eyes. They had arrived too late. Several police vehicles were already parked outside the hotel entrance.

The taxi driver twisted round in his seat to leer inquisitively at her. 'What's going on here?'

Without stopping to reply, she thrust a handful of notes at him, leapt out and raced into the hotel. The lift seemed to take forever to come down, but she waited. It would be quicker than running up three flights of stairs. At last she was ascending. Dashing out of the lift, she ran along the corridor. Two uniformed policemen were standing outside her room. Alain was trapped. She spun round and ran back towards the lift. A chambermaid was pushing a trolley along the corridor. In desperation, Lucy turned to a fire alarm and punched the glass. It broke with surprising ease. The bell was deafening.

'Fire! Fire!' Lucy screamed at the top of her voice. 'Fire! Save yourselves!'

The chambermaid took up the cry. Abandoning her trolley, she joined Lucy in running along the corridor, banging on doors and shouting. It was still quite early and many of the rooms were occupied. Within seconds several guests appeared in the corridor. Some looked as though they had only just woken up and were wearing dressing gowns or coats over their nightclothes. A few were barefoot.

'This way!' Lucy yelled. 'Hurry! This way! Follow me!'

'Follow that woman!' someone bellowed, and a few other people passed on the message.

Lucy sprinted back along the corridor, with a dozen people at her heels. 'This way to the emergency exit!' she cried out.

As she approached the room she was sharing with Alain, she halted. The door was open. The two policemen were still standing in the corridor with guns in their hands, hesitating. She guessed that Alain must be aiming his own gun at them, to stop them from entering. He would not be able to hold them off for long. The police turned, their eyes wide with surprise, as she gestured to the panicking hotel guests.

'This way!' she shouted. 'The police are here to show you the way! Go past the police through that door to the fire escape!'

'The police are here to help!' a voice rang out from the crowd of people behind her.

More hotel guests and another chambermaid had joined the small crowd that had gathered, alerted by the fire alarm. Without pausing to question why a guest was directing them, or how the police had managed to arrive on the scene so quickly, the queue of people pushed their way into the bedroom where Alain was trapped. The two policemen were swept into the room by the crowd. There was a sudden eruption of noise. It sounded as though everyone was shouting at once. All Lucy could do was slip away before anyone noticed her leaving.

With the fire alarm still ringing, several people were running down the stairs. Lucy joined them. By the time she reached the small entrance hall, it was crammed with hotel guests and staff heading for the exit. An officious concierge was standing on a low stool, waving his arms and shouting out instructions about where to assemble. No one appeared to be listening to him.

'Don't wait to gather up your belongings! Don't run!' he was calling out as Lucy hurried past.

Keeping her head down, she joined a group of young women. Jostling and chattering, they made their way out onto the street. As soon as she was out of the hotel, Lucy hurried across the road without looking back. She reached the Gare du Nord. If anyone had spotted her leaving the hotel, she would be difficult to distinguish as she manoeuvred her way through people crowding the pavement outside the busy station. A couple of fire engines roared past, sirens blaring. No one paid her any attention as she turned into a narrow side street.

All thoughts of finding Patrice forgotten, she hurried towards the café where she and Alain had breakfasted that morning, the one he had designated as their meeting place. There was only the slimmest of chances he would have given the police the slip amid the fracas of panicking people. She had done everything she could think of to help him, but his situation had been virtually hopeless. By far the most likely outcome was that the two police officers had taken him away, or even shot him as he tried to resist arrest. She hesitated to try his phone. He could be hiding somewhere. A ring tone might reveal his presence. There was nothing she could do but wait and hope he would come and find her. Miserably she skulked in the shelter of a shop doorway. Everything had gone horribly wrong. Patrice needed only to return to her flat. He would not have to spend long searching before he found his key. Once it was back in his possession, Lucy would lose any hope of negotiating Nina's release. Meanwhile, she was trapped in Paris, powerless to do anything to help Nina or Alain. Perhaps it was time to accept defeat.

27

As Lucy prevaricated, a voice whispered in her ear. 'I hoped you'd be here.'

She spun round, poised to run. Alain was standing in the shadow of the doorway. Without thinking, she flung her arms round his neck. He pulled away, smiling.

'Well, I'm glad you're pleased to see me, after you nearly got me banged up. Thank goodness I found you. When you let on to Joubert where I was, I barely managed to get out of there alive. Armed police came for me. They were at the door, but luckily there was some ruck at the hotel and I managed to give them the slip.'

'I know,' she giggled. 'I set off the fire alarm.'

'I might have known you were responsible. What were you doing going back there when you knew – oh, never mind. I can see it's not a good idea to let you go off on your own. I lose control of you for one morning—'

'You didn't lose control of me. You never controlled me in the first place.'

'I'm beginning to think someone should.'

'Talk about ungrateful. I just saved you from the police. If it wasn't for my quick thinking creating a diversion, they would have taken you away and locked you up.'

'You weren't exactly thinking quickly when you told them where to find me.'

'I didn't know then that Joubert was working for Patrice, did I?'

It appeared to have slipped Alain's mind that he was the one who had insisted Lucy go and see Inspector Joubert in the first place.

'Yes, well, I'm here now, and no harm done, so let's calm down. We don't want to draw attention to ourselves.' He glanced around the nearly empty side street. 'I could do with something to eat, but let's head back to your flat and pick up Patrice's key first, and then we'll find a safe place to rest and discuss what we're going to do with it.'

As they walked along side streets, avoiding the Gare du Nord, Alain smiled at Lucy. Joubert would not have kept him locked in a cell indefinitely, and would never have risked taking him to court on some trumped-up charge. There was really only one way his arrest could have ended. Yet nothing in his expression betrayed that he had just narrowly escaped capture and death.

'You realise if I hadn't got you out of the hotel, you would have ended up with a bullet in your head?' she said at last.

'Unlikely, I think. Bullets are far too suspicious. And they've already thrown one victim in the canal this week, and another in the river. I rather fancy I would have "committed suicide" by hanging myself in a police cell. There would have been a bit of a fuss over how I got hold of a belt in there, and some poor custody sergeant would most likely have lost his job over it, or his prospect of promotion. After that my death would have been quietly swept under the carpet.' He halted and stared at her seriously. 'Don't you think it's time you left this to me? It's dangerous.'

'I'm not giving up until I find Nina,' Lucy replied, 'even if I have to sleep on the street.'

She refrained from pointing out that so far she was the one offering protection, having saved her companion's life twice.

'I don't think it's going to come to that,' he replied. 'This isn't the first time I've had to stay out of sight. I have friends who can put us up.'

'How can you be sure you can trust them?'

'Oh, they won't blab. You trust me, don't you? Come on, there are enough people working against us as it is. If we can't trust each other, we're totally screwed. Now, let's get that key and then go somewhere off the radar where we can talk about what we're going to do with it.'

Having left all her belongings behind in the flat, Lucy had bought a new toothbrush and toothpaste, and other toiletries, on her way back from McDonald's on their first morning in the hotel. Now she had lost those as well.

'I'm sorry there wasn't time to pack your toothbrush and shampoo,' Alain said when she grumbled about it. 'Perhaps you've forgotten a small matter of two policemen pointing guns in my face.'

Lucy nodded miserably. He was right. Everything they had left behind was replaceable. Alain was lucky to have escaped alive. And with him on her side, at least she would have somewhere to stay. Patrice was clearly looking for her and she wanted to meet him on her own terms.

They made their way back to her flat, zigzagging along a warren of side streets. Approaching the end of the Rue Ferdinand Duval, they spotted several uniformed policemen patrolling the street. Without a word, Alain took her by the elbow and propelled her into a shop. Walking out again a moment later, they turned in the opposite direction and walked quickly away from her flat. It was too dangerous to try and go there.

By a roundabout route, they reached the Boulevard de Magenta and Lucy recognised the Quai de Jemmapes up ahead. As they reached the canal, she spotted the man Alain had referred to as Ferret, scurrying along the opposite pavement. He glanced up and their eyes met.

Lucy grabbed hold of Alain's arm. 'He's there. Over the road.' As she was speaking, Ferret must have realised that she was not alone because he spun round and hurried off.

'He's not getting away this time,' Alain muttered, turning and giving chase.

Disappearing from sight behind a small brick construction beside the canal, Ferret must have vaulted over the waist-high railings, because Lucy next caught sight of him racing down an incline on the other side of them. At the end of the slope, he ran down steps that led to a low tunnel where the dark water flowed under the road. Alain scrambled over the railings in pursuit. Lucy was not sure why Alain was so keen to catch up with him, but she clambered over as well, and hurried down the slope after him. Ahead of her, she could see the man they were following pause at the entrance to the tunnel. Looking over his shoulder, he saw Alain was gaining on him. With a low cry, Ferret stepped onto a narrow towpath beside the canal and disappeared through a metal gateway into the darkness beyond.

'No!' Lucy called out. 'He's not worth it. Don't go in there! It's too dangerous.'

Reaching the tunnel, Alain hesitated for only an instant before going in. A moment later, Lucy reached the entrance. Ahead of her, in the darkness, she could see a small beam of light jolting along slowly. She guessed that Alain was using the torch on his phone to light his way.

'Alain,' she called out softly. 'Alain, come back.' There was no reply. 'Alain!' she called more loudly.

The only response was a faint echo of her own voice bouncing off the dirty brick walls. The ledge she was standing on was very narrow. One false step and she would plunge into the dark water. Gingerly she edged forward, one hand pressed flat against the clammy wall to steady herself. The tunnel smelt foul, and it was cold down there.

Ahead of her, a thin voice reverberated eerily in the darkness. 'What the fuck do you think you're doing? Let go of me!'

'Shut up,' a second voice hissed, panting.

'Or what? You going to shoot an unarmed man?'

There was a confusion of blurred movement in the shadows, before the light abruptly went out. In the darkness Lucy heard a loud splash. Trembling, she took her phone out of her pocket and switched on the torch. In its narrow beam, she made out a single figure ahead of her on the towpath, standing with his back against the tunnel wall. A commotion of splashing and spluttering broke out in the black water below. As Lucy watched, a hand rose out of the water, waving and reaching out. The man on the path leaned forward. Lucy held her breath, wondering if there was anything she could do to help rescue the man who had fallen into the canal.

As she peered through the darkness, an unexpected muffled crack startled her so much that she almost lost her footing. For a second, she thought the roof had split and the tunnel was about to cave in. The reverberations faded into a silence that was absolute. As the solitary figure on the path straightened up, Lucy saw he was holding a gun fitted with a silencer. In the beam of light from her torch she watched in horror as he turned towards her. She did not know who had pulled the trigger, and whether she would be his next victim.

28

DESPITE HER PANIC, Lucy forced herself to move slowly and care-fully as she inched her way back towards the opening of the tunnel. It was not far, but she seemed to be creeping along for hours. At last she was out in the daylight. She could hardly believe there was no crowd of curious onlookers, and no sirens cutting across the quiet hum of traffic. It felt as though she was stepping back in time to the moment before she had followed Alain into the tunnel. It was hard to believe the shooting had passed completely unnoticed above ground. On shaky legs, she toiled up the slope as quickly as she could and climbed back over the railing onto the pavement, only dimly aware of a disapproving glance from an old woman who was passing.

'Lucy, where are you going?'

She halted and waited, trembling with shock, as Alain caught up with her.

'It's all right. He's gone. You're safe now. He can't hurt you any more.'

'You shot him!'

'Keep your voice down.' He glanced around. 'It was the only thing to do. He would've killed you if I hadn't stopped him.'

'What do you mean, he would've killed me? He was running away.'

'He would have come back. Would you prefer to spend the rest of your life looking over your shoulder for him? You know who that was.'

'You shot an unarmed man.'

'Of course he was armed. If I hadn't been there he would have had a gun at your head in a trice. How many times do I have to tell you. These people are dangerous. He'd kill you to get his hands on that key. I told you they call him Ferret. Well, he won't be after you again. Patrice has all sorts of hangers-on, and they have no respect for human life, none at all. Lucy, don't fool yourself you could have escaped. I saw it all. The guy had it coming. He won't be on my conscience.'

'You had a gun. He wasn't armed.'

'You don't know that. And I wasn't going to risk your life by waiting to find out. I wasn't going to take any chances. He would have shot you or knifed you in an instant, given half a chance. I wasn't going to risk your life. Now come on, we need to keep moving and lie low. Patrice is after you.'

Lowering her head to hide her shock, Lucy wondered what could have happened to make Alain feel such hostility towards the man he called Ferret. As far as she could tell, Alain had shot an unarmed man, but there was nothing she could do about that. The man was dead. She couldn't help thinking that at least she would always feel safe with a man who was prepared to kill to protect her, and she was dismayed at how rapidly fear had undermined her principles.

Telling Lucy that he was going to call in a favour from a friend who owned a few apartment blocks, Alain made a phone call. 'Bernard? It's me. I need a bed for the night. I don't suppose you've got an empty room? Anything will do. To be honest, I'm desperate and I can't go home at the moment. It's a long story. Have you got anything?' He listened for a moment, then his face broke into a smile. 'That's great. Thank you. I owe you one.' He listened again. 'Yes, I've got that. It's in the sixteenth, is it?'

After explaining to Lucy that he had helped the property owner get rid of his wife, he stood up. 'By get rid of I mean he divorced her,' he added with a grin.

Lucy did not return his smile.

The address they were looking for was in Rue Bellini in the sixteenth arrondissement, a fairly central area of Paris not far from the Eiffel Tower. They took the Metro to Trocadéro and walked a short distance to the block where Alain had been offered a room. Even in the shade of the tall buildings that flanked the road, the air was uncomfortably hot and stuffy. Reaching their destination, Alain rang the bell. After a delay, the door was opened by a shapeless old woman who stared at them, grinding her teeth.

'Madame,' Alain said, 'a relative of mine lives in this building.' The woman glared at him without speaking. 'He is staying in flat number four. I am his cousin, and this is my niece.'

The woman's eyes swivelled round to stare at Lucy who gave a nervous smile.

'Are you English?' the woman said at last.

'Yes. How did you know?'

The woman shook her head dismissively, and started to close the door.

'Didier is not here,' she grunted.

'I know he's not here. He has gone away for a few days. I am here on holiday in Paris, with my niece. My cousin said we can stay in his room until he returns.'

'Two of you?'

'Yes.'

The woman raised her eyebrows and rolled her eyes, muttering an insult.

'Offer her some money,' Lucy muttered.

The woman's eyes glittered as Alain took his wallet from his pocket.

'Because there are two of us,' Alain explained, withdrawing a note from his wallet.

The woman pointed at Alain's hand and made a beckoning gesture. He handed the money over. Slipping it somewhere in the folds of her skirt, she repeated the gesture. After they had gone through this pantomime a couple of times, Alain held up his hand.

'Enough,' he said. Before she could close the door he added that there would be more money the next day.

With a perfunctory nod, the woman ushered them inside. The door closed behind them. They were safe – or trapped. An old-fashioned lift with a metal grille for a door carried them, rattling and clanking, to the third floor. As they stepped out of the lift, the landlady produced a key from her skirt. Unlocking a high wooden door, she took them into a large room with a double bed. Everything in the room was painted white apart from a tall wooden wardrobe that stood in one corner beside an ornate metal fireplace. At the far end of the room, high shuttered windows opened onto a Juliet balcony not quite wide enough to stand on.

'Where did you say your cousin Didier has gone?' the landlady barked suddenly.

'He'll be back next week,' Alain reassured her.

The landlady grunted and turned to leave.

'Hold on a minute,' Lucy detained her. 'Where's the bathroom?'

The landlady led them back out onto the landing and showed them a tiny shower cabinet with a toilet and sink.

'You haven't given us the key,' Lucy said.

'Where's your cousin's key?' the landlady demanded, scowling at Lucy's outstretched hand.

Alain stepped forward and held out his hand. 'If you don't give us a key, you'll have to give me my money back,' he said, frowning fiercely.

The landlady did not seem intimidated. Lucy hoped she was not going to prove difficult. For all they knew, she might have a huge brute of a husband, and perhaps a son as well, or a vicious dog ready to chase off awkward tenants. Worse, she might call the police. Instead, she whipped a set of keys from her pocket.

'You can have one between you,' she said, slipping two keys from the ring and waving them from Alain to Lucy and back again. 'One set for the two of you.'

Lucy nodded and took the keys from her.

'This one's for the street door,' the woman pointed downwards. 'This is for the door to the apartment,' she pointed to the door of the room. 'Breakfast is ten euros.' She held up ten fingers. 'Each.'

Alain shook his head. 'We won't be wanting breakfast.'

The landlady went over to the bed and pulled at the sheets. 'It'll be another ten euros if you want me to change the sheets.'

'That's all right,' Alain said. 'You can leave the bed as it is. He's my cousin. We're family.'

With a grimace at Lucy, the landlady left. Alain closed the door behind her.

'This is perfect,' Alain said, looking around the room. 'We don't have to get involved in anything official like paying rent, or giving our names and showing our passports and all that, which could be risky. This way it's all kept casual and she won't ask any questions.' He grinned. 'I suppose you want the bed?'

Lucy scowled at him. 'I'll see if there's any clean sheets first.'

She opened the wardrobe and peered at a pair of jeans, a few T-shirts and a jumble of underwear.

'I tell you what,' she said, 'you can have the bed. You're welcome to it. I'll sleep on the chair. I'm not going to sleep in someone else's soiled sheets.' She wrinkled her nose in disgust.

Alain went and stood against the wall, peering down at the street.

'Well?' Lucy called out. 'Is the street out there teeming with police officers scouring the place for us?'

'Two police cars have gone by while I've been standing here,' he answered tersely. 'They're looking for us, without a doubt.'

Lucy shivered. Alain's vigilance no longer struck her as hysterical claptrap.

'So what now?' she asked.

They agreed to sleep on it, and discuss their next move in the morning. Alain was satisfied they would be safe as long as they stayed indoors, although he was not sure they should stay there any longer than one night. There was always a chance someone might trace them. He thought it was best to keep on the move. Lucy's relief that they had escaped the hotel had been short-lived. Settling herself on the only armchair in the room, she struggled against a growing sense of despair. Five days had passed since her flat had been broken into. She had seen how Patrice and his gang killed people whenever they felt like it, and she had no way of knowing if Nina was still alive. Haunted by her fears for Nina's safety, she resolved to get up early and go out before Alain woke. Now that Patrice knew she was still at large, she needed to act quickly. Having reached that decision, she drifted into an uneasy doze.

29

'WHAT DO YOU MEAN, you lost them?' Patrice's voice was steady, but his face was pale.

He was pacing up and down his living room while Joubert lounged in an armchair, his nonchalant posture at odds with his expression.

'How can you lose people?' Patrice demanded. 'They don't just disappear. Or is there a black hole in your police station? You had the girl I want right there with you. What the hell happened to her? How could you let her walk out right under your nose?' His voice rose in exasperation. 'What were you thinking of, letting her go like that?'

Joubert's features contorted in a ghastly rictus as he attempted a reassuring smile. 'They can't have gone far. We'll soon find them. There's no need to get so worked up about it.'

'You had her right there. What the fuck did you think you were doing?' The fury in Patrice's voice was no longer suppressed. 'I told you I wanted her. She's got something of mine, damn her. And damn you too. Why did you let her go?'

'I was afraid it might alert her companion if I detained her. As it was, neither of them suspected a thing. Lucy told me the name of the hotel they were staying in. If I'd kept her, I thought we might run the risk of her companion smelling a rat. He must have known she had come to see me. They had seen my name in the paper—'

'In the paper? What are you? A fucking film star?'

'They printed my name in connection with Angeline Colbert's death. I was quoted as saying it was an accident. I figured they must have arranged between them that she would come and see me. They could have agreed to meet afterwards at a certain time. If she failed to show up, he might have suspected something was wrong. I had her, but I risked losing him if I held onto her. I knew you wanted both of them, so I let her go back to him. That way I was confident I could apprehend them both at the same time in their hotel room. Remember, I knew where they were staying, and their room was on the third floor. There was no way out of there once armed officers were at the door. I had three cars there within minutes of her leaving the police station, and two armed officers knocking at his door minutes after that. In less than five minutes I had him trapped, and she was on her way back to be picked up as soon as she joined him. He couldn't escape from a room on the third floor—'

'But he *did* escape. They both did.' Patrice flung his hands in the air in despair. 'You had her and you let her walk, and you had him cornered with – in your words – no way of escaping. So? Where are they? What are you playing at? If you've double-crossed me, I'll have you exposed before you have a chance to end your miserable life. The scandal will finish your wife. She won't even get her hands on your pension.'

Joubert inhaled deeply, determined not to panic under the barrage of threats. He had heard them before. It was unusual for Patrice to lose his temper, because he usually got his own way. But Joubert was a trained police detective. Self-control had become second nature to him.

'Be logical,' he said calmly. 'They can't go back to the hotel. They'll have to go somewhere.'

'Somewhere?' Patrice fumed. 'What kind of an answer is that? I want them found, and I want them brought here, or you'll be sorry you were ever born. You have twenty-four hours.'

Joubert stood up and faced Patrice squarely. 'Are you threatening me?' he asked quietly.

'You're damn right I'm threatening you, and I'll threaten every member of your family too if I have to.'

'Leave them out of it.'

'Don't you tell me what to do, you imbecile.'

'That's a bit rich, after all I've done for you. Haven't I served you well? Where would you be now without my protection?'

'Your protection?' Patrice sneered. 'The protection of an incompetent fool. Have you forgotten that other English whore? How come you didn't realise she was the wrong girl? Didn't you ask her name when she was brought to your police station, after that idiot Marcel managed to lose her?'

Joubert shrugged. About to retort that Patrice had not realised he had abducted the wrong girl either, instead he attempted to be conciliatory.

'I can get rid of her for you, Patrice. You have only to say the word.'

Patrice shook his head and sat down, his anger spent. 'No. I'll hang onto her for now. She's going to be useful. She'll help me persuade Lucy Hall to give me what I want. But first we need to find Lucy Hall. See to it, Olivier. This has dragged on long enough. I want her found. Now get out of my sight. Oh, one more thing before you go.'

Joubert paused. Despite his attempt to stay cool, he was terrified.

'Don't be surprised if your wife and children aren't at home when you get there.'

'What have you done?'

'I haven't touched your family. Yet. They're nothing to me.' He snapped his fingers and the diamond in his ring glittered. 'Listen,

Olivier,' Patrice went on, dropping his voice and adopting a reasonable tone. 'You know you're far too useful for me to risk upsetting you unless I have to. But everyone's dispensable. Even you.' He sat down and leaned back in his chair with his eyes closed. 'You know my terms,' he added softly. 'You've got twenty-four hours.'

Muttering a curse, Joubert hurried from the room. As soon as he closed the door, he snatched his phone from his pocket and hit the speed-dial number for his home. The line was busy. He tried his wife's mobile phone. It went straight to voice mail. With growing dread, he sprinted to his car, trying to remember if this was one of the evenings when his wife went out, but he could not even remember what day of the week it was. He exceeded the speed limit all the way home. Dashing into the house, he screamed out his wife's name. She emerged from the kitchen, drying her hands on a tea towel.

'Olivier, what is it? What's wrong?'

'Why didn't you answer your phone?'

'What?'

'Your phone. Why didn't you answer it?'

She shook her head. 'It must be in my bag. I'm sorry. I didn't hear it. What's wrong?'

He shook his head, barely able to speak. 'Where are the boys?'

'They're in the backyard.'

He ran to the kitchen. Through the window he could see his two sons, kicking a football around.

'Olivier, what is it? What's wrong?'

'Nothing,' he murmured, putting his arms around his wife and pulling her close so she could not see the fear in his eyes. 'Everything's fine. But I'm going to have to work this evening.'

'Oh, Olivier, you said you'd be home.'

'Something's come up. I'm sorry. Don't wait up. I may be late.'

'Are you sure you're all right?'

'I told you, I'm fine. I'm sorry, but I have to get back. Tell the boys to come inside, and then bolt the back door. Do it now. Put the chain on the front door after I've gone, and don't open it for anyone until I get home, not even if it's someone you know.'

'Olivier, what's going on? What's happened? Tell me!'

Ignoring her anxious protest, he turned and hurried from the house.

30

ONCE AGAIN ALAIN WAS UP and preparing to go out before Lucy was fully awake.

'Here, take this,' he said, handing her a wad of notes.

Remonstrating feebly, she pocketed the money, promising to return it later. It was as well to be prepared for any eventuality.

'And this,' he added, holding out a small handgun. 'Don't worry, the safety catch is on. Go on, take it. You might need it for protection. But don't shoot unless you have to. You do know how to use a gun, don't you? No, I don't suppose you do. Look, you pull this, after taking off the safety catch just here.'

Lucy nodded. Too shocked to pay attention to his instructions, she slipped the gun in the pocket of her jeans all the same. It was surprisingly small, considering the damage it could wreak. Under normal circumstances she would never have taken it. She did not approve of guns. But these were not normal circumstances. Even though the safety catch was on, having the weapon made her feel safe.

As they crossed the hallway and left the building, Lucy glanced at her companion. His face was wan beneath its dark stubble. Even his friends might struggle to recognise him. They hurried outside and strode past several Metro signs, taking a zigzagging route through the city. After a couple of miles Alain turned and hurried down the stairs into a station, with Lucy scurrying at his heels.

'Where are we going?' she asked him when they were finally seated together on a train.

'I'm taking you somewhere safe.'

They changed trains. She followed him through the crowded station, involuntarily turning away from any cameras she saw. At 8.30 in the morning the stations were packed with Parisians going to work, crowded together with holidaymakers off on a day's excursion. A large group of Japanese tourists spilled onto the platform as Lucy and Alain waited for their next train. They kept their heads down, until finally they reached the Gare du Nord.

'What are we doing?'

Taking no notice of her question, he strode on.

'Wait here,' he said, suddenly darting away.

Standing at the side of the station, Lucy waited with increasing indignation. She was not sure what Alain was up to and by the time he eventually rejoined her, she was furious.

'What's going on?'

'Come on!' he muttered, heading off towards the Eurostar platform. 'You're getting on the next train. Here.' He handed her a passport. 'Your name's Maisie Smith. The photo's not a great likeness, but it's close enough. It'll get you back to London anyway. Here's your ticket. Go on, hurry. They're going through security already. Give me back the gun.'

'What are you talking about? I'm not going back to London.'

Taking her by the elbow, Alain steered her towards the departure lounge. With so many travellers milling about, their altercation went virtually unnoticed. They must have looked like a father and daughter having a row. In a low voice, Alain explained that it was time for her to return to London.

'No one knows we're here. This could be your last chance to get through passport control and onto a train. The longer you stay in Paris, the more the danger will escalate. You've been lucky so far—'

'What about Nina?'

Alain looked around with an impatient frown. 'Lucy, we haven't got much time. Tell me where you've hidden the key. I need to deal with Patrice once and for all. Don't worry, I'll do my best to rescue your friend. With her as a witness, the police are going to have to take this seriously. You must see that it's crazy for you to stay here any longer. Now we know Patrice has Nina, there's nothing you can do for her. Your only hope is to get back to England and alert the authorities there to what's happening. Get onto the British police and Interpol, write to your MP.'

Lucy had to admit what he was saying probably made sense, but he was talking about her abandoning Nina so she could persuade the English authorities to take action. At best there might be a delay of days, or even weeks, for political or bureaucratic reasons. Realistically, nothing at all was likely to happen in time to save Nina, if she was still alive.

'What if she's being tortured? We have to save her, Alain.'

'I'm sorry,' he said, propelling her forwards, 'it's too late for that. Patrice is a sociopath who kills on a whim. Now you've been to see Joubert, it's only a matter of time before Patrice learns he's got the wrong girl, if Ferret hasn't already told him. It's you he's after. Your friend's no use to him.'

'That means there's a chance he'll let her go once he knows he's got the wrong person.'

Alain shook his head. 'You have to stop this, Lucy.'

'So you're determined to see Patrice arrested, and you don't care about what happens to Nina.'

Alain stopped and turned to look at her. 'Is it so wrong to want to save other people from him?'

'If it costs one life, it's wrong. You've got no right to tell me to abandon Nina.'

'Surely you realise when you gave Joubert your name, you as good as signed Nina's death warrant? Patrice must know by now Nina can't help him. Why would he keep her alive, when she's a potential witness against him?' He glanced around and continued rapidly. 'Give me the code for the keypad to your street door, and tell me where you've hidden Patrice's key, and believe me, one way or another, Patrice will be finished. I should have done this a long time ago. He's the one we need to focus on now. You have to forget about Nina.'

'Would you be so quick to give up if it was your brother's life at risk? What if it was your life?'

'Lucy, listen to me—'

'No, I won't listen any more.'

Turning on her heel, she ran. At last she understood that Alain had never been interested in helping her rescue Nina. He condemned Patrice as a cold-hearted killer, but she had seen Alain himself shoot a drowning man. Now he wanted to force her to leave France. She had been a fool to believe a word he said. He was just another heartless killer. Trusting him had wasted precious time. All that mattered was finding Nina and, with Patrice's key in her possession, Lucy might be able to rescue her.

Glancing around, she hurried towards the exit. Joubert was bound to have officers out on the streets and stations looking for her, and he would have been able to give them an accurate description of her with dark hair. She must have been caught on CCTV entering the police station. Her picture had probably been circulated to every police officer in Paris. As she hurried outside, a gendarme caught sight of her. He started forward, bawling something about security.

With a stab of terror, she ran over to the line of people waiting for taxis and shouted to the woman at the front of the queue, 'I need to get to the doctor's. This is an emergency! I'm pregnant!'

She was not sure how she had managed to convince the woman. She hardly looked pregnant. Nevertheless, taken by surprise, the woman stepped back and allowed Lucy to wrench open the door of the first waiting taxi. A red-faced man ran forward shouting in protest at her jumping the queue. Lucy slammed the door in his face.

Frantic to get away from the Gare du Nord, she shouted out the first thing that came into her head. 'The Eiffel Tower!'

She hoped the driver had not heard her shouting that she was pregnant, but he nudged his way out into the heavy traffic without turning round. She sat back and tried to control her panic. Her phone rang. She checked the screen and saw Alain's number. She ignored it. Once she reached the Eiffel Tower, and was sure no one was following her, she would take another taxi to the street where Patrice lived. She had no idea yet what she was going to do when she finally met him face to face, but she was determined to rescue Nina. Patrice might be brutal, but he would have to listen to reason and release Nina in exchange for his key. As she closed her eyes, the sound of a siren cut through the buzz of traffic. Peering over her shoulder, she swivelled back to face the driver.

'Hurry!' she called out in a panic. 'I need to get there very quickly!'

She looked through the back window again. A police car was sitting in the traffic behind them.

'Hurry up!' she urged the driver.

Muttering an expletive, the driver swung the wheel and turned off the busy main street into a narrow side turning. Lucy looked out of the back window. The police car was still behind them. As soon as they approached the Eiffel Tower she determined to throw her money onto the front passenger seat, leap out and vanish before the police car reached her. Fishing in her pocket for her purse she felt Alain's gun, cold and hard. Not having wanted it in the first place, she was tempted to slip it down the side of her seat and leave it behind in the taxi, but she was afraid it would have her fingerprints on it. She wondered if she dared put it in her bag, but did not want to risk the driver spotting it in his mirror. Nervously she turned to look out of the back window. The police car was drawing closer.

31

As LUCY'S TAXI APPROACHED the base of the tower, the driver slowed down. Ahead of them she saw several other taxis and a couple of tour buses draw up.

'Here we are,' the driver called over his shoulder.

Lucy glanced behind her. The police car was only a few yards away. Without stopping to ask how much he wanted, she threw a fistful of money onto the passenger seat beside the driver and leapt out of the crawling vehicle, taking no notice of the driver's shout of surprise. She almost lost her footing as she reached the ground. The entrance to the tower was about a hundred yards away from the road. Recovering her balance, she raced towards a line of tourists leaving a tour bus, and slipped in among them. A couple of women cast puzzled glances at her, but most of them were so busy looking upwards as they made their way towards the base of the tower, they did not even notice her. It loomed overhead like a huge, grey electricity pylon. Passing a kiosk, Lucy thrust a fifty-euro note at the vendor, grabbed a straw hat and pulled it on. Ignoring the man shouting at her to take her change, she rejoined the group crossing the main concourse that led beneath the tower.

As she followed the crowd, Lucy gazed up at the iron construction, an impressive feat of human ingenuity. Despite its spectacular height, there was something harsh and uncompromising in its magnificence, the people below it dwarfed into insignificance. Glancing around beneath the brim of her new hat, she saw that several police cars had arrived on the road behind her. There was no way of knowing whether they were there as a matter of routine, or if they were looking for her. She wondered if they would arrest her in plain sight of all the tourists milling around. Spotting a gang of security guards immediately ahead of her, she slipped into the queue for the nearest ticket office. No one challenged her. The queue zigzagged slowly between low metal railings. Wherever she looked, uniformed guards were patrolling the main concourse. They could have been searching for someone. As the line shuffled forwards, she kept her face concealed beneath her hat. A security guard policing the queue barely glanced at her as he checked inside her bag to make sure that she was not carrying a glass bottle. It was lucky she had not been able to put the gun in her bag. The irony of it made her smile.

Keeping her head lowered, she bought her ticket without a hitch. She had escaped notice so far, but this was not a time for self-congratulation. She still had to get away from the place without being spotted, and find her way to Patrice's house. Instead of pretending to be a Hollywood scout, she might be better off simply announcing her real name. It was a risk to presume he would not recognise her. But then again, it might work, and there was no time to try to think of a better plan, so she decided to stick with it. In the meantime, she had to concentrate on escaping from the Eiffel Tower. Ignoring her phone ringing in her pocket, she followed the queue of people moving towards the lift. While other people manoeuvred their way to the sides, eager to see views of the city, Lucy stood as far from the glass walls of the lift as she could. It irked her to miss a clear view of the panorama below, but she could not risk being spotted by armed police patrolling the concourse and guarding the entrance. She had succeeded in slipping inside under their watchful eyes. It would be next to impossible to pull it off a second time and leave unobserved. Everywhere she looked, she saw police on the ground. The lift carried her upwards, further away from her pursuers, but there was only so far she could go. It was one of the stupidest hiding places she could have chosen. She had trapped herself.

On the second floor, visitors transferred to another lift that would take them to the top of the tower. Lucy felt relatively safe waiting in the crowd. Entering the next lift, once again she stayed in the centre. At last they reached the summit. The city looked wonderful from that high vantage point. Maps above the viewing spaces specified the distance to other major cities. London was less than three hundred miles away. It might as well have been three hundred light years. She turned and saw a guard watching the doors to the lift. Quickly she followed the crowd up a short flight of stairs that led to the summit. It was chilly at the top of the tower, despite the heat on the ground. The view was phenomenal, but she did not have time to stand gazing out, instead she had to watch out for people coming up behind her. If she blundered now, there would be no escape.

Going back down the stairs, she noticed a group of English-speaking schoolgirls crowded in front of a display.

'You've all been to Madame Tussaud's?' a woman was saying to them. Lucy guessed she was their teacher. 'This scene shows Gustave Eiffel. You can see a recreation of his office with the gramophone presented to him by Thomas Edison, and that's the figure of Eiffel's daughter in the background.'

Noticing a security guard hovering near her, Lucy removed her hat and tried to slip in among the schoolgirls without attracting their attention. She had reached the tower pretending to be a member of a bus tour. Perhaps she could escape in the same way, attaching herself to a group of students. They did not look very much younger than her.

'Gustav Eiffel,' one of the girls read the name aloud. 'Never heard of him.' She turned to her friends. 'Who is he anyway?'

'It must be his tower. It's the Eiffel Tower, innit?'

'I think he was the architect who designed it,' she mumbled at a girl who was standing on her own at the edge of the group.

Seeing her talking to the other girls, the guard lost interest and walked on. It was a good idea to stick to her new acquaintances for as long as she could.

'My name's Claire,' Lucy said, making a mental note to remember her assumed name.

As Lucy had guessed, the group of girls were on a school trip. They were younger than she had first thought, probably no older than thirteen, but several of them were as tall as her, and most of them did not look any younger than her. The girl at her side latched onto her. She introduced herself as Hannah. Lucy noticed that the other girls seemed to shun her. Gabbling excitedly, Hannah told Lucy they were staying with French students. While their hosts were at school, the English girls had been brought to the Eiffel Tower.

'This is crap. I thought it would be like the Tower of London,' one of the girls said, 'you know, with dungeons underground and torture chambers.'

Hannah sniggered. 'How could there be underground dungeons in a tower?'

'They got dungeons at the Tower of London, haven't they?' the other girl retorted. 'And before you start, no one wants a lecture from you about the history of the Eiffel Tower.' She turned to Lucy. 'Hannah's such a know-all.'

'It's perfectly reasonable to read up about the Eiffel Tower before coming here,' Hannah retorted.

'Oh, shut up, swot.'

Hannah's unpopularity was good news for Lucy, if not for Hannah. With Hannah's help she might be able to tag along with the group and get away from the tower.

'What else do you know about Gustav Eiffel?' Lucy asked. 'Was I right that he was an architect?'

Hannah linked arms with her and launched into a life history of Gustav Eiffel. As she was talking, a harassed-looking woman hurried over to them and began rounding them up. She gave Lucy a quizzical look.

'This is Claire, Miss Parker,' Hannah said.

'Not at school today, Claire?' the teacher asked.

Lucy responded with a shy nod. The teacher had mistaken her for a French girl. If Lucy replied, the error might become apparent. With a worried smile, the teacher continued assembling her charges, badgering them to stand still while she did a head count. Lucy heaved a sigh of relief.

'Come along now,' the teacher called out. 'Keep up, everyone. Don't straggle.'

The girls trooped back to the exit with Hannah talking to Lucy all the way down. Lucy did not blame the other girls for ignoring them. Hannah was no fun. Nevertheless, she served Lucy's purposes perfectly, and she so clearly enjoyed having an audience that Lucy barely felt guilty for taking advantage of her isolation. As one of the group of girls, Lucy walked away from the tower right in front of a row of security guards and police.

'Have you seen their guns?' one of the girls squawked.

'The security here is very good,' the worried-looking teacher said. 'Makes you feel safe. Now come along.'

Seeing so many police patrolling the area, Lucy considered

climbing aboard the bus with Hannah, but she could not maintain her subterfuge indefinitely and besides, she had no idea where they were going. At the last minute she slipped her arm out of Hannah's, darted out of sight around the bus and ran to a taxi that had just dropped someone off.

32

A ROUGH VOICE WAS SHOUTING HER NAME. Nina blinked. In the semi-darkness she made out the bulky figure of a man in the door-way of the cellar.

'Nina! Nina! Come with me!'

With difficulty she hauled herself up into a sitting position. She was confused. Somehow her captors had learned her name. Her head ached. She had been lying in one position on the hard floor for so long that her back hurt. Her wrists and ankles were tied tightly and she moved stiffly. Every movement stung the weals on her arms and back where she had been beaten for attempting to escape.

'You need to untie me if you want me to move.'

She raised her feet off the ground. The man glared at her and spat on the floor.

'Come with me!' he shouted.

Nina did not recognise him. Even in the dim light of the cellar she could see his hair was so thick and yellow it looked unnatural. Either he dyed it, or else he was wearing a ridiculous wig.

'I'll go with you, but you need to untie my legs so I can walk.'

He reached down and slashed the cords that bound her ankles with one quick swipe of a small knife.

'You follow me!' he yelled again. 'Follow me!'

'I'm coming as quickly as I can, but my legs are really stiff.'

'Come with me!'

'I'm being as quick as I can,' she repeated nervously.

She clambered to her feet, supporting herself with one arm pressed against the cold wall. Standing upright made her feel dizzy and sick. All the same, she staggered clumsily after the blonde man. It seemed to take her a long time to cross the cellar but at last she was following him up a stone staircase and along several corridors and more stairs, until he led her into a large dining room where the carpet felt soft beneath her bare feet.

Seated at a wooden table, Patrice did not look up when she entered the room. Her mouth watered at the warm salty smell of his steak and chips. He waved his hand, and Sacha darted forward to whip his plate away. Slowly, Patrice gulped from a glass of red wine, swilling it around his mouth before cutting himself a generous slice from a chocolate cake on the table. Engrossed in his task, he did not appear to have noticed Nina.

'She is here!' the yellow-haired man shouted suddenly.

Patrice raised his eyebrows and nodded without looking up. 'I've got eyes.'

Unhurriedly, he finished his cake and took another sip of wine, rolling it around his mouth, savouring the taste. At last he put his glass down. His blue eyes twinkled in a smile as he looked directly at Nina, but his voice was cold.

'Where do you suppose your friend, Lucy Hall, is hiding? I rather hoped to have found her by now. Where is she?' He thumped the table suddenly with his fist and shouted, making Nina jump. 'Where the fuck has she got to?' Scowling, he raised his glass. 'She must know where you are. It seems she doesn't care what happens to you. Or does she think she can play games with me and get away with it?' He took another sip of wine. 'No one gets the better of me.

No one. And certainly not some English whore. So I can tell you, whatever it is she thinks she's playing at, it's not going to end well for either of you.'

He leaned forward and cut himself a second slice of cake. Nina tried not to look at him. Aware that she was not going to be offered anything to eat, she struggled to hide her disappointment.

'Are you hungry?' he asked, smiling.

'No.'

His smile broadened. He knew she was lying. She pressed her lips tightly together and stared at the floor. The carpet was dark red with a complex design of intricate geometric patterns that seemed to squirm around as she stared down at them. She blinked, close to tears, trying to pretend it was only hunger that was making her tremble. But he knew it was fear.

'Soon,' Patrice said, suddenly brisk, 'you're going to phone your friend. You know what's going to happen to you if you fail to bring her here.' He sighed, shaking his head as though he regretted the situation that he himself had created. 'Sacha could break your neck with one hand. All I've got to do is give him a nod and he'll be happy to oblige, just to please me.'

Sacha took a step forward, eagerly.

Patrice waved him back. 'But then I ask myself, what's the point of that? One more dead whore isn't going to get me what I want. And I always get what I want. So, I'm going to give you one last chance to save your miserable life, at least for now. Call that whore, Lucy Hall, and tell her to come here tonight. When she hears your voice begging her to save your life, she won't stay away. If you want to live till tomorrow, just make sure she's here tonight.'

'I don't know anyone in Paris. I don't know what you're talking about. I don't know anyone called Lucy.'

Patrice's lips curled in a sneer. He saw straight through her pathetic attempt to protect her friend.

'You were staying in her flat, living with her. You even let me believe you were her. So stop thinking you can fuck me about. She's going to come here. And if she doesn't come tonight, the police will find her and bring her to me soon enough. That won't be very pleasant for her, but you won't be around to see how they treat her.' He smiled. 'They're right bastards, aren't they, Sacha? They make us look like good Samaritans. But whatever happens, neither of you walks out of here until I get what I want.' His voice softened. His cajoling tone made her cringe. 'If you help me, we can finish this tonight. I'll have no further use for you, and you can go home. But if you refuse to help me . . .' He broke off, shaking his head again.

Remembering the woman in the red dress, Nina shivered. Patrice would never let her go. She had seen too much. Fear made her bold. Staring straight ahead, she was surprised by the strength of her own voice.

'No way am I going to ask her to come here. Threaten me as much as you like, but I'll never help you to find her. Never ever ever! I won't be a part of it!'

Patrice glared at her, his large face flushed with anger, his high-backed wooden chair creaking beneath his shifting weight. Nina's legs shook until she could hardly stand. Watching Patrice intently, the yellow-haired thug stirred. The atmosphere in the quiet room grew oppressive with menace. Suddenly, Patrice flung his huge head back and laughed. His accomplice stepped back, glaring at Nina. She was afraid she was going to collapse at Patrice's feet. Only the thought that her fear would amuse him gave her the strength to stay upright.

'I won't break your friend's neck if she returns what she stole from me,' Patrice said softly.

'She's not a thief. She never stole anything,' Nina shouted hoarsely, but her voice had lost all conviction. She had no idea what Patrice was talking about.

At a nod from Patrice, the yellow-haired man approached Nina. Seeing him draw something from his pocket, she let out an involuntary whimper. The image of the woman in a bright red dress flashed across her mind once more. In that instant of terror, she was conscious only of her desire to live. She would have told Patrice anything he wanted to know. Her legs shaking uncontrollably, she watched Sacha take a packet of cigarettes from his pocket. He lit one and handed it to Patrice who leaned back in his chair, gazing upwards.

'Isn't this beautiful?' he asked her, waving his hand in the direction of the ceiling. 'Don't you think it's beautiful?'

Nina looked up at the high ceiling, as ornate as the ceiling in a grandiose palace. Normally she would have admired the stunning artwork. As it was, she barely grunted.

'And what's really beautiful about it is that it's all mine,' Patrice went on, seemingly in an expansive mood. 'All of it. An ignorant whore like you wouldn't know it's a replica of a segment of the Sistine Chapel in Rome. Tourists travel from all around the world to see that, but I can look at it any time I want. You think this is impressive, but the villa I'm building is going to be a hundred times bigger and better.' He grinned, showing yellowing teeth. 'Sadly you won't get to see it, but I can tell you, it's going to be fantastic. There's no space here for decent-sized grounds, and I need space. My dogs like to run around. Those dogs love me. You know why? Because I'm good to them. Aren't I good to those dogs, Sacha?'

His accomplice nodded his head.

Patrice carried on. 'I made this house myself, from nothing. I wasn't born with a silver spoon in my mouth. No, I was born with fuck all and I built this house with my own hands. But it's nothing compared to what I'm going to build next!'

Nina looked up in surprise. 'You built this house yourself?'

'Yes! With my own money—'

'Stolen money,' she muttered, lowering her head.

'Don't insult me.' He banged the flat of his hand on the table, making her flinch. Her reaction made him laugh. 'When I clap my hands, men tremble. Do you want to know why?' She didn't answer. 'I'll tell you why. I'm the power today, the real power. Politicians, huh!' he snapped his fingers. 'They depend on the support of other people. The owners of large corporations, the heads of banks, all of them, they rely on the support of other people. They're no more free than you are, and do you want to know why? Because they must all be seen to follow the rules. Don't be caught breaking the law. Don't do this. Don't do that. This isn't allowed. That's not allowed. Their hands are tied, as tightly as yours are. You've got that in common with the President of France himself. But not me. All these so-called powerful men depend on other people. Everyone does, but not me. I'm the only one who understands the secret of real power, and it's so simple.' He smiled at her, a genuine smile that lit up his whole face. 'I hold your life in my hands. That's true power. No one can stop me from doing whatever I want. And no law's ever going to control me. I've got real power, and I'm not afraid to use it.'

He rose to his feet and turned to Sacha. 'It's time.'

Nina's legs threatened to give way, but once again his companion did not draw a gun. Instead he held out a mobile phone.

'Call this Lucy Hall and tell her to come here,' Patrice barked. 'She knows where I live. And you can tell her she has to come here tonight if she wants to see you alive. Do it.'

With trembling fingers, Nina dialled Lucy's number. She knew it off by heart. The phone rang but there was no answer.

'It says the line is no longer in use,' she whispered.

'Try again. I'm not waiting around forever,' he said, raising his voice impatiently. 'Call again. If you don't speak to her, you'll never see her again. In fact,' he continued more quietly, 'you'll never see anyone again.'

33

THE TAXI DRIVER TOOK LUCY across the river through the sixth and fifth arrondissements, to the Rue Saint-Séverine. She waited until he had driven off before she turned and made her way along the road, searching for the lane that led to Patrice's property. Recognising the place, she sat on the grass and rehearsed what she was going to say. As long as her American accent was convincing, Patrice would hopefully have no inkling who she really was. She planned her speech until the sun set and she could procrastinate no longer. Alone in the gathering darkness, she was beginning to suspect it had been a mistake to wait until so late in the day. She would have done better to have waited until the morning to contact Patrice, but Nina was in trouble. Realistically, there was probably nothing Lucy could do to rescue her friend; guilt was driving her to pursue a reckless course.

As furious as she was with Alain for betraying her trust, she bitterly regretted having left him. At least he had been willing to protect her. Now she was on her own, lost, and it was growing dark. His concern for her welfare had been genuine, she was sure of that. Fiercely dismissing her regrets, she reminded herself that Alain was a cold-blooded killer. Morally he was no better than Patrice. She was better off on her own. But recalling how he had looked after her, she felt bereft.

Reaching the corner, she was relieved to recognise the grassy area of trees where she had walked with Alain. She strode on with renewed confidence. The lane was not completely dark. Pale street lamps illuminated the path at intervals. As the lights became less frequent she hesitated, tempted to turn round and make her way back to the river. Once she found a Metro station she could go to the British Embassy near the Avenue des Champs-Élysées. Even without her passport, she could appeal for help there, claiming that she had been mugged and had lost everything. But the embassy would not be open until the morning. The sensible course would have been to accept Alain's offer to get her on a train out of France. She could have been in London by now, with a serviceable false passport in her pocket. Yet even if the authorities in the UK had accepted her story, she doubted she would have been able to mobilise them in time to save Nina. She had no option but to press on and speak to Patrice. There was a chance she could save Nina. She would never be able to live with the guilt if she backed out now.

It was not too late in the evening to attempt to lie her way into the house by masquerading as a film scout, and effect an escape for the two of them. Only as a last resort was she going to reveal her true identity. Her mind seemed to be operating on two levels, her reason telling her it was crazy to continue, while her emotions drove her on. However scared she felt, she clung to the thought that she and Nina were going to walk away from this together. In the meantime, she could not stand there dithering all night. She gazed around. The last glow of daylight vanished. There was no moon. In the darkness, nothing looked familiar. She was not sure whether she had taken the wrong turning and was completely lost, or was going in the right direction, stumbling in darkness towards Patrice's house and whatever dangers awaited her there. Taking a deep breath, she walked on.

Catching her foot on a tree root, she cried out in alarm. Her heart raced. Leaning back against the trunk of the tree, she reached out behind her to touch the bark. Rough and warm against the palms of her hands, the solidity of the trunk was somehow reassuring. The tree had probably been growing there before she was born. Impervious to her terror, its leaves rustled softly in a night breeze blowing high above her head. Closing her eyes as she waited for her pounding heart rate to slow, she inhaled a faint scent of grass and damp earth. She had no idea how long she stood there, paralysed with indecision. Whichever way she turned, she faced uncertainty and menace.

A sound carried on the still air. She opened her eyes a slit. Darkness. It reached her again, a whisper in the air, a footstep, all but inaudible. She closed her eyes and held her breath, listening. This time there was no doubt. Someone was walking towards her along the lane. A twig cracked not far behind her. Hearing a muttered curse nearby, she opened her eyes. She could not see anyone. An instant later a beam of light flashed on the ground ahead of her. Whoever was walking along the path had tripped and switched on a torch to light the way. Lucy began edging her way around the tree, out of sight. Before she could hide, the beam of light spun round.

'Who's there?'

Blinded by the torch shining in her face, Lucy shut her eyes. She had not been able to see who was behind the light, but the voice was unfamiliar. Too late she darted behind the tree. Alone and defenceless, she had nowhere to hide. The light approached, footsteps shuffling cautiously on the uneven ground. Circling the trunk, the stranger stood in front of her, shining his torch at her face. Fumbling in her pocket, she felt the hard cold metal of Alain's gun. Slowly she drew it out. As if in a dream, she raised her trembling hand. The stranger blurted out a curse. The beam of light from his torch wobbled as he took a step back.

'Who are you?' Lucy called out, past caring that her shaking voice might betray her fear. 'Are you Patrice? Answer me!'

The figure lowered his torch.

'Who are you?' Lucy repeated. 'What are you doing here?' The gun shook in her hand. 'Answer me before I shoot you right between the eyes.'

She hoped the stranger would not realise that not only could she not see him clearly, but she did not have the foggiest idea how to use a gun. All her instincts screamed at her to drop the weapon before there was an accident, but she clung on to it, frantically picking at the safety catch as Alain had shown her. Nothing happened. Through her terror, she was only dimly conscious that she had gained control of the situation. The stranger must be far more frightened than she was. He did not know her threat to shoot him was mere bluster.

'Answer me!' she insisted, her voice becoming firm. 'Answer me before I shoot you.'

For a long moment they stood confronting one another in silence. Lucy struggled to keep her hand steady, aware that she had just threatened to shoot a complete stranger dead. She had not stopped to consider whether he was armed. If she killed him, she would be no different to Alain who had shot a man, possibly with the gun she was now holding. Her hand shook. With a sudden cry, the stranger raised his torch and shone it directly at her eyes. Blinking, she fell back. Before she could recover her balance, he lunged forward. A strong hand grabbed her by the wrist and twisted her arm painfully up behind her back.

'No. Let go. You're hurting me.'

There was a deafening report as the gun went off and fell from her grasp. Terrified that she had shot herself, she was dimly aware of the man swearing, but he was not crying out in pain. Dazed with shock, she moved her legs in the darkness and was relieved to discover she was uninjured. The man was shouting at her. Given that she had nearly put a bullet in his head, it was hardly surprising that he sounded furious. The gunshot right by his ear must have frightened him as much as it had her.

'I wasn't going to shoot you, not really. I've never shot anyone in my life. I don't like guns. I think they should be banned,' she babbled in panic. 'It's not my gun. I don't even know how to use it. I don't know why it just went off like that. I thought the safety catch was on. The safety catch should've been on.'

Still swearing in fright, the stranger bent down to retrieve the weapon she had dropped. There was no doubt he knew how to use it. With his torch no longer pointing directly in her face, dazzling her, she could see him glaring as he turned Alain's gun on her.

'I'm sorry, I'm sorry,' Lucy cried out in terror, holding her hands up in the air. 'Please don't shoot me. I'm here to speak to Patrice Durand. I don't want to hurt anyone. I just want to speak to him.'

Seizing her roughly by the arm, the man shoved her forwards. Stumbling and tripping, she staggered along the path. She had no choice. Even if the man had not been armed, there was no way she could overpower him or outrun him. They walked on, the silence of the night punctuated by their shuffling footsteps, and the low hoarse wheezing of her companion's breathing. In the passing torchlight, trunks of tall trees emerged and vanished again into the darkness. The path she had followed to Patrice's house with Alain had not seemed nearly as long as this.

After they had crossed seemingly endless rough terrain, the ground smoothed out into a gravel path bordered with trees and a wide grass verge. This was more like the approach to Patrice's house that she remembered. She took a deep breath and marched in front of the man with growing optimism. She was about to meet Patrice and persuade him to let Nina go. After all that had happened, everything was going to be all right. She had been right to persevere.

Metal gates appeared in front of them, looming high above the path, impossible to breach. Their approach triggered Patrice's security system, flooding the path in front of them with light, illuminating the wrought-iron fence topped by vicious spikes. With the view on the far side of the railings obscured by thick hedges, the property was impenetrable. They walked up to the gate. The man pressed a button and spoke into an intercom, before grunting at her and pushing her forward. Lucy cleared her throat, preparing to announce herself.

'Who are you, and what do you want?'

Just in time Lucy remembered she was posing as an American. Hoping her escort would not think it odd that she had pulled a gun on him, she spoke up. She had nothing to lose by sticking to her plan. 'My name is Angie Baker,' she called back, hoping the man accompanying her would not comment on her sudden change of accent. 'I work for a Hollywood film production company as a location scout. We're on the lookout for a villa near Paris, France.' She had heard Americans refer to her own home city as London, England, and was sure there must be a town called Paris in the United States. 'We need somewhere we can film without interruption. There are household names involved in this project, so we have to have a closed set, somewhere the paparazzi won't be able to pester our stars. Of course, we'd provide full security. We value our privacy as much as you value yours. It looks as if your villa here might be sufficiently discreet, although I can't say whether it would meet our requirements until I've taken a look around. You'd be generously remunerated for your trouble,' she added. 'I represent one of the biggest Hollywood film studios. This is a blockbuster with a budget that runs to millions of dollars. And of course we'd leave the house and grounds exactly as we found them. You wouldn't be inconvenienced by our visit.'

The voice on the intercom called out, 'Come in! You, Angie,' the disembodied voice went on, 'you can come in too. But be careful to follow Louis. As long as you stay on the path, you'll be safe. If you stray off the path, you'll soon know about it.' The speaker broke off, laughing.

Lucy shuddered as the man beside her joined in the laughter. There was no need to ask the nature of the threat. As the high gates swung open, the quiet of the night was shattered by loud barking. Only a stranger stood between Lucy and several guard dogs, each one large and powerful enough to rip her throat out and tear her limbs from her body.

34

'WHAT DO WE DO ABOUT THE DOGS?' she enquired anxiously as the man stepped through the gate. 'Those are Rottweilers. They could kill us.'

Like beasts in a nightmare, two huge animals bounded up to them, one on either side, growling and snarling. Others waited for them further along.

'Beau!' the man called out. 'Duc!' He talked to the creatures as though they could understand him. The dogs continued to gnash and growl, straining on their chains. Lucy's legs shook so badly she could hardly stand, let alone walk, as her guide strode away from her towards the house. His stocky figure shadowy in the security lights, he led her between two slavering beasts, neither of which could quite reach him. Centimetres away from him on either side, they snarled and whined in frustration.

Lucy almost turned and fled. Remembering why she had come, she started after him, before he was too far away for her to follow. She understood the slightest deviation from the safe track between the dogs could prove fatal, and it would not be a quick death. Keeping her eyes fixed on the man walking away from her, she tried to ignore the beasts. It was difficult to block out their deep-throated growling. Her legs felt weak, but it was too late to retreat. She would not be able to stick to the safe route all the way back. If she stepped too far to the side in either direction, a vicious dog would seize her and shred her flesh as though she was made of paper. In any case the gates had probably swung shut by now. She dared not turn round to look. Her only hope was to keep going. Thinking of Nina, she forced her legs to move.

The man strode steadily on and ascended wide white stone steps that led to the front entrance. With pointed grey roofs on top of two turrets, one at either end, the villa had been modelled on a French chateau. Reaching the top of the staircase the man turned to watch Lucy toiling across the grass, while the dogs lunged at her. One of them snapped at her. Feeling hot breath on the back of her hand she snatched it away, almost veering to the other side straight into the jaws of another beast. Shuddering at a streak of saliva dripping from her hand, she pressed on and reached the foot of the stairs where the man was standing, grinning at her discomfort.

'We're here!' he called out.

Hearing the wild excitement in his voice, she realised that he too had been terrified of the dogs. She wondered what might make him choose to walk that path. As she tottered up the steps, the massive front door creaked open. There had been no need to announce their arrival. After the racket of howling and yelping, their approach had not gone unnoticed. A gigantic man stood framed in the doorway, his huge shoulders nearly spanning its width. Lucy paused on the top step. Her legs felt like jelly. Her teeth were chattering so hard she could not speak. Concentrating on breathing deeply, she tried to calm down. She was finally going to meet Patrice. The master could not be as terrifying as his dogs.

Her escort reached the door. Lucy swallowed hard. Once she was inside the house, she might be one of those people who simply disappeared. Her boss would assume she had done a runner.

Eventually her parents would report her absence to the police, who would discover that she had gone on the run the day after her flat had been broken into. It would look very odd, but no one would ever find out exactly what had happened. Her body would probably never be found. Her bones would lie scattered around the grounds, her flesh gnawed away by huge dogs. Lucy's parents would go to their deaths waiting for her to return. But she could not back out now. All she had to do was hold her nerve and play her part. She was Angie Baker, Hollywood film scout, on the lookout for a likely location for a new high-budget film. Lucy Hall did not exist.

'Sacha!' the man who had brought her there shouted.

The huge man stepped forward. 'Louis!' he replied, a wide grin plastered across his broad face.

The big man held out his arms and Louis disappeared in his gorilla embrace. After a moment they stepped back and Sacha turned to glare at Lucy, demanding to know who she was, and what she was doing there.

'I'm Angie Baker,' Lucy said quickly. 'I'm a location scout from a Hollywood film studio.'

The words were out of her mouth before she had time to think. She was not sure if the post of location scout actually existed, but she did her best to sound confident. Alain had warned her that Patrice was a vicious criminal who would stop at nothing to get what he wanted. Concealing her identity could mean the difference between life and death. She hoped her dyed hair and accent would provide her with sufficient disguise, added to the fact that Patrice would not be expecting her to have the effrontery to come to him.

'Come.' Sacha gestured towards the vast house.

Lucy followed the two men inside. The front door slammed shut behind them. As Louis and Sacha muttered together, she looked around. Despite her apprehension, she was impressed by the palatial hallway. On the far side of an ornate marble floor, a double staircase with an elaborate white balustrade was illuminated by a gold chandelier. An arched passageway below the stairs led to a large window with a view out over a landscaped courtyard.

Sacha strode over to a door leading off the hall. 'Wait in here.'

Muttering a silent prayer that she was about to see Nina, she entered an empty living room. Although the weather was mild, logs were glowing in a red-tiled fireplace. A large furry rug lay in front of it and a massive mirror with an ornate gilt frame hung above the mantelpiece. Along one wall there was a lush red velvet couch, surrounded by several matching high-backed armchairs. Comfortable and warm, the room had an air of vulgar opulence. Lucy perched on the edge of the chair furthest from the fire, sinking into its soft upholstered seat. Without warning the door was flung open and two naked women dashed in, their breasts wobbling. Intoxicated or high, they were clutching each other, giggling and shrieking. Catching sight of Lucy, their scarlet-painted lips parted in surprise. Shrieking with hysterical laughter, they ran out, banging the door behind them.

A few minutes later the door opened again to admit Sacha, the huge man who had met Lucy and her escort at the front door. He was followed by a stocky man, clean-shaven, with a receding hairline that made his broad forehead look massive. Together with his square shoulders and huge hands, it gave him an air of brutish force. Although he was not particularly tall, he seemed to fill the doorway. He strode over to the sofa and sat down, arms crossed, legs spread wide. When he moved, brilliant colours flashed from a huge diamond on his finger. He stared at Lucy without speaking. Nervous under his scrutiny, she broke the silence.

Attempting to speak brightly, she was vexed to hear her voice trembling. 'I'm Angie Baker, a film scout from Hollywood. Are you the owner of this house?'

Sacha approached the sofa and leaned down to speak to the seated man in a rapid undertone. Lucy could hear little of what he was saying. She caught only a few words: 'American' and 'Hollywood', and something about the dogs which made them both chuckle.

'So, you're called Angie Baker,' the seated man said at last.

Putting his hands on his knees, he leaned forward, studying her face. His eyes slid upwards to stare at her recently darkened hair. She shifted uncomfortably in her chair.

'That's right. Are you the owner of the house?'

'Yes, I'm Patrice Durand, and you're Angie Baker, and you've come all the way from Hollywood to speak to me?'

Something in the tone of his voice suggested he was humouring her. The subterfuge had seemed reasonable enough when she had first thought of it, and her American accent was passable, especially to a Frenchman. As long as none of his household were actual Americans, she had been confident she could get away with it. Yet on Patrice's lips her story sounded far-fetched.

'I'll be visiting several locations. I didn't come here only to check out your place.' Afraid he might ask her where else she was going, she carried on quickly. 'I'm looking for a property to use as a setting for our next film, and I think this might be just perfect. But before I can be sure, I'll need to have a look around the house and grounds, so I'll have to ask you to lock your dogs up while I'm here.'

To her relief, Patrice did not seem suspicious of her fake identity after all. He sat back, smiling easily at her, and she relaxed. Her impression that he was sceptical had sprung from her own anxiety. Her plan was very simple. She would insist on wandering around the property by herself. Once she found Nina, they would work out an escape route together. Without the dogs, when the gate was opened for Lucy, Nina would be able to slip out behind her. They would be gone before anyone noticed they were missing. With Nina's eyewitness testimony, they would make sure he was arrested and convicted of theft and kidnap, if not murder.

She was impatient to start searching for her friend, but Patrice did not seem in any hurry to let her go.

'So you're Angie Baker,' he repeated, grinning. 'And you came all this way to see me, Angie. I'm flattered.'

His repetition of her false name was beginning to rekindle her unease.

'But it's not me you came here to see. You want to look around my house. I hope you like what you've seen so far.' There was something faintly obscene about the way he leaned back, with his legs spread wide.

'This is a very comfortable room,' Lucy agreed.

'There's plenty more to see. Come, let me show you around.'

Lucy followed him across the hall and into a dining room with a large wooden table. The furniture was basic, but the decor was splendid.

'Look up,' Patrice said. His diamond ring flashed as he waved his hand at the ceiling. 'What do you think of that?'

'It's beautiful,' Lucy agreed.

Having given her time to admire the decor, which he told her was based on the Sistine Chapel in Rome, Patrice led her back to the front room.

'Well, what do you think of my house so far?'

'It's beautiful.'

Uncertain how to move the situation forward, Lucy waited to hear what he would say next.

'This is an unexpected visit,' Patrice repeated, sitting down on the sofa again, 'and I'm wondering what made you want to come here. I mean, why would a film scout risk walking past my dogs just to speak to me?'

Lucy decided to resort to flattery. He was obviously very proud of his house. 'Someone told me your home is magnificent, and it's true. I've never seen anything like it, outside of a museum or a palace. Now if I could just take a look around, that would be brilliant. From what I've seen so far, it's all beautiful. I can't wait to see the rest of the house and gardens, after you've locked your dogs away, that is,' she added, forcing a laugh.

Patrice inclined his head at the compliment.

'And now, Lucy Hall,' he replied very quietly, 'what made you think you could get away with your clumsy pretence?'

35

'MY NAME'S ANGIE,' Lucy stammered, clambering to her feet. Her legs felt weak. 'My name's not Lucy. It's Angie. Angie Baker.'

'Baker? Because you've been cooking up a story for me?' Patrice chuckled at his joke.

'No. Well, yes, all right then. You're right. But how do you know who I am?'

'I know everything that goes on in my city. Now, let's start with your phone.'

'What?'

'Your phone,' he repeated. 'You must have a phone. Everyone has a phone, even if they refuse to answer it when it rings. Your friend Nina has been trying to get in touch with you. And now, here you are. It's almost as though you knew she was trying to summon you.'

'But—'

Patrice nodded at his accomplice who stepped forward, grinning and licking his lips. Feeling sick, Lucy took the phone Alain had given her out of her bag and handed it to him. Nina would not have had that number. If Lucy had received a call from her earlier, she would have done her best to reach her friend sooner. She dreaded to think of the state Nina must be in.

'Now let's sit down comfortably and talk.'

He pointed at one of the armchairs grouped around the hearth and smiled at Lucy as she sank into it. So far Patrice had not behaved aggressively towards her. She was still hopeful she could persuade him to listen to reason.

Although he spoke gently, Patrice's next words were direct. 'You've got something of mine and I want it back.' Smiling, he held out a large hand. 'Come on. You've kept me waiting long enough.' His veneer of civility slipped as he leaned forward and hissed at her, scowling. 'Where the hell did you get to? I've had guys out there looking everywhere for you. You think you can just walk away with what's mine?' Recovered from his brief outburst, he sat back again, smiling. 'The only question now is whether you want to suffer before you give me what I want.'

'That's hardly fair. I came here to talk to you. I didn't have to come.'

About to tell him his key was safely hidden away, she paused, remembering the violence she had witnessed. Entertaining the possibility that she might have made a terrible mistake, she hesitated. If Alain was right, she could end up knifed or shot, or worse, and so could Nina. She had to think carefully about what she was going to say to ensure they were released.

'You thought you were clever enough to get me nicked,' he said and laughed. 'You thought you'd turn into a big-shot celebrity with what you've got on me. What you don't know is how many people have tried to bring me down, bigger and more influential people than you. No one's managed it yet, and no one ever will. Certainly not some English whore. I can have you disappear any time I want. Isn't that the truth, Sacha?'

'Anything you say, boss.'

'Listen, you've got this all wrong,' Lucy protested. 'I don't want anything that belongs to you. I never did. This is all one huge misunderstanding, and it has nothing to do with Nina. She just happened to be visiting me when you searched my flat.' She smiled nervously.

Patrice's voice hardened. 'Don't try your tricks on me. I can see straight through your lies.'

Lucy cursed herself for squeaking in alarm as she denied his accusation.

'You know what I want,' he continued, his tone even, as if he was ordering new curtains. 'And your friend isn't going anywhere, not till I've got back what's mine. And after that . . .' He grinned and shrugged his shoulders. 'Just give it to me!' he yelled suddenly.

Disconcerted by his rapid changes in mood, Lucy struggled to remain calm. She stood up, and glanced at the door. Sacha was blocking her exit, and beyond him she could hear the dogs howling. 'It's time for me to leave,' she said in a panic, 'and I'm taking Nina with me. This is all just a mistake. And besides, we're British citizens. You can't keep us here.'

Patrice raised his hand and Sacha stepped forward. Out of the corner of her eye, Lucy saw him leering at her. Sick with fright, she sat down again.

'You know what I want,' he said.

Keen to return Patrice's key to him as quickly as possible, Lucy forced herself to speak slowly. 'Listen, you can have it back, but it's not here. I never wanted it in the first place. I don't even know what it's for. But before I do anything, I want to see Nina's safe.'

'What is your obsession with that girl?'

'She's my friend.'

Frowning, Patrice turned to Sacha. 'Fetch the other English whore.'

Sacha turned and left the room. For such a bulky man, he moved rapidly. Patrice leaned back in his chair and closed his eyes. For a second, Lucy wished she still had Alain's gun in her pocket, not that she would have known how to use it, but at least she could have threatened Patrice with it.

A slight creaking behind her alerted her to Sacha's return. She turned to see the door swing open as he came in. A scraggy old woman shuffled into the room behind him. She stood bent over, her head bowed down over her chest. Her hands were tied, her jeans and shirt were grubby and torn, and her filthy feet were bare and bloodstained. Patrice clapped his hands sharply. At the sound the creature raised her head, her bloodshot eyes devoid of expression.

Lucy started forward, aghast. 'Nina? Is that you?'

Slowly Nina turned her head. Her face was streaked with dirt, and she seemed to be in a daze. Her voice was no more than a dry whisper. 'Lucy?'

'Oh, my God, Nina. What have they done to you?'

'What are you doing here?'

Lucy could scarcely speak through her tears. 'I've come to take you home.'

A sob burst from Nina's cracked lips. 'I won't be going home. He'll never let me go. You shouldn't have come. It's too dangerous. Go away.' She shook her head. 'Go away.'

'I had to come and get you. I couldn't leave you here.'

'Go, for God's sake. Run while you still can.'

'I'm not leaving without you.'

'Forget about me. Save yourself.'

The sound of slow handclapping interrupted their exchange. 'Very touching. Two whores, each prepared to sacrifice their own life to save her friend. It would be entertaining to put that to the test, wouldn't it, Sacha? Oh, don't look so disappointed,' Patrice added, grinning at his accomplice, 'there are plenty of whores upstairs. You can take your pick.' Patrice turned back to Lucy, his expression serious again. 'The time for games is over. You've got less than a minute to give me what I want. If you don't, your friend goes

– what's that expression you English people use? – Oh, yes, your friend goes to the dogs.'

Lucy glanced from Patrice to Sacha and back again. It was hard to believe the two men could be serious. Sacha was watching Patrice constantly, his tiny eyes alert to every gesture, every nuance in the other man's voice. Patrice stood up and stretched, before resting one of his hands on the back of a chair and gazing around the room with a proprietorial air. Nina was staring at the fire, giving no sign that she was even listening to the macabre conversation. Lucy shivered. The whole situation felt surreal.

At last Lucy could bear the silence no longer. 'Are you just going to stand there and say nothing?' she burst out, glaring at Nina. Too angry to restrain herself, she turned on Patrice. 'Do you really expect us to believe you're going to kill Nina over something she knows nothing about? That's insane! What the hell would you gain from killing either of us?'

'I didn't say I was going to kill her. I've got no intention of killing her.' Patrice smiled. 'I'll leave that to my dogs.'

Horrified, Lucy shook her head. 'That's inhuman.'

'But effective.' His soft voice was beginning to make her skin crawl. He gave a careless shrug before turning to Sacha. 'I'm bored of this. She talks too much. Take them away, both of them.'

Nina hung her head and stood, immobile, as Sacha grabbed her arm, but Lucy was not prepared to submit without putting up a fight.

'Let go of me!' she shouted. 'What are you doing? Where are you taking us?' Incensed, she struggled to escape his grasp.

'You know what I want,' Patrice said quietly. 'If you think you're walking out of here without telling me where it is, you're even more stupid than I thought. Now shut up and listen. Do you think I'm going to be outsmarted by a whore? You stole something that belongs to me. Tell me where it is, or you won't live long enough to be sorry you ever thought you could get one over on me.'

Helplessly she stared at his glittering blue eyes, fighting to control her panic. Once he had his key back, she would have no influence over him. He would probably kill her and Nina as well. She needed to think of a way to persuade Patrice to release Nina before she returned his key.

36

HIS BROAD FACE TWISTED IN A SCOWL, Patrice flung himself down on the sofa and held out his hand.

'I told you I haven't got it here.' Lucy took a deep breath. However menacing he was, she refused to let him see she was intimidated. 'Before I do anything, you've got to let Nina go.' His silence gave her confidence. 'As soon as she calls me to say she's safely back in England, you can have what you want. I'll need her to send me a photo to prove she's really there, so don't try and trick me.'

Patrice waved his hand dismissively. 'I'm getting bored of this nonsense.'

Stepping forward, Sacha seized Lucy by the arm and dragged her over to where Nina was standing, hunched over, staring at the floor.

'What are you doing? Let go of me at once!' Lucy yelled.

As she squirmed, trying to break free of Sacha's strong grip, a second man joined them. Seizing Nina round the waist, he hoisted her up and flung her over his shoulder, leaving Sacha free to clasp one of Lucy's wrists behind her back in one large hand, twisting it upwards until she was afraid he would dislocate her shoulder. Nina flinched as Lucy screamed in pain.

'All right,' Lucy cried out, 'I'll come with you but please, stop—'
She broke off as Sacha gave her arm another tug.

'He's just playing,' Patrice said. 'But don't touch her, Sacha.
Not yet.'

'OK, boss,' Sacha replied cheerfully. 'But this one's mine.' He
leaned down and whispered in Lucy's ear. 'I won't forget.'

Lucy was shaking too much to answer. Her bold defiance had
evaporated. Trying not to speculate about what had already happened to Nina during her captivity, she let Sacha drag her from the
room. As they were crossing the hallway, the two women Lucy had
seen earlier came down the stairs towards them.

'He's waiting for you,' Sacha called out to them. 'In there.' He
jerked his head in the direction of the room where they had left
Patrice.

The older woman nodded. Dressed in a red silk kimono to
match her shoes, she tottered down the last few stairs, closely followed by her younger companion who was still stark naked.

Frantically, Lucy seized her chance. 'Wait! You've got to help us!'

The woman in red laughed as Sacha clouted Lucy on the side of
her head, making her ears ring painfully. The younger woman did not
react. From her glazed eyes and impassive expression, she was clearly
off her face on drugs. The two women trotted past them, the older
one chattering and laughing, the young girl wide-eyed and silent.

Following the man who was carrying Nina, Sacha dragged
Lucy down a narrow wooden staircase. At the bottom, he propelled
her along a shadowy corridor. The air smelt musty. Away from the
overheated house and the mild Parisian night outside, it was chilly.
Turning several corners, they passed a number of doors. It was like
a maze. At last they stopped. Taking out a huge metal key, Sacha
unlocked one of the doors with a loud scraping noise. On the other
side, a narrow stone staircase led them down to a dark tunnel. Lucy
touched the wall. It felt damp and clammy. Reaching the end of

the passageway, he unlocked yet another door. Pushing her inside, Sacha let go of her. As she walked through it, she could have fallen off the edge of the world into oblivion, it was so dark.

A putrid stench made Lucy gag. In the darkness she heard Nina whimper. With a click, a bright electric light bulb illuminated a dirty, whitewashed cellar, empty apart from a row of manacles attached to one wall, a few metal chairs arranged along another wall. The filthy floor sloped gently down towards a large drain encrusted with brown scum. Beside it, a pool of congealed blood glistened thickly in the bright light. Lucy stared at it, horrified. Nauseated by the stench, she made an involuntary movement towards the door. As she did so, the light went out. The door slammed and a key scraped in the lock. Trembling, Lucy reached out and took Nina's arm. For a moment they stood in silence, side by side.

'I told you,' Nina whispered. Her voice sounded hoarse. 'You shouldn't have come. You shouldn't be here. Why are you here? You shouldn't have come. It's what he wanted. He always gets what he wants. There's no way of stopping him.'

'That's nonsense,' Lucy interrupted her sharply. 'No one gets their own way all the time. Now stop worrying. I'm going to take you home and everything's going be all right.'

'I'm going to die here, and you're going to die too.' Nina began to cry. 'Why is he doing this to us?'

Lucy's mind was spinning in confusion. She had not yet fully recovered from her shock. But she had to remain calm and plan their escape. Nothing else mattered.

'Stop crying, Nina,' she said gently. 'We can't stay here. We need to think.'

Beside her in the darkness, Nina's hoarse voice answered. 'Try not to think. It's better that way.'

Lucy spoke as firmly as she could. 'Nina, I'm going to get you out of here.'

In the silence that followed her remark, she heard a faint skittering.

'I hear them in the night,' Nina whispered, 'squeaking and scampering around. I can't see if they're mice or rats.' She let out a guttural moan.

'If we shout and stamp our feet, we can scare them away,' Lucy suggested. 'They're more frightened of us than we are of them.'

She had no idea if that was true, but somehow she doubted it. In any case, they could not shout at vermin all night. Struggling against an almost overwhelming despair, she allowed Nina to pull her over to the wall beside the door where they sat with their backs to the damp brickwork, gazing into darkness. Lucy had never felt so helpless, or so frightened. Afraid of the men more than of the odious rodents that shared their cell, her worst fear was that she would end up like Nina, too shocked to think. That was what Patrice expected. With a shiver, she tried to stop Nina's words repeating themselves in her mind: 'He always gets what he wants.'

37

DAZZLED BY THE LIGHT, bewildered by the warmth of the fire and the softness of the carpet, Lucy sank into a chair. She felt sick. The reality of the stinking cellar was already evanescent as a nightmare. Only the stench clinging to her clothes persuaded her that she had been locked in a subterranean dungeon. Forcing herself to stay alert, she focused on the terrible truth that Nina was still locked in the cellar.

'I'm not giving you anything until Nina's safely back in London,' she said, speaking as firmly as she could, 'so you might as well let us both leave right now.'

'I'm getting tired of this. Everyone does what I tell them in the end, so you can make this quick, or you can drag it out a bit longer. Either way it makes no difference.' He held out his hand. 'Now hand it over or I'll take it off you.'

'I told you, I haven't got it here.'

'Then you're no use to me.' He stood up. 'Sacha, I think you like this girl? You can have her. Do what you want with her, then throw her to the dogs. But search her first. Thoroughly. Give me anything you find.'

Lucy shivered. Sacha came further into the room and walked around behind her chair.

'No! Wait!'

Patrice sat down again, smiling easily. 'I thought you'd change your mind. Now hand it over. And God help you if it's been tampered with.'

Lucy thought quickly. She was going to have to hand the key over to Patrice to save Nina's life, but she knew now that Alain had been telling her the truth. Patrice was a sadistic psychopath. The key she had been given could lead to proof of his crimes, some of them no doubt violent. She could not turn her back on this opportunity to punish him for what he had done to Nina. And if she and Nina were destined to die, before she was killed at least she would do her best to prevent Patrice from torturing and killing anyone else.

'I told you I haven't got it here. But . . .' she hesitated. 'I know where it is. I'll go and get it, but first you have to let Nina go. This has got nothing to do with her.'

'You're in no position to bargain with me.'

'On the contrary, if I really do have something you want, then I think I'm in a very strong bargaining position.'

Patrice glared at her. Then he threw his head back with a bark of laughter. 'You – in a strong position!'

Behind her, Lucy heard someone else laughing. She shuddered, trying not to think about Sacha. She wondered if she was being an idiot to insist on Nina's release. Perhaps she ought to just concentrate on getting herself out of there so she could try and have Patrice arrested.

'You stupid whore,' Patrice said. 'You've got no idea who you're dealing with, but you'll find out soon enough.' He waved one hand in the air and his diamond ring flashed. 'All this belongs to me. How do you suppose I acquired my wealth? I started with nothing. You think I got here by waiting patiently for everything I wanted to drop into my lap?' He held out his hand. 'Now give me what's mine.'

'I told you I haven't got it here. It's hidden where you'll never find it,' she lied. 'That's why you didn't find it when you searched my flat. It's not there. It's not anywhere you could possibly think of.'

Patrice's eyes flickered with anger. 'Where is it?'

Lucy shook her head. Somehow she had to convince him to let her go and fetch it for him. Carefully she repeated her story that the key was safely hidden.

'If I go missing for one more week,' she lied desperately, 'it will be found.'

'Do you think I believe your bullshit?'

She met his gaze levelly. 'I can't make you believe me, but can you afford to risk ignoring what I've said, knowing what might happen?'

Their eyes met. 'So you *do* know what it is,' he said, very softly. 'Don't play games with me. I never lose.'

'If your secret was out, it would have been in the news. The police would have come knocking on your door by now. Nothing's happened, because it's still safely hidden away. And I'll get it for you if you let Nina go. If not, within a week, everyone in Paris will know about it.'

'Tell me where it is and I'll let you both go.'

She wondered whether to believe him.

'It's not that easy.' She shrugged. 'I can't explain exactly where it is, but I'll recognise the exact place when I see it. I need to go there and see it for myself.'

It was an unlikely lie, but he seemed to accept it.

'Your friend stays here,' he said. 'Sacha goes with you. If you're not back here by tomorrow night, you won't see her alive again.'

'If I bring you what you want, will you let her go?'

Patrice's wide face relaxed into a smile. 'Bring me what I want and you both leave here. You have my word.'

'Very well.'

'If she tries to get away, let me know,' Patrice said, as Sacha reached for the door handle. 'And I'll tear the other English whore apart. Slowly.'

With a grin, Sacha held the door open for Lucy.

'Remember if you're not back here in by midnight tomorrow, your friend dies,' Patrice called after her. 'And it won't be a quick death.'

38

LUCY WAS NERVOUS getting into the car beside Sacha, but there was no avoiding it. Aware of his eyes on her, she sat as far away from him as she could, pressing her shoulder against the door. After a tense journey, they pulled up outside her apartment block in the Rue Ferdinand Duval. The instant the car stopped, she wrenched the passenger door open and leapt out, eager to put more space between them. By the time she had tapped in the code, and entered the courtyard, he was at her side again. Reaching the front door of her flat, she stopped.

'I haven't got my key,' she muttered. 'You'll have to open it.'

Hoping Sacha would pick the lock carefully, she stood poised to dash past him and slam the door behind her. If she was quick enough, she might succeed in wedging the door shut. She needed to delay Sacha for long enough to allow her to grab Patrice's key and escape through the kitchen window. It did not take him long to unlock the door. He held it open for her to go in, his bulk preventing her from shutting it. As she walked into the living room, she was aware of him following her. It was strange walking back into her flat. For an instant she felt as though she had imagined the whole terrifying episode. The untidy state of her apartment confounded that hope.

She ran into her bedroom and closed the door. Seizing her jewellery case from the drawer, she turned it upside down and shook the contents out on her bed. Sliding out the lining, she closed her fist around the key that had been the cause of so much violence, just as Sacha pushed the door open. She spun round to face him, stuffing the key in the back pocket of her jeans. Whatever happened, she was not going to give up the key without a fight. Once Sacha got hold of it, there was no knowing what he might do to her. She was alone in her bedroom with a sadistic criminal.

'The key's not here,' she said firmly. 'I just came back to pick something up. Come on, let's go and get what Patrice wants.'

Sacha took a step into the bedroom.

'We need to get going,' she said quickly. 'We don't want to upset Patrice.'

Sacha moved towards her, a grin spreading across his huge face. For all she knew, he was a serial rapist and a killer. She could not hope to overpower him. Her only chance was to catch him off guard. She stared about wildly for something she could use as a weapon. He was probably armed, but in any case one swipe of his massive fist would be enough to shatter her skull. Before he realised what she was doing, she grabbed her deodorant, darted forward and aimed the spray directly at his eyes. He staggered back, yelling in pain. While his hands were still covering his eyes, she ducked beneath his elbow and squeezed out of the room. She dashed for the kitchen. Before she had a chance to scramble up onto the sink, she heard heavy footsteps pounding after her. Shaking, she grabbed the bread knife from the draining board and turned, just as Sacha ran into the kitchen.

Not noticing the knife in her hand he charged towards her, crowing in triumph, his arms outstretched. Resisting her instinct to turn and run, she launched herself at him. With a shriek of terror, she plunged the bread knife into the side of his neck. Taken by surprise, he staggered backwards. Blood flowed from his wound, spreading in a dark pool by his feet. An expression of disbelief crossed his face as he collapsed on the floor. His eyes closed, and he lay still. Horrified, Lucy heard the knife clatter to the floor. She drew back, too shocked even to cry out. She was a murderer. She might be able to convince the police that she had slashed at an intruder in self-defence, but the fact remained that she had killed a man.

Alone in her flat with a dead body, she knew she had to get out of there fast. If she was apprehended for questioning she might not be released in time to return to Patrice ahead of the deadline and Nina would be killed. Meanwhile she had to call an ambulance. The man on her kitchen floor might still be alive. Panicking, she ran into the living room, away from the sight of her dreadful crime.

39

NINA THOUGHT ABOUT LUCY'S VISIT and shivered. Overall, it had been a disturbing experience. She was glad to be back in her cell. As long as everyone left her alone, she could block out the memories of her former life. If she could only find a way to ignore her physical pain, she would be content to hide in her corner of the cellar and hope they would leave her alone. Uncomfortable though it was to be chained up in semi-darkness, this was where she now belonged. There was no point trying to get away. She had learned that lesson the hard way. Whenever she moved, agonising lesions on her back and arms reminded her of the consequences of trying to resist Patrice.

Until a few days ago she had been full of fight, but that had been beaten out of her. With a tremor of fear, she remembered her efforts to escape. At one point she had even believed she was free. She had been driven to a police station where she should have been offered protection. But she had not known then what she knew now: there was no escape from Patrice. At least he ignored her when she was chained up in her cell. She had grown accustomed to the rodents who scampered around at night. As long as she stayed awake, she could scare them away. Exhaustion helped her to sleep during the day, which was better than watching what happened in her cell when the men arrived to carry out their barbarous acts. Crouching in her corner, her head in her hands, she shut them all out of her mind.

Once her life had been very different. She had not always lived like a blind beast, chewing fetid scraps of gristle that made her want to vomit. She blinked, peering through the darkness of her cell, trying to remember what had happened when Lucy had arrived. It was hard to recall the exact sequence of events after she had been escorted into Patrice's presence by one of the men who terrorised her daily. To her amazement, Lucy had been waiting for her, sitting with Patrice. To begin with, Nina had kept her head down, pretending not to recognise her friend. She was aware that Patrice wanted something from Lucy, and figured it might endanger her friend's life if Patrice discovered who she was. She had wanted Lucy to leave before he discovered her identity, but Lucy had given the game away at once, telling Nina she had come to rescue her.

Lucy had not yet learned that no one could get the better of Patrice. Nina understood that only too well. Patrice always got what he wanted. Lucy had been a fool to think she could help. She should not have come. Nina had wanted to explain that she only wanted all this to end. Death was no longer the worst she had to fear. Patrice was never going to let her go. And if he did, what future could she face? After the horrors she had witnessed, she could never return to her previous life. The person who had lived that life no longer existed. Lucy had seen how her mind had been corrupted by her experience. Evil had tainted her. She would never be normal again. That was why Lucy had abandoned her, after coming to find her. Lucy no longer wanted to be her friend. It was understandable. Nodding her head in agreement, Nina realised she was crying. She struggled to recognise her own mind in this morass of twisted thoughts.

Lucy had been brought down into the dark, stinking basement. Nina closed her eyes and tried to remember what Lucy had said to her. Shuddering, she recalled Lucy had disagreed with Patrice. Lucy was not the first person to have challenged him. Nina had watched a young man try to stand up to him. She had no idea what they had been arguing about. The disagreement had not even become heated when Patrice had tied him up and attacked him with a whip. All the time he was torturing the young man, Patrice had been laughing and chatting with his accomplices. Starving and sick, she struggled to recall exactly what the man had done to provoke Patrice, but her memories swirled around uncontrollably until she could no longer remember what she had been thinking about. It was better that way.

She recalled Lucy coming to see her. Lucy had been with her in the cellar. In a way when Lucy left again, it was worse than if she had not come at all. Nina should have warned her about Patrice, but she had been too traumatised to think clearly. She ought to have told Lucy that Patrice killed people for no reason. Nina was haunted by the memory of the woman in the red dress. Her murder had appeared so casual. The woman had not wanted to defy Patrice. On the contrary, she had been doing her best to placate him. But he had killed her just the same. It made no difference whether people argued with him or tried to ingratiate themselves with him, he killed them anyway. That was the most frightening aspect of it all. In the end he killed everyone. She wondered if he had ever murdered someone and then regretted it afterwards. Either way it made no difference. One day he would kill her. Far from regretting her death, he would not even remember it by the following day. Clasping her knees to her chest, she realised she was crying again. Although she did not want to carry on like this, tied up in a filthy cell, living a life that was no life, she did not really want to die. She wanted to be saved.

40

TREMBLING, LUCY KNEW THAT SHE HAD to get out of there. She hurried to her front door and leaned against it for a moment to recover her breath. If she panicked, she would never be able to cope with the knowledge that she had killed a man. Straightening up, she was almost knocked off her feet by a painful blow on the side of her head. Powerful hands grabbed her, lifting her off the floor, pinning her arms to her sides. A deep voice growled unintelligibly in her ear, and she felt a rough chin scraping against her cheek. Still muttering, Sacha threw her to the floor. The gash on his neck was bleeding, but he was clearly not as badly hurt as Lucy had assumed. Despite his injury, Lucy was horrified to feel his fingers grappling with her clothes. While he was fumbling with her belt, she reached for the metal umbrella stand beside her front door. It was too heavy for her to shift with one outstretched hand but her fingers closed on an umbrella Nina had brought with her from England. Raising it in the air, she brought it down on the back of Sacha's head, swinging it with all her might. At the same time, she struck him forcefully with her knee, right between his legs.

Sacha grunted in surprise and grabbed at her face, his arms flailing. Panicking, she hit him repeatedly with the umbrella, raining down blows on the back of his head while he was still stunned by the impact from her knee. With a groan, he collapsed on top of her. Crawling out from beneath him, she grabbed a scarf from the coat stand and bound his wrists tightly behind his back. She tied his ankles together as well. Only when she was sure he could not move did she step back, panting with fear and exertion, avoiding a pool of blood that was soaking into the light-green carpet. With all the shouting and crashing around, it was hardly surprising that Lucy heard voices outside her front door. Now she would no longer welcome any interference, several of her neighbours had come to investigate the noise coming from her flat. Someone tapped on her door.

'Is everything all right?'

She drew in a deep shuddering breath. 'Everything's fine,' she called out. 'I just fell over, that's all. Sorry to disturb you.'

Someone called back, complaining about the racket. Then there was silence. Lucy hurried into the living room to fetch her bag. Glancing at the mirror, she saw blood smeared over her face and hair. It was not hers. The full horror of what had happened nearly overwhelmed her. Unable to think, she ran to the bathroom and locked the door. Shuddering, she sat on the toilet seat, struggling to control her tears. Although she was in a hurry to get away, she showered. The sight of Sacha's blood disappearing down the plughole made her feel sick.

Clean, and in fresh clothes, she felt slightly better. She slipped the key into her purse, zipped it shut, and was ready to go. She could hear Sacha thrashing about and shouting. Having regained consciousness, he was calling out, hitting the floor with his elbows and lifting his feet and banging them down in an attempt to attract attention. It was lucky Lucy's flat was on the ground floor. When she stepped into the hall, he bellowed with fury and pulled himself up onto his knees, bloodshot eyes glaring malevolently while he raged at her. Relieved that she had tied him up securely, she darted round behind him and shoved him suddenly in the back as hard as she could. He pitched forward onto his face and lay still. Lifting his heavy head with difficulty, she bound another scarf around his mouth to silence him before she left.

Out on the street, the terror of her recent struggle began to fade. A feeling of triumph swept through her. Traumatic as the encounter with Sacha had been, she had single-handedly subdued him. She was a survivor, and she was going to save her friend. Not even Patrice was going to stand in her way. For a few moments, euphoria overwhelmed her. Recovering from her excitement, she began to examine her feelings. Opposed to violence, she had never understood why other people were entertained by fighting in films. The idea of people hurting one another appalled her. Yet she had just tried to kill a man, and had exulted in the success of her own violence. Alain claimed to have killed Ferret in self-defence. Lucy was shocked to discover for herself how easily fear could explode into violence.

It was warm outside and the pavements were crowded. Spotting Sacha's car, her first impulse was to try and drive it away, but she did not have the key. She was tempted to smash the windscreen, but that would make a terrible din, especially if it set off a car alarm. She could not risk attracting attention. Instead, she slipped off her socks, rolled them up in a tight ball, ducked down and shoved them as far up the exhaust pipe as she could. Her feet were less comfortable, but her socks were all she could find to sabotage Sacha's car at such short notice. She considered going round the car smashing all the lights, but was afraid of being spotted. Meanwhile, every moment she lingered increased the risk she might be caught. She walked away quickly.

41

As Lucy passed one of her favourite patisseries at the end of her road, the plump owner called out to her cheerily from the doorway. With a cursory nod Lucy strode on, barely pausing to acknowledge the greeting. Normally she would have liked nothing better than to have gone into the shop for a pastry and a chat, but such pleasantries belonged to another world now. Looking out for a taxi, she walked in the direction of the Gare du Nord. The pavements became busier. It was disconcerting passing so many strangers, any one of whom could be a member of Patrice's criminal gang. Several times she thought she caught someone staring at her as she hurried past, but no one challenged her.

Walking cleared her head and she recovered some of her composure. Thinking over what had happened, she was not sure what to do. Much as she abhorred Sacha, she did not want to leave him to die, tied up in her hall. As she dithered, someone hissed her name. She held her breath and turned. Alain was standing behind her, half concealed in the shadow of a doorway. Startled, she hurried over to him.

'How did you find me?'

'I've been following you since you left your flat. Where did you get to earlier?' he demanded. 'I went to the café and waited for you.

Where have you been? In the end, I went to your street and waited there for you there. What's going on?'

Lucy shrugged. 'It's a long story.'

'Why did you run off like that? And why didn't you answer your phone?'

Lucy wanted to go somewhere they could sit and talk properly. There was a lot to tell him, and it was going to be an awkward conversation.

'I haven't got my phone any more. I'll tell you all about it, but can we go somewhere we can talk?'

'I was going out of my mind, worrying about you,' he said.

Lucy was not sure whether to believe him, but she was too tired to care.

'I don't suppose you know somewhere we can grab a few hours' sleep?'

He nodded. 'A friend of mine lives not far from here. We can rely on her to be discreet. We could go there for tonight as long as we're sure no one sees us. I was outside for a while and I didn't see anyone watching the flat. I don't think you're being followed, but we need to keep a lookout.' He hesitated. 'Before we go, is there anything I need to know?'

'Quite a lot. But do we have to go into it here? It's going to take a while.'

She followed him along the streets, skirting the station. They walked for a long time, seeming to go round in circles, until she had no idea where they were. At last Alain led her to the side door of a large block of flats.

'No one followed us,' he said, looking around before ringing one of the bells. 'Let's hope she's in. Otherwise, we're going to have a long walk ahead of us.'

Lucy sighed. She felt as though she had been walking forever. 'Couldn't you have phoned her first?'

'I never phone her. I can't risk leaving any trace of our connection. That way she's protected, and her flat's a safe place for me to stay when I need it. To be fair, I hardly ever call on her for help. It's only ever happened once before. But I can see you're exhausted.'

While he was speaking, he rang the bell again. This time, the entryphone crackled and a voice called out.

'Who's there? What do you want? It's late.'

'Liza? It's me. I know it's late—'

A buzzer sounded. 'Come on up.'

Lucy followed Alain up two flights of stairs. On the second floor, a woman with long fair hair was standing in an open doorway. She was wearing a pale-blue towelling dressing gown and pink slippers. Behind her glasses, her eyes looked kind. As she closed her door Alain introduced the two women, and Lucy thanked Liza for her hospitality.

'That's perfectly all right,' Liza replied. 'It's the least I can do.' She linked her arm in Alain's. 'You're lucky I was awake and heard the bell.'

Alain smiled at her. 'We all deserve a bit of luck now and then.'

Liza turned to Lucy. 'He helped me out when I was in terrible trouble. I had to get rid of a real son-of-a-bitch who was threatening to ruin everything for me. If it wasn't for you,' she smiled at Alain, 'I don't think I'd be here now.'

'I was only doing my job,' Alain said, but Lucy could tell he was gratified by Liza's appreciation.

After a bowl of home-made vegetable soup with a hunk of baguette, Lucy felt a lot better. It was a relief to be back with Alain, fed, and with a safe place to stay for the night. Liza said goodnight and left them to it. Lucy was exhausted, but before they went to sleep she owed Alain an account of where she had gone after she had run off at the Gare du Nord. Sitting at the table, she launched into her story, determined to tell him everything. When she reached the part where she had gone to Patrice's house, Alain interrupted her. To her relief, he seemed curious rather than angry.

'How the hell did you manage to get away?'

Lucy explained why Patrice had sent her home. Hearing how she had left Sacha tied up in her flat, Alain laughed.

'I've got to tell someone,' she added. 'We can't just leave him there to starve to death.'

'Never mind that,' Alain replied. 'He deserves whatever he gets. The important thing now is to get hold of that key and work out what it's for. Then we can deal with Patrice.'

Reaching a decision, Lucy unzipped her purse and pulled out the key.

Alain stared at it in surprise. 'Is that what this is all about? Where was it?'

'I hid it in my bedroom after Patrice had searched the flat. When you came round, we had to leave in such a hurry that I didn't have a chance to go and get it.'

'So it's been there all this time?'

She nodded. 'They'd already searched my flat, so I suppose it never occurred to them it might be there. That's why I had to get away from Sacha. I couldn't let him get the key and take it back to Patrice. That would have been the end for Nina. Patrice wants this key back, and he's given me until tomorrow night to return it to him. If I don't, he's threatening to kill her.'

They sat staring at the key for a moment. It was strange to think that such a small object had been the catalyst for so much destruction.

'How the hell are we supposed to find out what that key opens?' Alain burst out, without taking his eyes off it.

'I need to tell someone about Sacha,' Lucy insisted. 'I can't just leave him like that, locked in my flat.'

'He's a vicious scumbag,' Alain muttered. 'It's no worse than he deserves.'

'I don't care who he is,' Lucy insisted. 'He's a human being. If we leave him there to die, we're no better than they are.'

'He wouldn't do the same for you.'

'That's exactly my point,' Lucy muttered. 'I'm not the same as him.'

'Someone will find him, sooner or later. Let's hope it's later.'

'But I left him tied up in my flat! He might not be found until it's too late to save him.'

'That's his hard luck. We're not risking our liberty for him. You can forget that. Think about it, Lucy, getting away from Sacha buys you some time while Patrice thinks you're being watched. If you call the police, Joubert's going to hear about it, and then Patrice will know you've escaped and start hunting for you again. Next time, you might not get away. Now, let's take a look at that key.' Alain studied it. 'What the hell does it open?'

Lucy shrugged. She had no idea. All she knew was that they had less than twenty-four hours left to find out. After that, she was taking it to Patrice.

'Come on,' Alain said, 'you look done in. Let's have a few hours' kip, and then we'll get started. Tomorrow we'll find out what that key is for.'

42

EXHAUSTED, LUCY SLEPT VERY WELL. She would have carried on sleeping if Liza had not woken her up, telling her that Alain wanted to set off soon. After a quick breakfast, they left and walked back towards the city. With no particular destination in mind, Alain was keen to keep moving. It was a beautiful sunny morning, with a hint of autumn in the breeze. Lucy had showered and borrowed fresh underwear from Liza. In the bright light of morning, she felt far more optimistic than she had been the previous day.

'All we need to do is persuade Patrice to exchange Nina for this one little key,' she told Alain. 'Let's do it soon. Can you imagine if I lost it before I gave it back! Come on, we have to get Nina out of there. She looked terrible.'

'Don't you want to see what it's for first?'

'Honestly, I don't care. I just want to get Nina out of there.'

'The trouble is, once Patrice has that key, what guarantee have you got that he'll let her, or you, go?'

'Why wouldn't he?' Lucy replied, although she knew he was right.

Avoiding main streets and public transport, they kept moving as they talked. If they could discover what the key opened, they might be able to go to the police with incontrovertible evidence against Patrice. Nina would be released, and they would both be safe. But first they had to figure out what the key was for. The fob looked as though it might open a garage or a car-park barrier, so Alain thought it could be a car key. If he was right, his theory would help to narrow down their search. He suggested they visit a contact of his who was a car mechanic.

'Another grateful ex-client whose life you saved?' Lucy asked with a smile.

'No, Theo's the guy who fixes me up with a car when I need one.'

They walked to a vehicle repair shop on the way to Clichy. Crossing the forecourt, they entered a workshop where several men in greasy blue overalls were fixing cars. Alain asked for Theo and was directed to the far corner of the workshop. Theo was a tall gangly man with a very large mouth which broke into a smile when he saw them. Wiping his hands on an oily rag, he greeted Alain like a long lost friend.

'After some wheels?'

'No,' Alain replied. 'We need to ask your advice. Can we step outside for a moment?'

Theo followed them out of the workshop. In a corner of the forecourt, Alain nodded at Lucy who took out the key.

'Can you identify this, or tell us anything about it?' Alain asked. 'What make of car is it for?'

Theo took the key and turned it over a couple of times, squinting at it. 'If this is a car key, it's for no car I've ever seen,' he said at last.

'I thought the fob might open a garage,' Alain explained.

'It might,' the mechanic replied, handing the key back to Lucy. Alain frowned.

'Are you saying it's definitely not a car key?' Lucy asked.

Theo shrugged. 'Not one that I recognise.'

'I didn't think it was for a car,' Alain said.

Disappointed, Lucy did not remind him that they had only gone to see Theo because Alain had suggested it might be a car key. Still, at least they seemed to have eliminated that line of enquiry. In an Internet café, they sat side by side at terminals, looking up images of keys. Lucy was worried when she could not find anything that matched the one she had been given. The key had wards on both sides of the pin which she discovered was fairly standard. It looked like the kind of key used to open desk drawers, but the top part, the bow, was a slightly unusual diamond shape, with a narrow slit for the key ring to pass through. The majority of the keys she found online had round bows. Diamond-shaped ones were not uncommon, but none of them had the same slit in the top.

'I don't suppose you've got any contacts who are locksmiths?' she asked.

Lucy took the key off the fob before handing it to the first locksmith they found. Alain had suggested they have a copy made so that they could split up and work twice as fast, but none of the locksmiths they asked could do it straightaway. It seemed the key had a slightly unusual design, and none of the locksmiths they visited had the right kind of blank in stock. It was frustrating, but there was nothing they could do about it and they spent the rest of the day traipsing along side streets, going from one locksmith to another, hoping to find a clue to what the key opened.

Even though Patrice had given Lucy until midnight to get back to him, they were careful to avoid CCTV cameras whenever they could. Where they had to pass one, they turned their faces away. Lucy was amazed that Alain seemed to know all their locations.

'Do you know where every CCTV camera is in the whole city?'

'Pretty much,' he replied. 'Of course I don't always know which ones are actually working. Probably half the detours we've taken weren't necessary, but it's impossible to tell if the cameras are recording or not.'

It was a tiring and frustrating day, because no one they spoke to was able to offer them any help at all.

'It belonged to my aunt who died recently,' she explained each time she handed the key over.

A couple of the locksmiths thought the design was old-fashioned, but that did not help them to identify where the key might come from.

'It's funny that it doesn't have any numbers on it,' one of the men they spoke to commented.

'What does that mean?' Lucy asked with a sudden burst of hope.

He shrugged. 'I don't know that it means anything. There's no knowing. Your key looks pretty old. The identifying numbers might have just worn off.'

'I need to get back to Patrice tonight,' Lucy told Alain as the shops began to close.

'We can't pass up on the opportunity to find out what he's so keen to hide,' Alain insisted. 'It could be his loot. We could get him arrested and put away for life. He's a dangerous monster, Lucy. We can't just ignore the chance we've been given.'

'I can't risk Nina's life.'

Alain turned to face her, his expression dark. 'Face the facts, Lucy, your friend's going to be killed, whether you return this key to him or not. She's probably already dead. Now he's flushed you out, he's got no further use for her. In his warped mind, people are expendable. He has no respect for human life, none at all. It means nothing to him. You have to understand, Lucy, he's a psychopath. He doesn't think about people in the same way that we do. He's completely insane. Once he knew he'd abducted the wrong girl, he was only holding onto her until you showed up. If you give him back the key, there's nothing to stop him getting rid of you as well.' His voice rose in exasperation. 'Don't throw your life away like that.

At least if we keep hold of the key, there's a chance we might be able to avenge your friend's death by getting Patrice locked up.'

'I can't take any risk with Nina's life,' Lucy insisted. 'Even if there's just a slim chance she's still alive, I have to keep trying to rescue her.'

They had reached an impasse. Alain glared at her, but Lucy was determined to do whatever she could to free Nina.

'He only wants the key,' she insisted, aware that she was trying to convince herself. 'He told me he'd let Nina go if I gave it to him. There's no reason for him to hold on to her once he's got what he wants. And it'll be better if he knows we couldn't find out what the key opens. If we don't know anything, we're no threat to him.'

'We know he locked Nina up.'

'I have to take that chance. I'm sorry, I know you don't agree with me, but I'm going back to his house and I'm going to get Nina out of there. If you'd rather not come with me, that's fine. I'll go and see him on my own.'

'At least arrange to meet him in a public place,' Alain replied. 'If you go to his house, I don't suppose you'll ever leave there alive, you or your friend.'

Pleased that Alain had finally agreed with her, Lucy nodded. She could see the sense in meeting somewhere public.

'OK. The deadline is midnight tonight. Let's give it another couple of hours and then I'll send him a message.'

'How are you going to contact him now that you've got rid of Sacha?'

'I'll call Inspector Joubert. Patrice will get the message, won't he?'

'Good idea. But let's not phone him from here.'

Now that she had got her own way about returning the key in exchange for Nina's life, Lucy was willing to agree to whatever else Alain suggested. 'Where do you think we should go to make the call?'

'Let's go to a hotel. We go in, make the call, and leave straight away. We don't take any chances. As soon as you make contact he'll know you've got the key, and start looking for you in earnest. Him and his tame police inspector. We'll be up against the full force of the police, so we're going to need to move fast and keep out of sight.'

43

NOW THAT THE ORDEAL WAS NEARLY OVER, Lucy felt shaky. Nina had been held by Patrice for nearly a week. It felt like years.

'If she's still alive,' Alain commented tersely when Lucy mentioned how she was feeling.

'Stop saying that. It doesn't help. She's alive. She has to be. Why would he kill her now, after all this? She was alive when I went there yesterday, and he promised he'd let her go once he got his key back.'

As they walked along a side street near the Gare du Nord, Lucy tried to work out what to say to Inspector Joubert. Nina's life might depend on her words.

'What if he's not there?' Alain asked.

'They'll put me through. They have to. I'll insist. Even if he's not at work, they'll have a number for him. He's a police inspector, they must be able to contact him. I'll tell them he has to get the message before midnight. They have to listen.' She hoped she was right.

Before she made the call, Alain took her to a dingy café in a back street for a late snack. She agreed it was important that she keep her wits about her when talking to Joubert, and she was beginning to feel light-headed after their stressful day. She had not realised how hungry she was. Smelling food, she remembered they had not stopped for lunch. The pizza was unexceptional, but she wolfed it down.

'I was starving,' she said, when she had finished.

Alain grinned. 'Me too.'

It was gone eleven when they left the café. Instead of phoning Inspector Joubert from a hotel, where they might be seen, Alain decided it would be safer to walk down a side street and make the call from a deserted spot. He seemed to have an endless supply of cheap pay-as-you-go phones.

'Whatever you think. You're the expert,' Lucy said, pleased that Alain was going along with her plan.

He led her into a narrow side turning.

'Surely it's more important to try and stop him altogether, than . . .' He broke off. 'Who knows how many more people he's going to torture and kill if he isn't locked up?'

'You think stopping Patrice is more important than saving one life,' Lucy finished the sentence for him. 'In theory I suppose you're right, but you must see there's nothing else I can do. Nina's my friend. I've known her nearly all my life. It's my fault she's in this trouble in the first place. I can't just abandon her. Think what you would do if you were in my place and it was your brother's life at stake. Can you honestly say you'd desert him, knowing he was almost certainly going to die and you were the only person who might be able to save him? Listen, there's no need for you to be dragged into it, really. I know I came to you for help, but you've done more than enough. If this is going to be dangerous, you don't have to come with me. It's not fair on you.'

He laughed and told her to stop gibbering. 'It's good of you to concern yourself with my safety, but I'm committed to helping you. After all, you saved my life.'

'You're forgetting it was my fault you were in danger in the first place.'

'Come on, enough arguing. You need to make that call before midnight.'

They turned off the side street into an alleyway. There was just enough room for them to pass two huge trash bins.

'This is an unregistered phone. Use it and then we'll destroy it to make doubly sure. Even the police won't be able to trace where we are, as long as you don't stay on the line for long.' Alain handed her a phone. 'Here, let me hold your bag.'

'Thanks.'

Lucy's fingers trembled as she dialled the number. 'My name is Lucy Hall. I have a message for Inspector Joubert,' she said, speaking as clearly as she could. 'It's very important that he gets it straight away. It's very urgent.'

'Would you like me to put you through?'

'Please be quick. Tell him it's for his friend Patrice.'

'What is it?' Alain hissed from behind her. 'What's going on? What are you doing? You can't mention his name.'

'Shh. They're putting me through to Joubert.'

'It's taking too long.'

'I can't—' Lucy broke off as a voice interrupted her down the line.

'You wish to speak with Inspector Joubert? This is he.'

'I have an urgent message for Patrice,' she gabbled. 'It needs to reach him before midnight tonight. Tell him he can have what he wants. I've got it.'

'Where are you?'

'Tell him I'll bring it to him tomorrow.'

'Good. He will be waiting for you.'

'No, wait!' Lucy cried out before he could ring off. 'Tell him I won't come to his house. I'll meet him in a public place.'

The inspector barely hesitated. 'Come to L'Ours Doré tomorrow at midday.'

Lucy had intended to choose where they were going to meet, but she was afraid to remain on the line any longer in case he was able to trace her call. She hung up. Annoyed with herself for allowing Joubert to choose the meeting place, she turned to tell Alain what had happened. She was alone in the dark alley.

'Alain?' she whispered. 'Alain? Where are you?'

There was no answer. Lucy waited a moment, but he did not reappear. Looking around the shadowy alley, she saw her bag lying on the ground. Frowning, she picked it up and made her way gingerly past the bins, back the way she had come. Peering round the corner, she saw a deserted street.

'Alain?' she whispered.

There was no answer, and no sign of him. If he had been mugged, not only would Lucy have heard a scuffle, but her bag would have gone. He must have lost his nerve and run off, leaving her to deal with Patrice alone. Perhaps that had been his intention all along. Cursing him under her breath, she made her way back to the main road. While she was bitterly disappointed that he had abandoned her, she was more upset that he had run off without a word. She had given him ample opportunity to tell her he was not going to accompany her any longer. He could at least have wished her luck.

With a sigh, she walked back to the Gare du Nord, and found the hotel where she had stayed with Alain.

'I don't have any papers with me, but it's just for the night.'

The woman at reception shrugged and told her how much it would cost. Desperate for somewhere to stay that night, Lucy agreed the price, but she could not sleep. She might as well have spent the night walking around the streets and saved the money.

44

IN A SMALL ROOM ON THE TOP FLOOR, Lucy lay on the bed, thinking. Her bag was under the pillow, with Patrice's key in her purse. The mattress felt knobbly and the bed stank of sweat. She kept her clothes on and tried not to touch the sheets. Wriggling around to find a comfortable position, she deliberated over what she was going to say to Patrice. Every time she rehearsed the meeting in her mind, she came up with a different speech. Patrice was a psychopath alleged to have the blood of many victims on his hands, yet he had never been arrested. Even when it seemed impossible for him to get away, against all the odds he had contrived to vanish like a shadow at sunset. Lucy doubted whether Inspector Joubert could really be powerful enough to have protected Patrice so completely all by himself. There must be other powers at work.

She was beginning to wonder if she had been a fool to trust everything Alain had told her. In any case, an investigative journalist was probably better off working alone. At the same time, she was at a disadvantage living in a foreign city. Paris was certainly a beautiful and exciting place but she was, basically, friendless here. She had many acquaintances, some of whom were likely to become real friends in time, but there was no one in whom she could confide.

Perhaps her isolation had driven her to trust Alain too quickly. She knew very little about him, and that was only what he had told her himself.

Her knowledge of Patrice's history was also limited, and most of what she knew about him she had learned from Alain. But she had observed for herself how Patrice surrounded himself with vicious thugs, all of whom seemed eager to do his bidding. If so many violent criminals were scared of Patrice, it was hardly surprising that he had reduced Nina to a quivering wreck within a week. The more Lucy thought about it, the more nervous she felt about the coming meeting. It was frustrating that yet again Patrice was likely to evade prosecution, but she could not afford to be distracted by his fate. Her sole concern was to save Nina. As the only bargaining chip she possessed, it was essential she keep the key hidden until Nina had been released.

After everything that had happened, she was determined to show Patrice that he could not frighten her. That way she hoped to stand a better chance of achieving her goal. And if she was going to die, at least she would do so with dignity. That was her intention, at least. She lay awake for most of the night fretting about the meeting. She had promised to take the key with her, but if she did, there was nothing to stop Patrice from simply taking it from her. On the other hand, if she broke her promise, Patrice was unlikely to keep to his side of their bargain.

Her thoughts went round in circles for most of the night. It was a pity she had allowed Joubert to choose the location for their meeting, but there was nothing she could do to change that. At least it was a public place. She wished she had insisted on seeing Nina at the meeting, but it was too late to request her presence now. Patrice would probably have taken no notice of her demands anyway. It was possible she would never see Nina alive again, but she tried to remain optimistic.

To add to her fears about meeting Patrice, she was anxious about having left a man tied up in her flat. Recovered from her initial sense of triumph, she was troubled. If no one arrived in time to save him, Sacha would starve to death, bound and gagged in her hallway. Lucy did not care what happened to him, but she did not want to end up in serious trouble if a trussed-up corpse was discovered in her flat. Her own lack of interest in his fate as a human being disturbed her. It was late when she finally drifted into an uneasy doze.

She woke early, feeling tired and irritable. Telling herself that everything would work out, she went to the bathroom. Poorly lit, it smelt dank and unpleasant. After checking the door was bolted, she opened her bag and took out her purse. The fob was still in her purse, attached to the ring, but there was no sign of the key. In a panic, she emptied her bag on the grimy floor in case the key had fallen out of her purse. It was not there. She was sure she had put the key away safely. No one could have come in and removed it during the night. She had hardly slept, and her bag had been beneath her pillow, zipped shut, all the time. The only possible explanation was that Alain had taken the key while she had been on the phone to Joubert. He had offered to hold her bag. Behind her back, he must have slipped the key from the ring and made off with it.

Sitting on the toilet seat, her head in her hands, Lucy tried to think. She felt sick. Alain had gained her trust only to betray her. He had sacrificed her and Nina for Patrice's key. All she could do now was throw herself on Patrice's mercy and beg him to let Nina go. She did not hold out much hope that he would release either of them, even if she told him who had taken his key. She looked around the squalid bathroom in desperation. Catching sight of her reflection in the cloudy mirror, she was startled to see how pale she looked. She could have been gazing at a corpse.

45

NINA TENSED, HER EYES WIDE OPEN, straining to peer through the suffocating darkness. Although she could not see anything, she could still hear. Footsteps were stomping along the corridor on the other side of the door, accompanied by muffled voices. Every morning a solitary man shuffled down the stairs to bring her food and drink. His arrival indicated that another night was over. She had lost count of the days and nights she had spent in the cellar. Now there was more than one man in the corridor. What she could hear was not the sound of her food arriving. Stifling a whimper, she crouched down in her corner and closed her eyes tightly. Whatever was happening, she did not want to see it. With her hands tied together, she was unable to cover both her ears. All she could do was press one of them against her shoulder.

The footsteps were just the other side of the door now. It sounded as though as many as three or four people were outside, waiting around while the door was unlocked. Either she was about to witness another murder, or they were coming to kill her. The prospect of death did not frighten her as much as it would once have done, in the days when life had seemed beautiful and precious. Those feelings seemed distant now. It was hard to believe she had ever felt truly happy. Even her anger had passed. Drained of energy, she watched her life slipping away as she waited to die.

The door opened with a creak. Faintly illuminated in the beam of light from a torch, she caught a glimpse of something scampering across the floor. With a muffled yelp she wrapped her arms round her knees and pulled her feet closer towards her. She could not tell if it was a mouse or a rat. But she was more frightened of the men who entered the cellar. The light flicked on and she opened her eyes a slit, making herself as small as possible. A man she had not seen before was shoved forwards before the light went out and the door closed, leaving her locked in darkness with a stranger.

Hardly daring to breathe in case he heard her, she considered her options. She did not know whether he had noticed her. If he had, he would know roughly where she was in the room. It might be safer to shift her position, rather than wait for him to find her, but she would need to move soundlessly. Cautiously she stood up. Not even by a whisper could she dare betray her presence. Holding her breath, she lifted one foot and took a step. She took another step. And another. The man would never find her now as long as she kept moving silently.

Remembering the rats that roamed around the cellar at night, she wondered whether she should try and sit down with her back to the wall again. She turned, and felt the heat from a body against her arm. With a thin scream she sprang back, but she was too slow. His fingers closed around her elbow, holding her too tightly for her to wriggle free.

His voice was quiet. 'I'm not going to hurt you. Who are you? What are doing here?'

She did not answer.

'Is your name Nina? Don't be afraid. I want the same as you, to get us out of this dreadful hole. It isn't exactly a comfortable place to spend the night, is it? And it can't be healthy either. It stinks in here.'

Nina was only half listening to what the man was saying. All the time he was speaking, he kept tight hold of her elbow. He was gabbling very fast, and her French was not good enough for her to understand everything he said. He was talking about getting away, but she knew that was impossible. This was a room where people came to die. She had seen blood on the floor. People had been killed in there, many times, like the woman in the red dress whose neck Sacha had snapped. The stench of death hung in the air, damp and sickly.

Immediate danger made her alert. Her muscles tensed as she waited for a chance to slip from his grasp. As soon as she was free, she would make a dash for the far wall of the cellar. With any luck, the stranger would be too disorientated in the darkness to try and follow her. If he came after her, she would be able to hear him coming and dart away again when he got too close. If he followed her again, she would keep running. Whatever happened, she would not let him get her. With a visceral thrill, she understood that she was not ready to die after all.

'What's your name?' he asked.

She did not answer. He was trying to trick her. As soon as he loosened his hold on her arm she sprang back, spun round, and sprinted over to the wall, stepping as quietly as she could.

'Stop,' he called out. 'Where are you?'

Silently she lowered herself to the floor and leaned back. The cold wall pressed against her sore shoulders, but the pain did not bother her. It would help her to stay her awake through the dark hours.

'Where are you?' the man called out. 'I don't want to hurt you.'

Nina concentrated on breathing silently. He would never find her.

46

GATHERING HERSELF TOGETHER, Lucy stood up and repacked her bag. She was certain the key could not have fallen out in the room where she had spent the night. All the same, she went back and spent nearly an hour hunting inside and underneath the bed, checking and rechecking everywhere. She pulled off the sheets and removed the pillowcase, shaking everything in case the key had somehow slipped out of her bag. She could not find it. As she searched, she became increasingly convinced that Alain must have taken it. Nothing else made sense.

She wondered whether Alain had wanted the key for himself all along, or if Patrice had paid him to take the key from her. Perhaps Alain was not looking for the stolen treasure at all, but was prepared to sacrifice Nina in order to bring Patrice down, so saving other lives in the future. Who was he to decide who was to live and who was to die? It was worse to be let down by someone she had trusted than to face open hostility. But there was no time to fret over Alain's betrayal. She had to decide what to do when she faced Patrice again. Somehow she had to convince him to release Nina before she revealed that the key had been stolen. She would have no scruples about disclosing who had taken it.

Unable to find her destination without a smartphone, she went downstairs and asked the woman behind the reception desk for directions to L'Ours Doré. The woman raised pencilled eyebrows at the name.

'Keep going straight past the Galeries Lafayette. But are you sure you got the right name?' She tapped the screen with a long scarlet nail and squinted up at Lucy. 'You sure that's what you want? It's very pricey there.'

Lucy did not bother to reply. After settling her bill in cash, she set off. L'Ours Doré was not hard to find. Walking away from the area around the Gare du Nord, she saw the seedy hotels, cafés and small shops give way to more upmarket outlets, Rolex and Dior, Louis Vuitton and Chanel. She reached L'Ours Doré with two hours to spare. From the outside it looked magnificent, with high white pillars and marble steps leading up to a vast revolving door in a golden frame. A man in smart red and gold livery was standing outside. She hesitated in front of the entrance. Aware that drinks there were likely to be very expensive, she walked on and found a bar where she sipped bitter coffee and picked at a croissant. It would be as well to have a good breakfast, but she was too nervous to eat. The minutes seemed to crawl by as the pastry crumbled between her fingers. At last it was time for her to stride up the steps of the hotel, her head held high as though she was feeling perfectly relaxed and confident.

Reaching the top of the marble stairs of L'Ours Doré, she entered a palatial foyer. As she glanced around at the marble and walnut decor, a concierge in a smart red uniform approached her.

'Miss Lucy Hall?' She nodded dumbly, surprised that he knew her name. 'Would you like to come with me, please.' It was not a question. 'Monsieur Durand has reserved a room for you.'

Suppressing the urge to turn and run, Lucy followed her uniformed guide across an opulently furnished bar area. Passing a white grand piano, they reached an imposing monogrammed glass door where they were joined by a tall man with fair hair and broad shoulders. He held the door open for her and she entered a narrow corridor, bare apart from a long table with a massive vase of lilies, their sweet perfume overpowering in such a small space. As the door closed behind them, the man stepped forward briskly, seized her bag and pulled it off her shoulder. Before Lucy could protest, he frisked her. There was no point in remonstrating. In the face of such an aggressive reception, Lucy tried to remain calm. Out of the corner of her eye she could see another man checking her bag. She felt as though she was suffocating in the heavily scented air. They appeared to be checking for weapons, patting her pockets quickly and glancing inside her purse.

At last one of the men opened another door and pushed Lucy through into another room.

'Can I have my bag back?'

One of the men handed it to her. Slinging her bag over her shoulder, she gazed around an elaborately decorated lounge. A few upholstered chairs stood grouped in front of a high marble table with intricately carved gilt legs. A massive chandelier winked and sparkled in the centre of the room, its light reflected off mirrors that reached up to the ceiling, which was decorated in a delicate gold design. Long gold-coloured velvet drapes were drawn across the windows. Distracted by the splendour, for a moment she did not notice Patrice seated on a high-backed chair in front of the fireplace. He rose to his feet and strutted towards her as though he owned the hotel. Perhaps he did. He was flanked by two bulky men who looked like bodyguards. Patrice was not a small man, but he was dwarfed by his companions. Nevertheless, his presence seemed to command attention.

'You missed the deadline.'

'I sent you a message before midnight yesterday.'

'True.' He glanced around. 'Where's Sacha?'

'He was delayed.'

Lucy held her breath, but Patrice did not pursue the matter.

'What do you think of this place?' he asked. 'Not bad, is it? This room's modelled on the Salon de la Paix at Versailles, and do you know who that is?' he added, pointing above the white and gold fireplace to a large full-length portrait of a rosy-cheeked woman in a long gown. 'It's Madame de Pompadour, mistress to a king.' He grinned. 'She was a whore, and look where she ended up, living better than a queen.' He laughed.

Lucy bit her lip and glared at him. Patrice appeared to have reserved the room. With the curtains closed, they had complete privacy. Only Lucy, Patrice and his four accomplices were present. Two of the men stood by the door, like bouncers, while the others remained close to her. They appeared ready to pounce if she made a move, as though she could pose any threat to Patrice.

Meanwhile Patrice returned to his chair, his feet making no sound on the thick carpet. Sitting down again, he smiled up at her and held out his hand.

'Come on then. Time to hand it over. And then I'm going to have it carefully checked to make sure you haven't made a copy.'

Wondering how he would have been able to tell if the key had been copied, Lucy cleared her throat. Before admitting she no longer had the key, she wanted to see Nina safely out of the building, at least.

'Where's Nina?'

'Who? Oh, yes, the other English whore.' Patrice scowled. 'The way you harp on about her, it's not natural.'

'I told you, she's my friend.'

He held out his hand.

Lucy took a deep breath. 'I won't tell you where it is until you let Nina go.'

Patrice's face flushed with anger. 'Give it to me right now, or I'll put a bullet in her myself and you can watch her die.'

Realising she could not stall him any longer, Lucy spoke as firmly as she could. She could feel her legs shaking. 'I haven't got anything of yours.'

Patrice stood up. The chair he was sitting on fell over with a soft thump. One of his accomplices darted forward and set it back on its feet. Patrice ignored him. His eyes never left Lucy's face.

'What the fuck do you mean? That's what you came here for, isn't it? Why else are you here? Now hand it over before I run out of patience with you.'

Lucy met his gaze. 'I told you, I haven't got anything of yours. If I had it, I'd give it to you. What would I want to keep it for? I don't even know what it's for, and besides, we had an agreement. Why else would I have even come here? But I haven't got it any more.'

'What the fuck are you playing at? I was told you were coming here to give it to me. You're here, aren't you? So hand it over.'

'It's true I had what you want when I left that message with Inspector Joubert, but it was stolen from me last night.'

'What do you mean, it was stolen?' Patrice asked, his voice low with menace. He turned away and walked over to the fireplace where he stood for a moment with his back to her. 'I've no idea what the fuck you're talking about,' he yelled, turning suddenly and running up to her. 'What the fuck do you mean?'

'It was stolen,' she repeated, struggling to breathe.

Staring at him, Lucy registered the rage in his blue eyes, and hesitated. She owed Alain nothing. But somehow she could not bring herself to name him. Patrice was going to kill her and Nina. She would not be responsible for any more deaths.

'Enough of your games!' he roared. 'I'll make you sorry, you stupid whore. No one fucks with me. No one.' He paused, and his eyes narrowed in a sadistic glare. 'We may have to take you somewhere else after all.' He waved his hand in the air in a circular motion. 'The carpet in here's too beautiful to spoil. Of course we could work on you without spilling your blood, but it would be easier to persuade you to cooperate if Fabien could be given a free hand.'

One of the bodyguards at the door grunted, and Patrice smiled. 'Fabien can do things with a knife that you wouldn't imagine in your darkest nightmares.' He smiled at her suddenly. 'Don't worry. You'll be able to admire his handiwork for yourself soon enough. He's been practising on your friend. Let's show her, Fabien. That'll loosen her tongue. And if it doesn't, you can loosen it for her.'

To illustrate his meaning, he stuck out his own tongue and made a slicing movement in the air with his hand. Behind her, Lucy heard the other men laughing.

47

PATRICE TURNED AWAY FROM HER and sighed, as though exasperated. 'This is a nice place, isn't it? I thought we'd all come here for a celebration. Shame I can't invite you to stay for tea after all.' He burst out in noisy laughter and his accomplices joined in. 'Come on,' he snapped, and the laughter stopped suddenly, as though a soundtrack had been switched off. He glared at Lucy. 'When you see Fabien's work, you'll change your mind, and that's a promise. Like I told you, he's been practising on your friend. He's quite an artist.' He turned to one of his accomplices. 'Bring her back to the house, Marcel. She thinks she can be stubborn, but it won't take long to break her. She'll snap just like a twig. They all do, sooner or later, and this whore's not going to hold out for long.' He raised his hand again, and clicked his fingers. 'She'll break as easily as that. Fabien's going to be disappointed. He likes them defiant. It helps him work. It's – what's your English expression? It's an ill wind that blows no good to anyone? If everyone did exactly as they were told, straight off, Fabien might start to feel his artistry lacked purpose. Of course, skill like his doesn't need any justification apart from artistic merit. Even so, he likes to feel he's working for a reason. It makes him feel useful.'

Lucy stared down at the carpet and pressed her lips together to stop herself crying. She had a horrible suspicion that what he was telling her was true, and Nina had been tortured. She hated him not only for what he had done to her friend, but for what he was turning her into. It was uncomfortable to think that, under the surface, she was no better than Patrice, her morality a fragile veneer. This was no longer a question of self-defence. She wanted to kill him.

'Now, Lucy,' Patrice went on, sitting down and speaking in a reasonable tone. 'I'm going to give you one last chance. You know what's going to happen to you if I don't get what I want. So hand it over, nice and calm, and no one gets hurt.'

He nodded at one of his accomplices who stepped forward, one hand outstretched. Lucy stared at a large face framed by straw-coloured hair. His dark eyes made her uneasy. He looked pitiless. She wondered if this was Fabien.

'You can give it to Fabien,' Patrice said in answer to her unspoken question. 'Fabien won't hurt you, as long as you give him what I want.'

Lucy glanced at the portrait above the fireplace, and wondered how the red-cheeked Madame de Pompadour would have responded to such sadistic posturing. It was strange, but she was growing used to the idea that every breath she drew might be her last. It was oddly liberating to feel that she actually did not care. She was going to die one day anyway. If her life was cut short by a maniac, so be it. She drew a deep breath, noticing the brightness of the golden curtains and the softness of the carpet beneath her feet. Moments seemed to pass incredibly slowly as they all waited for her response. At last she turned and stared directly into Patrice's blue eyes.

'I haven't got anything to give you. I told you, it was stolen.'

Her voice sounded unnaturally loud, seeming to echo around the large white and gold room before being swallowed up by the silence that followed her statement. Fabien stood immobile, his large hand reaching out towards her, palm upwards. His smile appeared fixed to his face, but his eyes blazed with anticipation. For a second, no one moved. Not for the first time, Lucy felt as though she had stumbled onto a film set, only now she was not in an action thriller, but in Walt Disney's *Sleeping Beauty* at the point when everyone falls asleep for a hundred years. Just as the tension grew intolerable, Patrice's features shifted around on his face.

'Bring her back to the house!' he snapped, and life resumed its normal pace. 'She'll soon change her mind. But first, give me that bag she's clinging onto.'

'I told you, it's not here,' Lucy protested as her bag was seized yet again.

Taking out a pistol, Patrice aimed it at Lucy, and let out a little grunt.

'I don't want to use this,' he said softly, his eyes narrowed in anger, 'not here anyway. Guns make such a mess, and it's all over so quick. But they have their uses. Where would we be without them?'

'We'd all be a lot safer,' Lucy muttered.

Patrice laughed. 'You would say that. You're not the one holding a gun.'

Fabien and one other man strode from the room, leaving another man at the door, and Marcel watching Lucy. She looked at her minder, trying to figure out the best way to attack him. Her speculation was hypothetical. She had succeeded in overpowering Sacha in her small flat, but that had been a very different situation to the one she now faced. She knew where everything was in her own home. It had been easy to grab hold of a bread knife, and a stout umbrella, and she had known where to find enough scarves to tie up her adversary. She was not stupid enough to start a fight with two hefty thugs, plus Patrice, in a strange place. The other two bodyguards might return at any moment. The odds were stacked in Patrice's favour. They always were. He made sure of that.

Meanwhile, Patrice had taken a seat. With his back to her, he was emptying everything out of her bag onto an ornate table. After a while, he stood up. His vexed expression had cleared and he looked smug. Once again, time seemed to hang suspended. Like the woman in the painting, Lucy stood poised, watching, unable to speak. She noticed a faint ticking from the heavy gold watch on Patrice's wrist. A tiny gnat hovered in the air above his head, oblivious to the drama playing out underneath it. With a flutter of invisible wings, it disappeared. Patrice's smile never wavered as they stood waiting in a silence that grew almost unbearable again. For a crazy instant, Lucy was tempted to provoke him to shoot her and get it over with, but that would not help Nina. Besides, she did not want to die.

Patrice slipped the gun inside his jacket pocket as a hotel waiter came in.

'Are you ready to order, sir?' he asked, holding out a menu.

It was hard to believe the waiter did not notice anything amiss. Lucy glanced around. Nothing was out of place. To a stranger, they must look like a family group having a quiet conversation.

'Thank you, but we're leaving,' Patrice replied.

'Some tea would be nice,' Lucy cried out, desperate to detain the waiter. Somehow she had to convey the message that she was being held against her will. If she could only communicate her feelings to the waiter, there was a chance he might help her.

'Another time,' Patrice said.

As the waiter slipped out of the room, Lucy felt as though her last hope of rescue had gone.

48

'Where the hell's the van?' Patrice asked, drumming his fingers impatiently on the arm of his chair. The ring on his finger sparkled with the movement.

As he was speaking, one of his gang returned. He sounded breathless. 'We're ready, boss.'

Marcel seized Lucy by the elbow. She tried to shake herself free, but it was pointless. Apart from Patrice, who was armed, there were two strong men in the room with her. In any case, even if she could escape, Nina was still in Patrice's house. She lowered her head in submission as she was led out. Forcing herself to remain positive, she shuffled along the corridor between Marcel and another thug. Any hope she might have harboured of attracting attention to her plight on the way out of the hotel was scuppered as she was shepherded into another room where two more men were waiting, together with the concierge who had greeted Lucy on her arrival at L'Ours Doré. There was no way she could make a run for it with five minders and Patrice accompanying her across the room and through a fire exit. She glanced around as they left the building, but before she could get her bearings she was bundled into the back of a black van. The door slammed shut and the van began to move. All she could do was pray that Alain had taken the key in order to expose Patrice's criminal exploits. If he succeeded, she and Nina might yet be saved. But time was running out.

Slumped against the side of the van in darkness, Lucy had the impression they were weaving through traffic. Stopping and starting, swerving round corners, they made their way across the city. At last the van slowed down, accelerated one last time, and came to a halt. They had arrived. The door opened. Blinking in the sudden daylight, she clambered down onto a gravel pathway. Hearing dogs baying, she suspected where they were, before she saw the turrets of Patrice's villa. The gates were locked behind them, and she could hear the dogs barking frenziedly nearby. At least she was going to be reunited with Nina. Desperately, she told herself they would plot their escape together.

'The boss is letting the dogs out,' Marcel grunted.

Grabbing hold of Lucy's arm, he dashed towards the stairs. Patrice laughed at his panic.

'You can laugh,' Marcel yelled over his shoulder. 'I seen them tear a man to pieces. If they come near me, I'll shoot them, every one of them.'

'You touch my dogs and I'll tear you to pieces myself, with my own bare hands,' Patrice snarled, as he followed them into the house and shut the door.

'Just don't let them near me,' Marcel growled. 'Where are we taking her?'

Patrice looked at Lucy, his eyes sharp. 'Put her in the front room,' he said. 'Then go and get the others.'

Marcel shoved Lucy through the door of the room where she had first met Patrice. Pushing a naked woman off the settee, Patrice sat down. The woman fell on the floor and rolled over onto her back, legs apart, eyes closed.

'Get this whore out of here,' Patrice snapped, nudging the woman with the toe of one shoe.

The woman did not stir, even when a man ran forward and lifted her off the floor. She moaned softly without opening her eyes as she was carted out of the room. Lucy looked round. Standing guard by the door, a dark-haired, wiry man was staring at her. Even in his own home, Patrice seemed reluctant to go anywhere without at least one companion to protect him. The room was unpleasantly warm. Lucy edged forward and sat down on a chair as far away from the fire as possible.

There was a brief disturbance outside, and the door flew open. For an instant, Lucy thought a rescue team had arrived. Her hope vanished as two filthy figures staggered into the room, a man and a woman. They were holding hands. Had she not known the woman was Nina, Lucy would not have recognised her. One side of her face appeared bruised. Looking more closely, with a tremor of horror Lucy saw that Nina's cheek had been scored by three crude circles, one inside another, like a rough target.

'Isn't she a sight? A work of art!' Patrice crowed, bouncing on his seat. He clapped his hands. 'Didn't I tell you Fabien's a fucking genius? Every time she speaks, the circles move! Lovely, isn't it?'

'Nina is lovely,' Lucy replied carefully, struggling to keep her voice even. 'She always was and she always will be.'

At the sound of Lucy's voice, Nina's wretched companion spoke. 'Lucy?' he croaked.

'Alain? I don't understand. What are you doing here? I thought—' She broke off in confusion, but anger overcame her circumspection. 'How much did he pay you for the key?' she shouted. 'How much to betray me?'

'Don't be so stupid,' Alain mumbled without looking at her. His voice sounded strange, as though he was whistling through his teeth. 'I brought him the key to stop you coming here. It was the only way I could think of to make you stay away. I wanted to protect you. Stupidly, I thought I might be able to get him off your back and rescue Nina at the same time. But it didn't work out that way. You still came here, and he didn't even want the key anyway.' He paused. 'He made me swallow it—'

Patrice interrupted him. 'What would I want with a key when I don't even know what it's for? How the fuck am I supposed to find out? Go round every lock in Paris to see if it fits?'

Lucy was baffled. 'What do you mean, he didn't want the key? What else has this been about?'

But she had a horrible feeling she knew. As realisation dawned on her, Patrice held out his hand. The key fob was lying on his palm. He had taken it out of her purse at the L'Ours Doré.

'You had the camera in your bag the whole time, you lying whore,' Patrice hissed.

Lucy let out a sob that turned into hysterical laughter. She and Alain had spent hours agonising over what the key was for, and all the time it had only been used to help disguise the fake fob. There was no hidden treasure. The key fob was a miniature surveillance camera. She would never know what had been concealed on its film. Evidence that would destroy Patrice had been right in front of her all along. If she had simply worked out how to access the film, she could have uploaded the recording onto YouTube before handing the camera to the police. Since her informant's death the evidence had been hidden away in her flat, and then inside her bag. She had even slept with it under her pillow. Free to discover its significance at any time, she had run around Paris with it in her bag, barely even glancing at it. And now it was too late.

'No!' she cried out. 'We can't let him win!'

At the sound of her anguished protest, Alain raised his head to reveal that one of his eyes was bruised and swollen, and his nose looked misshapen. His bottom lip had been split, his jaw looked swollen, and when he opened his mouth to speak, she saw that one of his front teeth was missing. She felt sick. Registering her expression, Alain looked down, concealing his battered face from her.

'You must agree that Nina looks interesting,' Patrice sniggered. 'Your other friend is not such a pretty sight. Clumsy, clumsy, clumsy. Not Fabien's work, of course. But effective all the same.'

'You didn't make me talk,' Alain muttered between clenched teeth.

'Oh, I'm not really interested in anything *you* have to say,' Patrice answered brusquely. 'You're only here as a demonstration. Lucy is the one who is going to talk to me. I want to hear from her.'

'Let her go. She has nothing to tell you,' Alain said. 'She never even looked at the film. We didn't know—'

As he was speaking, one of the guards hit him, deliberately slapping the injured side of his face. Alain cried out and Nina moaned in sympathy. Tears coursed down Lucy's cheeks.

'Let them go and I'll tell you anything you want to know,' she cried out. 'Just let them go, please.' She was sobbing in earnest now. Pulling herself together with an effort, she continued. 'If you don't let them both go, I won't tell you anything. I don't care what you do to me, I won't say a word if you don't let them go. Not one word.'

Patrice laughed. 'Fine words,' he said, with a hint of admiration in his voice. 'You know, you're working for the wrong people, Lucy. I need tough women. All the whores that hang around here are pathetic. You're more of a woman than all of them put together.'

He sprang from his chair and took her hand in his. Lucy pulled herself free.

'Get off me!'

Nina began to sob. Letting out a roar of rage, Alain yelled at Patrice to leave Lucy alone. If anything, Patrice appeared to find the outcry gratifying.

'You're a fascinating woman. You're brave, and you inspire loyalty. You know, I could make your life better than your wildest dreams.'

Lucy shook her head. 'I don't know what you're talking about. I don't want anything from you, except for you to let all three of us go. You've got what you wanted. You don't need us any more.'

'Fuck them. They don't matter.' Patrice snapped his fingers.

'They matter to me. They're my friends.'

'How you do keep on about it. Friends, friends, friends, what have your friends ever given you?'

'They don't need to give me things. But you wouldn't understand. The people you surround yourself with are only here for your money, or because they're afraid of you.'

Patrice shrugged. 'Works for me.'

'Your way of doing things can't last,' Alain cried out. 'You'll be stopped one day, and it can't come soon enough.'

'Shut up before I rip your tongue out. No one's going to stop me doing what I like. No one's even going to dare to try—'

'So what about that film you've been so desperate to get your hands on?' Lucy asked. 'Someone dared to try and stop you. And whoever it was, there'll be others.'

Patrice turned to her, his voice suddenly soft. 'So you admit Jérôme told you about his film.'

'No,' she replied, trying not to panic. 'I didn't know there was a film. I didn't even know it was a camera until you told me just now. I thought you were after the key.'

'Like hell you did. You thought you could pull the wool over my eyes, so you sent your monkey along with a key to try and trick me.' He walked over to Alain and slapped him on the injured side of his face. 'Did you really think I'd believe you? Do you think I don't know when someone's lying?'

'She didn't know what it was,' Alain gasped. 'Neither of us knew.'

'There's no point in persisting with your lies.' Patrice turned to Lucy. 'Before he died, your friend Jérôme confessed that he'd told you all about his film when he gave it to you. Why would he make that up?'

'Because you were torturing him,' Alain replied. 'He would have sworn black was white to make you stop.'

'If I'd known about the film, it would have been all over the Internet by now,' Lucy said.

'You thought you could fool me. No one does that and gets away with it. No one.'

'You mean no one has yet. That doesn't mean no one ever will,' Lucy muttered angrily.

'Let them try. They'll end up like Jérôme. He thought he could get the better of me, and look what happened to him.'

Patrice turned away from her and paced the room. Lucy, Nina and Alain followed him with their eyes, while the two gang members watched them. After a while, Patrice stopped and gazed around the room. There was something magnetic about his arrogance. Despite her terror, Lucy could not help staring at him.

'Enough of this,' he announced, sitting down. 'I've got what I want. I don't need them any more.'

There was silence for a moment.

'You mean we can go?' Nina whispered.

'Go? Go? Where the fuck do you think you're going, looking like that?'

Lucy stepped forward and the bodyguards stirred. 'You told me you'd let us leave once you got what you wanted.'

Patrice laughed. 'I'll let you leave all right. You think I want to keep you here? You're a fucking nuisance, all of you. You think I want you cluttering up my cellar? She was bad enough.' He glared at Nina who cringed and hung her head. 'But three of you? No way. This isn't a hotel.'

257

'Come on, let's get out of here before he changes his mind and goes back on his word,' Lucy said.

'Not so fast. I won't go back on my word, you stupid whore. I said you'll be leaving and you will. You're going away in a body bag.' Patrice threw his head back and laughed. 'But first,' he went on, serious once more, 'I need to know who else you told about this and who you showed it to.'

Lucy was trembling so much she could barely speak. 'I didn't tell anyone about it. I didn't even know what it was.'

'You've tested my patience long enough. Tell me who else knows about this, or I'll have the rest of his teeth out.' He grinned at Alain. 'Don't look so miserable. You won't be needing teeth where you're going.'

He nodded at one of his accomplices, who stepped forward, knife in hand. Patrice held up a hand to stop him. 'Not here, you idiot. Do you want to ruin the carpet? Oh, don't look so sullen, Fabien. You'll have your chance to show off your skill with a knife.' He turned to Lucy. 'You can watch. Only remember to admire Fabien's handiwork, or he'll sulk.'

49

LUCY GASPED. As she ran forward she was halted by Marcel, who grabbed her by the arm.

'Let go of me!' She turned to Patrice. 'You've got what you wanted.'

'Not so fast. I want you to tell me who else has seen this. It's more important than you know.'

'I never told anyone. I didn't breathe a word about it to anyone. How could I when I didn't know what it was? Please, you have to let us go.'

Lucy bit her lip. Her chance of walking out of here alive was looking remote. Nina and Alain were standing behind her. She wondered if they realised her earlier desperation to find a news-worthy story was costing them their lives.

Patrice understood. 'You thought you'd found yourself a scoop,' he sneered. 'Paris gangster in snuff video. Well, fuck you. That's why you kept it to yourself. It was going to make your reputation as a reporter.'

'If I'd known that there was a film, everyone would know about it by now. I told you, I never watched it. I thought it was just a key fob. That's what it looks like. How was I supposed to know it was a camera?' Lucy replied, nearly crying with fear and rage.

Alain stepped forward to stand beside her. 'Why do you think I risked my life to come here with that key? I did it to save Lucy. We didn't know about the key fob. None of us did. She and Nina haven't done anything to threaten your freedom, so you can't keep them here. They don't know anything about you. They don't even know who you are.'

Patrice grinned at him. 'They might not have known who I was once, but they do now. I understand exactly what you were playing at. You came here with your stupid key because you wanted to save her, just so she could use the film to bring me down. Well, you tried to destroy me before, and you failed then. This time, it's game over.'

He took out his gun and stroked the barrel gently. Lucy watched him in horror. Turning, she cast a frantic glance at Alain. He was staring at the floor. Nina's eyes were tightly closed, as though she could shut out what was happening.

'I won't say a word. None of us will,' Lucy cried out, turning back to Patrice.

'You know I can't take that risk,' he replied softly.

He took the key fob out of his pocket and put it down on the hearth. Lucy stared at it, defeated. She had come so close to destroying Patrice, and she had failed. Now he was going to kill Nina and Alain too, and it was all her fault. Taking careful aim, Patrice shot at the fob, which shattered. Gathering up the pieces he could see, he turned to Alain.

'I think they'd go well with the key, don't you?' He laughed.

'Whatever you say,' Alain muttered, his square jaw jutting out.

Changing his mind, Patrice tossed the black scraps into the fire and stood for a moment watching them curl and melt. There was a smell of burning plastic.

'No one crosses me and gets away with it,' Patrice said complacently, as he turned away from the fire and went to sit down on the sofa. He stared up at Lucy. 'Your time has almost come.'

260

'I've no idea what you're talking about,' she stammered. 'That doesn't even make sense.'

He smiled. He knew she understood exactly what he meant. Patrice looked around the room. For a few seconds no one spoke.

Alain broke the silence. 'You're a deluded maniac if you think you'll get away with this!' he shouted.

Fabien stepped forward, growling like an animal.

Patrice waved him back. 'Leave him.' He turned to Alain. 'You're the one who's deluded. Many idiots like you have tried to stop me, yet here I am. No one has, and no one ever will, because I'm too clever for them all. The police, the government, no one can touch me. No one even comes close. No one's ever going to stand in my way.'

Fabien grinned. Another of Patrice's gang members shook his fist at Alain.

'You think they haven't tried?' Patrice asked. 'I'm telling you, no one can stop me.'

Alain adopted a reasonable tone. 'Kill me, if you must, but you'll never get away with killing them. You might be able to bribe your way past the law here, and get rid of a few whores and low-lifes, but the British government won't ignore the murder of two British citizens. They'll be all over Paris as soon as our bodies are discovered. They'll track you down, and the whole history of your life will unravel.'

Patrice nodded indulgently at him, as though humouring a child. 'What makes you think your bodies will ever be found?' he asked quietly.

The ensuing silence was broken by a burst of raucous laughter as the door flew open and the two women Lucy had seen before ran in, giggling and shrieking. The slender one was still naked. Wearing what looked like a crimson curtain draped around her ample curves, the older one teetered through the door on her bright red stilettos.

'Help us!' Nina called out suddenly in a hoarse voice. 'Help us!'

The older of the two women turned to her, beaming kindly. 'What you after, dearie? I got some skank, and Marianne here's got some smack will blow your head clean off.'

'I'll give you a smack if you don't fuck off out of here!' Patrice yelled. 'Can't you see I'm busy?'

Mumbling incoherently, the younger woman cowered away from him and fled from the room.

'Wait for me,' her companion called out as she tottered after her. The edge of her billowing shawl caught under one of her sharp heels. As she clutched at it, her ankle twisted and she fell head-long, landing on her hands and knees. With a yelp of surprise, she gathered up the fabric and wound it around her body. Clambering awkwardly to her feet, she pulled off her shoes. If her own situation had not been so precarious, Lucy would have found the clumsy interruption entertaining.

'Help us!' Nina repeated feebly.

'Oh, go fuck yourself,' the voluptuous woman snapped as she limped from the room, shoes in hand.

Nina wailed, as though being abandoned by two spaced-out prostitutes was the final straw. Alain remained standing very up-right, his undamaged eye shut. Lucy scowled and looked at the four men who had regrouped, two at the door, two on either side of Patrice. Alain and Nina were incapable of defending themselves. They looked as though they could barely stand. Alain could hardly see. By herself, Lucy was helpless against five men.

'Yes,' Patrice said softly, 'your time has come.'

'You can't kill us,' Lucy said. 'We've done nothing wrong. It was Jérôme Meunier who filmed you, not any of us. It's got nothing to do with us. You can't punish us for what he did!'

Fabien dashed forward and grabbed her, twisting her arm behind her back.

'You see what happens if you dare to cross me,' Patrice crowed.
'Let the English whore go, Fabien.' He turned to Alain and stared
coldly at him. 'You really think their deaths will be investigated by
the British police? Your pathetic attempt to frighten me is futile.
With nothing to investigate, there will be no investigation.' He
leaned back on the sofa and continued as calmly as though he was
inviting them all to go on an outing. 'I can see we need something
less obvious for you than a trip to the Seine. Rivers and canals can be
dredged, and you're going to have to vanish without trace. Oh, don't
look so worried. It's simple. A child could manage it. Just as well,
really, as I'll be arranging it myself, since Joubert killed himself last
night. Hung himself in a police cell.' He shrugged. 'Poor Joubert,
he couldn't cope with the stress of his job any more. Losing him is
a nuisance, but he can be replaced. A man who's lost his nerve has
outlived his usefulness. He fussed like an old woman when I asked
him to carry out the simplest task. You see, Lucy Hall, not even a
police inspector can defy me and live.'

Lucy hung her head. She and her companions were going to die,
and there was nothing she could do to prevent it. Patrice had won.

50

'Put them in the back of the van. We need to get them away from here.'

'Where are we going?' Lucy asked.

'Are we going home?' Nina whispered.

Lucy squeezed her friend's hand reassuringly.

'I don't get it,' one of the men said. 'What's going on, boss?'

'We're taking them somewhere we can get rid of them, discreetly,' Patrice answered.

'Why don't we just go downstairs, like we usually do?' Marcel wanted to know.

Patrice shook his head. 'Didn't I just say we've got to be discreet? This one here's got a big mouth.' He scowled at Lucy. 'I don't know who she's been talking to. That's why we've got to get them right away from here. The last thing we want is anyone sniffing around, trying to find out what's happened to these two whores.' He glared at Lucy. 'You've been a fucking nuisance right from the start.' He turned back to Marcel. 'With what I've got in mind, we can get rid of all three of them in one go without leaving a shred of evidence, not so much as a scrap of skin or bone.'

'How are we going to do that, boss?'

'We're going to take them all out on a boat.' His shoulders shook as he laughed suddenly, showing yellow teeth. 'We might even go fishing.'

'Fishing?' Marcel repeated. 'What the fuck?'

Patrice grinned more widely. 'We might attract a few sharks with this bait.'

Nina whimpered. Marcel took hold of Lucy. She winced. Her arm felt tender where he had grabbed it before; it was probably bruised. Behind her, Alain had seen what was happening and was trying to put up a fight. His attempt at resistance was pointless. Lucy watched in silence as both his arms were yanked behind his back and two hefty men hustled him roughly out of the room in front of her. They shoved him across the hall, with Nina propelled behind him by a third man, and Lucy was pushed along after them by Marcel. Vainly attempting to pull back against him, she stumbled towards the front door, her head spinning. As the front door opened, the howling of Patrice's dogs reminded her that escape was impossible.

A black van was waiting for them outside the house. Helplessly, Lucy watched as Alain was hoisted up and thrown in head first. He lay sprawled on the dirty floor, groaning. Nina was tossed in next. She submitted without protest to the rough treatment, her arms and legs flopping in the air like a rag doll, before she too fell in a heap on the floor of the van. Finally, Lucy was lifted off her feet and shoved inside. Behind her the door clanged shut, leaving them in darkness.

Unable to see and afraid of kicking one of the others, Lucy crawled forwards, feeling her way to one side of the van. Reaching the edge, she propped herself up in a sitting position and listened. The sound of someone shuffling around was accompanied by a low moaning. All at once a dazzling beam of light illuminated a strip of floor. Alain had switched on a torch concealed at the end of a pen. In the narrow beam of light, Lucy saw Nina spreadeagled on the floor. Alain was sitting, hunched over, his knees pressed up to his chin. He shuffled further along so his black eye faced the door. With his good eye he stared wretchedly across at Lucy and Nina.

'How on earth did you manage to keep hold of that?' Lucy asked him, nodding at his torch.

He smiled weakly. 'I nicked it off Marcel. It was sticking out of his pocket. I hadn't planned to take it. I was making a bit of a fuss, asking why he needed to search me when I'd just come from Patrice's cellar, and while he was distracted, I pocketed his pen. A sort of reverse frisking.' His smile broadened into a grin. 'I didn't realise it was one of these, with a torch on the end.'

'We're not too hot at recognising what things are,' Lucy muttered. 'Still,' she added more cheerfully, 'it's lucky you've got it.'

'I took it because I could. I think I had some vague notion that I might try to use it as a weapon.'

'The pen is mightier than the sword,' Lucy said.

'But probably not very effective against a gun. Still, it's nice to have some light.'

Lucy grunted in agreement. During this exchange Nina had not moved.

'Nina,' Lucy called out gently. 'It's all right. Don't worry. We're going to get out of here.'

Hearing Lucy address her, Nina raised her head. Seeing the others sitting up, she hauled herself over to the side of the van where she could prop herself up next to Lucy.

'You heard what he said,' she mumbled tearfully. 'They're going to kill us all. They're going to feed us to the sharks.'

'That's bullshit,' Lucy told her. 'Apart from anything else, there aren't any sharks where we're going.'

'How do you know?'

'Trust me,' Lucy said vaguely. She had no idea if her claim was true. She did not even know where they were going. 'At least there aren't any dogs in here,' she added, and Nina gave a feeble smile. 'There are three of us, Nina. You're not on your own any more. Now we're together again, we'll think of something.'

While she was speaking, Alain had crawled over to the door on his hands and knees. He rattled it loudly, but it was no use.

'Alain can get us out of here,' Lucy went on brightly. 'He can open doors, even when they're locked. So don't worry, we'll be OK.'

But the door was barred on the outside and there was no way Alain could reach the lock to even try and open it. The van jolted and began to move. They spun around corners, revving and braking, until Lucy felt dizzy.

'We're going west,' Alain said when it no longer felt as though they were travelling in circles, but seemed to be speeding along in one direction. 'We're going pretty fast, so I'm guessing we're on the N13.'

'What does that mean?' Nina whispered.

'I think they might be taking us to the coast. I'm going to turn out the light. We don't need it right now.'

Before Alain switched his torch off, he and Lucy exchanged a worried glance. They knew why Patrice was taking them to the sea.

'What is it?' Lucy asked, hearing Nina snivelling in the darkness.

'Sorry about the dark,' Alain said. 'I want to save the battery.'

'It's not that,' Nina said. 'I don't mind the dark. I prefer it, really. Wouldn't you, if you looked like me?' She paused. 'They're going to kill us, aren't they? And even if they don't, how can I go home, with a face like this?' She began to cry more loudly.

Lucy reached out and took her hand. 'Don't worry. Your face can be sorted out once we get back to England.'

The thought that they would probably never get there hung unspoken in the stuffy air.

'How do you know we're going west?' Lucy asked after a pause.

For a long time, Alain did not answer. She could imagine him shrugging his shoulders in the darkness.

'You brought this on yourself,' he said at last. 'You should have gone back to London when you had the chance.'

'I had to stay and help Nina. And anyway, you didn't have to take the key to Patrice. You walked straight into this mess too. You had even less reason to get involved than I did.'

'You came to me for help. What was I supposed to do? Abandon you when it all started to get out of hand? I hoped that if I took him the key he'd leave you alone. It was a gamble, but what else could I do?' He sighed. 'The guilt of my failure had been eating away at me for years, but I was too much of a coward to go after him.'

Lucy knew he was thinking about his brother.

'And then you came along, and you gave me the strength to start again,' he said.

'What do you mean, I gave you strength? What did I do?'

'You refused to give up.'

'It was different for me. Nina was alive. There was no need for you to go after Patrice when you knew your brother was dead.'

'What difference does that make? He was still my brother.'

The van sped on. Nina rested her head against Lucy's shoulder and seemed to be sleeping. Lucy tried to keep still so as not to disturb her. It felt as though they had been travelling for days.

'How far is it to the coast?' Lucy whispered.

'It's over a hundred miles,' Alain answered.

'We've been driving for ages.'

'Almost two hours. Another half-hour or so and we could be in Le Havre. We've been travelling north-west most of the way.'

Nina sat up. 'There are ferries from Le Havre.' She sounded vaguely excited.

'If we can get on one.'

'I think I know why he's taking us to the sea,' Lucy whispered, recalling what Patrice had said about their bodies disappearing.

'I know,' Alain replied quietly.

They travelled on in silence.

51

At last the van jolted to a halt. Lucy screwed up her nose at the stench. Somehow the smell seemed stronger now they were no longer moving. The floor beneath her felt slightly damp. She was not sure whether she had wet herself or not. Her neck was painfully stiff from lying awkwardly propped up against the hard metal side of the van and her buttocks and thighs ached.

'Are you all right?' she whispered.

No one answered.

With a loud clang the door of the van was thrown open and they were bathed in blinding sunlight. Lucy shut her eyes. At her side she felt Nina stir. Opening her eyes slowly, Lucy squinted around. Her companions looked disgusting. Under any other circumstances, the sight of them would have repulsed her. They could have stepped straight off the set of a horror film. But their disfigurements had not been created using stage make-up. In the bright light, Nina's mutilated face looked grotesque, while Alain was sitting very upright on the other side of the van, his open eye glaring balefully from a face pale and pinched with pain. One side of his face had been pummelled mercilessly, every inch of skin bruised and split, the purple and black contusions laced with dried blood.

Two of Patrice's accomplices were standing at the door, waving handguns and shouting at the prisoners to get out quickly. Lucy recognised Marcel. She was sure she would have remembered his companion if she had seen him before, because he was extraordinarily ugly. With a large snout-like nose and tiny eyes, a wide mouth and bristly facial hair, he looked just like a pig. Under other circumstances she might have felt sorry for him. Without speaking, they clambered out of the van. Lucy glanced around, but there was nowhere to run. Apart from the fact that she was not prepared to abandon Nina after everything she had suffered, their guards were armed. It would be suicide to attempt a getaway.

Descending a deserted slope, they made their way at gunpoint through a gap in a fence and scrambled down to the water's edge. Patrice was waiting for them, accompanied by Fabien and another man. Lucy thought it must be a dreary existence, never daring to set foot anywhere without an entourage of thugs for protection. Breathing in the smell of the ocean, with the breeze blowing on her face, she despised him for believing his wealth had bought him freedom.

Not far out at sea, a smart yacht was lying at anchor. A small motorised dinghy was making its way towards the coast, heading straight for them.

'Is that your boat?' Lucy asked, looking out over the water towards the yacht.

With a grin, Patrice told her he was borrowing it.

'Only I may have forgotten to mention that to the owner,' he added, laughing. 'He'll be in for a surprise next time he wants to use it.'

As it drew near, Lucy saw that the dinghy was bigger than she had first thought, large enough to carry a dozen people in comfort. Frantically she glanced around, hoping to spot someone who might come to their aid, but that rocky stretch of coast was deserted. Still at gunpoint, they were hustled into the dinghy. Along with the man at the tiller, the three prisoners and Patrice, four more men embarked and they sped out to sea. Reaching the yacht, they saw a fixed metal ladder leading up onto the deck. When Nina complained her legs were too stiff for her to climb up, Marcel raised his gun and pointed it at her face.

Patrice shook his head, smiling indulgently at his accomplice. 'Don't be impatient. The whole point of bringing them here is to dispose of them out at sea. The sharks will clean up any mess.'

'There aren't any sharks in the English Channel,' Lucy declared. She hoped that was true.

'Oh, all right,' Nina grumbled. 'It's not like I've got any choice, is it?'

Lucy watched Nina crawl up the ladder. She moved like an old woman, seeming to rely on her arms to pull her up, while her legs dragged feebly. Lucy could not help feeling it was her fault her friend had been reduced to that state.

Reaching the deck, the three prisoners were escorted down a second ladder into a narrow cabin where Marcel and the ugly man she'd seen earlier shackled their hands behind their backs. Lucy gathered that Marcel's porcine companion was called Eugène. With their prisoners secured, the two guards went back up on deck, shutting the door behind them. Although the curtains were drawn across the portholes, enough light penetrated the flimsy fabric for them to see around their prison clearly. All the fittings had been ripped out. The walls were a jumble of paintwork interspersed with bare plaster where cupboards must once have been attached. A long bench ran along one side of the cabin, while on the other a wide strip of unpolished floorboards at the edge of the dusty carpet showed where cupboards had once stood. The interior of the cabin formed a stark contrast with the yacht's spruce exterior.

Lucy struggled against an almost overwhelming despair. Every time she moved, metal manacles dug sharply into her wrists. She tried to keep still. Just as maddening as the pain was an itch on the side of her face. She tried shaking her head but it made no difference. There was nothing she could do to relieve the irritation, which seemed to grow worse the more she tried to ignore it. Closing her eyes, she tried to block out the motion of the boat, rocking gently on the water. It was making her feel slightly sick. She could hear someone shuffling around, voices shouting above her head, and footsteps pounding on the deck. All of a sudden the engine roared, the floor vibrated, and the boat began to move. She opened her eyes.

'Where are they taking us?' Nina asked.

'We're not going anywhere,' Alain replied tersely.

Nina turned her disfigured face to him. 'I don't understand.'

Before Alain had a chance to explain, Lucy interrupted. 'Alain, have you still got that pen?'

'What are you proposing to do? Send a message in a bottle? I know you're relentlessly positive, Lucy, but even you must see that it's over. He's beaten us.' He hung his head.

'If you can get at that pen, I was thinking you might be able to pull it apart and use a bit of it to unpick the locks on our handcuffs. It was just an idea.'

Alain sat up, his voice trembling with suppressed excitement. 'I don't know. It all depends on what kind of lock it is. I can't make any promises, but I suppose we could give it a go. But I don't think I can reach it.'

He leaned right over to one side, straining to push his hands up towards the pocket of his jacket. Lucy jumped to her feet. As she stood with her back to him, he too got to his feet, bent his knees, and manoeuvred his pocket towards her outstretched fingers. Once she had the pen, she gave it to him and he fidgeted with it behind his back.

'We might be able to use the metal clip on the end, if I can just break it off,' he muttered. 'It's a bit like a slim jim.'

'What's a slim jim?'

'It's technically known as a lockout tool. It's just a thin strip of metal, really, usually steel, used to unlock car doors without a key. The trouble is the pen clip won't have a hooked end, and it's not metal so it might just snap.'

'But there's a chance it could work?' Lucy persisted.

Alain shrugged. 'It's better than nothing, I suppose. It feels like it might be thin enough.'

'It's got to be worth a try,' Lucy insisted. 'We can't just sit here doing nothing. If they're going to kill us all, the least we can do is try and put up a fight.'

'Yes, let's take some of these bastards with us, starting with Fabien,' Nina said.

Lucy was startled by the venom in her friend's voice. She had known Nina for years, and had always found her to be soft-hearted and timid. Over the past week she had changed so much that Lucy hardly recognised her any more. Lucy was different too. If they survived, she wondered if either of them would ever really recover from their encounter with Patrice.

With a faint snap, the clip broke off. Alain said that as he was most able to defend them, they should work on releasing him first. Lucy said nothing about having overpowered Sacha in her flat. She was not sure she would be able to repeat her performance. Certainly Alain was physically the strongest of the three of them, and in such a small space his partial blindness might not be too much of a problem. She no longer harboured any suspicion about his commitment to helping her. He had risked his own life to protect her by taking the key to Patrice himself. It was ironic that his gesture had turned out to be so utterly pointless.

Sitting back to back, Alain handed her the pen clip and they wriggled around until Lucy was able to feel his handcuffs with her outstretched fingers. Several times she lost her grip on the pen part and they had to scrabble around looking for it. Alain swore whenever the point of the clip slipped and dug into him. She fiddled around, trying to insert the point into the aperture of the lock, while Alain gave her an unhelpful running commentary.

'I'm trying, I'm trying,' she kept repeating in exasperation.

Just as she was beginning to think that her efforts were futile, there was a click and the lock on Alain's handcuffs sprang open. He waved his hands in the air with a muted cry of triumph. Lucy handed him the improvised lock pick, and he set to work on her manacles. He seemed to be working behind her back for hours, but at last she was free. It was a relief to be able to move her arms again. Even after so short a time, her shoulders ached from being pulled backwards, fixed in one position. With a sigh, she scratched the side of her head and stretched her fingers, examining the angry red lines where the bracelets had been chafing her wrists. Before long her flesh would have been raw, but the skin, although red, was still intact. Smiling grimly, Alain turned his attention to Nina who sobbed quietly while he worked. He held his head on one side so he could focus on the manacles with his one open eye. Engrossed in the task, neither Alain nor Nina heard the bolt slide across the door at the top of the stairs.

'Someone's coming,' Lucy hissed. 'Watch out!'

There was no time to issue any more warnings before the door opened and a pair of huge dirty trainers appeared. Their owner descended backwards down the ladder, his face to the rungs. With a loud bang the door swung shut behind him. Without making a sound, Alain took one long stride across the floor of the cabin and stood still, poised to strike. As the back of the man's head came within reach, Alain sprang forwards and grabbed the gun from his hand. With an angry growl Eugène spun round, his swinish eyes wide with fury. In that instant Alain struck the side of his head with the butt of the gun. Eugène staggered, dazed by the blow, but did not collapse. With a roar he lunged at Alain who leapt aside and struck him again, hitting his skull with a muffled crack. Eugène crashed to the floor, hitting his head on the side of the metal ladder.

'One down, five to go,' Alain said, pocketing the gun.

'You made a bit of a racket,' Lucy whispered. 'It's lucky the door's shut or they'd all have been rushing down here to investigate.'

Alain tapped his pocket where the gun was stashed, and grinned. 'Let them come. We'll be ready for them.'

'Is he dead?' Lucy whispered, nodding at Eugene, whose face had turned horribly pale.

'As a door nail,' Alain replied cheerfully.

He returned to Nina and resumed working on her handcuffs. He had to proceed carefully as her wrists were bleeding, but at last there was a click. Nina's hands were free.

'I'm sorry it took so long,' Alain said. 'Sometimes they open really easily.'

With a nod of thanks, she took the small metal strip and slipped it in her pocket.

'Get him right in the eye,' Alain muttered.

Lucy was unnerved by the manic expression on Nina's face as she nodded at Alain, but there was no time to worry about that. Their hands were free, Eugène was dead, and Alain had a gun. The situation no longer felt completely hopeless. Alain looked around and pocketed a pair of handcuffs. Lucy wondered whether he intended to use them to shackle the guards, or kill them. The sharp metal could be an effective weapon if used with sufficient force. With a shudder she slipped a pair of handcuffs into her own pocket.

52

THEY WERE SITTING IN A LINE, examining their injuries and rubbing their wrists, when the door was flung open and they heard voices coming from the deck. Someone complained that the door was not bolted, and another voice replied that Eugène had gone down to the cabin and had not yet returned. A third voice remarked that he had been gone for a long time. Lucy glanced down at the body lying at the foot of the ladder. It was too late to move it. The door was open and another guard might come down the stairs at any second. In any case, there was nowhere to stash Eugène out of sight. Even if they managed to prop him up to make it appear that he was sitting down watching them, his companions were bound to call out to him. When he failed to respond, one of the other guards would come down the stairs to investigate. Even a moron would not have to look too closely to see that Eugène was dead. Alain slipped his hand in his pocket.

'Might be best not to let them know we're free until we've planned what we're going to do,' Lucy whispered.

Alain nodded and put his hands behind his back as though he was still manacled. Lucy and Nina did the same.

'We could say he fell down the stairs,' Lucy whispered.

Glancing down she saw Nina's handcuffs on the bench beside her. She shifted along to hide them as a pair of feet came slowly into view. Watching, she recognised a brilliant diamond flashing at her from one of the hands holding onto the rails. Patrice was already halfway down the ladder. He was descending slowly. Even so, in less than a minute he would reach the bottom. Without stopping to think, she grabbed the gun from Alain and sprang to her feet. Before Patrice's feet touched the floor, she gripped him in a head-lock, pressing the gun against his temple. Patrice swore ferociously and waved his arms, trying to grab onto her. In one bound, Alain was at Lucy's side and had Patrice's gun in his hand.

'Turn round slowly,' Lucy said quietly. 'If you call out or make a sound, you're dead.'

'What the fuck? You can't do this. Let me go. I'll crucify you.'

'Shut up,' Alain hissed. 'If you open your mouth again, I'll put a bullet in your brain quicker than you can utter a word. Don't think I won't do it. The only thing stopping me from killing you right here, right now, is that a quick death would be too kind for you.'

'Here,' Lucy thrust the gun she was holding at Nina. 'I don't know what to do with it. You've seen one of these before, haven't you?'

White with shock, Nina took the gun, shaking her head and mumbling about her uncle owning a farm. For a second, Lucy was afraid her friend might start shooting indiscriminately, she appeared so disturbed. But Nina stood perfectly still. Only the gun trembled in her hand. Meanwhile Alain was pointing his gun at the side of Patrice's head. Slipping it round to aim at Patrice's eye, he suddenly jerked it forward to touch the iris. Blinking, Patrice recoiled with a strangled cry, mumbling about making Alain regret what he was doing.

'The only thing we're going to regret is treating you too gently,' Lucy replied.

'You could've damaged my eye, you fucking bastard,' Patrice protested.

'I hope I did,' Alain retorted, slapping his hand over the gang-ster's mouth.

'You're hardly in a position to complain about someone inflict-ing physical pain,' Lucy said.

Alain leaned forward to hiss in Patrice's ear. 'Scum like you don't deserve the mercy of a quick death. I'm going to make you suffer worse torments than you put Nina through, and she's going to sit here and watch.'

'Let me go,' Patrice cried out, breaking free of the hand gagging him. 'You can't do this to me. Get your fucking hands off me, or you'll be sorry.'

'I thought I told you to shut up,' Alain hissed. He was sweat-ing, and there was a frenzied look in his eyes. 'One more word and you're a dead man.'

Patrice blinked, scowling. Pressing his lips together, he stared at the gun in Alain's hand through half-closed eyelids.

With his free hand, Alain gestured towards the stairs. 'Get up there and send your gorillas away.'

'And remember, no tricks,' Lucy warned Patrice. 'Alain's jumpy enough as it is.'

'If any of your gang is still within sight of the boat five minutes from now, you're a dead man,' Alain added.

'They won't desert me.'

'Haven't you noticed a man you tortured is holding a gun to your head?' Lucy said.

Alain's voice shook but his hand was steady. 'Enough talking. Get up those stairs and send them all away. I'd rather shoot you than keep you alive, if that helps to make things clear. After what you did to me, believe me, my fingers are itching to pull the trigger.'

Patrice climbed the ladder slowly with Alain at his heels. Lucy followed them and after her came Nina, gun in hand. With Eugène dead, four gang members remained on deck, one steering the boat, the others waiting to carry out Patrice's orders. For a second none of them noticed the gun at their leader's head. They stared in surprise as the three prisoners emerged from the cabin, following Patrice. He called out to his accomplices by name, ordering them to pay attention. Marcel started forward. Catching sight of the gun Alain was holding against the back of Patrice's head, he froze. Raising his voice, Patrice yelled at them to assemble on deck. The man at the helm left his post and they all made their way hurriedly to the deck.

'Take the dinghy and go,' Alain shouted, 'unless you want me to put a bullet in his head right now. And you'll be next.'

'Get rid of them! Feed these whores to the sharks!' Patrice screamed in a frenzy.

Patrice's accomplices only hesitated for a moment before making their way to the dinghy at the stern of the yacht. With her gun trained on Marcel, Nina gestured at him to move. Grumbling, he followed the others and clambered down the ladder to the dinghy.

Patrice was alone on the boat with the three people he had taken captive and tormented. Alain grinned at him, but Lucy watched Patrice warily. She did not trust him. With his gun still pointing at Patrice, Alain glanced over his shoulder to check that the dinghy had gone. As they watched the small boat drawing away from them into the gathering darkness, none of them noticed Marcel hauling himself back up over the edge of the deck until it was too late.

With a roar, Marcel flung himself at Alain and grabbed him round the waist, knocking the gun from his hand. It clattered to the deck and slid over the side to vanish in the dark waters. Nina and Marcel were holding the only guns left on board. Nina raised her hand, aiming her weapon at Marcel. It was a difficult shot, with Alain and Marcel grappling on the deck. Nina fired. One of the wrestlers shrieked. It was impossible to tell which of them had been hit. Eyes blazing, Nina turned the gun on Patrice. As she pulled the trigger, Lucy darted across the line of fire, crying out Alain's name.

53

DASHING FORWARD, Lucy ran straight across the trajectory of Nina's bullet. If the gun had not run out of ammunition, she would have been shot. She felt physically sick. Struggling to control her shaking, she turned to face Nina who was staring at her, white with shock.

'I'm sorry,' Nina gasped. 'I didn't see—'

'Get him off me!' Alain yelled, heaving himself out from under Marcel's writhing figure.

Unaware that Lucy had almost been shot, he crawled to the edge of the deck where he dragged himself to his feet and leaned against the rail, panting. He was holding Marcel's gun in his hand. Meanwhile, Marcel lay on the deck, groaning and clutching his shoulder where Nina had shot him. Patrice ran over to him, exhorting him to hand over his weapon, unaware that Alain had already disarmed him. Ignoring the injured man, Lucy went and stood beside Alain who looked down at her with his one good eye.

'Just give it to me!' Patrice was shrieking in a frenzy. 'You'll be the first to get a bullet in your brain for holding out on me like this.'

Marcel cried out in pain as Patrice kicked him. Glancing around, Lucy saw Patrice struggling to force Marcel to his feet. She turned back to Alain.

'I still don't understand what made you hand the key over to him.'

Alain shrugged. 'You came to me for help. I don't like to walk away from an unfinished job.' He frowned. 'I thought if I could give Patrice what he wanted, you'd be safe and it would all be over for you.'

'For me perhaps, but what about you? What did you think would have happened to you, if he had let Nina and me go after you took him the key?'

Alain gave a tired smile. 'It would have been worth it. At least I would have been able to save you. But my plan was doomed from the start, because he wasn't after the key at all.'

'I know. All that time we spent trying to find out what it was for! I wonder what was on Jérôme's film. A record of Patrice torturing some poor soul to death, I suppose. You realise we had proof that could have put him away, and we missed it completely. He's going to carry on now, isn't he? And whoever he hurts or kills from now on, that's going to be on our consciences for the rest of our lives, unless we can stop him. We have to make sure he doesn't escape justice this time.'

Alain took a deep breath and gazed out over the sea with his one good eye. A loud scream made them both turn to see Patrice stamping on Marcel's injured shoulder.

'I should kill him,' Alain said. 'That would save a lot of other people from suffering and death.'

'But if you do, you'd be no better than him. He has to stand trial.'

'What if he gets off? He's destroyed the incriminating evidence.' Alain glanced down at the gun he was holding. 'I could end this right now and no one else would ever know.'

'I'd know, and so would you. But there must be other evidence. We'll think of something. We can't take the law into our own hands. We have to be better than him, or what was this all about?'

Throughout their whispered discussion, Patrice had been pre-occupied with Marcel. Now he turned his attention to Lucy. His eyes seemed to sear into her brain as he taunted her.

'You'll never get one over on me. You had enough to get me banged up for life and you couldn't do it. Now I've destroyed the film it's all over. You missed your chance. So much for you and your friends. Soon *my* friends will be here—'

'I don't think anyone's coming back for you,' Alain answered. 'They all seemed very happy to get away and save their own skins.'

'They'll be here. You'll see. They always come through for me. We've survived a lot together, me and my gang. On their own they're nothing, and they know it. They need me.'

'Yeah, I bet you tell them that all the time,' Alain said.

Lucy turned to him. 'I think it's time we sent this all-important gang leader to sit in state in the cabin. After we've handcuffed him.'

'And gagged him,' Alain agreed. 'And he can take his devoted disciple with him.' He kicked Marcel, who groaned.

Patrice took a step back, his face twisted in an unexpected expression of terror.

'No! You're not going to lock me down below! You stay here if you want to, but I'm leaving.'

'No one's leaving,' Lucy replied.

'Not to worry,' Alain said. 'It might take a while, but we're going to take you back and hand you over to the police so you can stand trial.'

'Which is more than you deserve,' Lucy added.

'Shut the fuck up!' Patrice shouted. His face was pale and he was sweating. As he stepped forward, Lucy saw that he was shaking. 'You're wasting time. I need to get off this boat right now. There's a lifeboat on the other side of the deck. Lower it into the water. You can all stay here, with him.'

He gave Marcel a vicious kick before he ran and pressed a lever that set the mechanism in motion to lower the lifeboat.

'Oh, we've got plenty of time,' Alain said, leaning back against the rail. Lucy watched him lift his head to feel the wind blow his fringe off his face. He looked almost happy.

'You don't get it,' Patrice shouted, his voice suddenly shrill with fear. 'I'm not staying here. I need to get off this boat!'

'You're the one who doesn't get it. We're taking you back to France, where you'll stand trial,' Lucy said.

'You can count yourself lucky you're escaping with your life.' Alain glanced down at the water and smiled. 'Unless I think better of letting you live.' He held up the gun he had taken from the bodyguard.

Marcel raised himself up on one elbow. Alain kicked his arm from under him and he fell back to the floor, moaning.

'You don't understand. I have to leave the boat,' Patrice repeated urgently. 'There's a bomb on board, and it's set to go off in less than ten minutes. You'll all be blown to smithereens.' His eyes lit up with a maniacal zeal. 'Brilliant, isn't it? You're all going to disappear without trace. There will be no investigation, because no bodies will ever be found.'

'We have to stop the bomb!' Lucy cried out.

'Don't look so worried,' Alain said. 'Do you think he'd risk his life coming on board if he couldn't control the explosion?' He raised his gun. 'Do it, now!'

Patrice laughed. 'Shoot me and you're all dead. I'm the only one who knows the code.'

'Do you know anything about bomb disposal?' Lucy asked Alain.

'You can't do anything to the bomb itself. The whole boat is wired up. It can only be stopped on the computer.' Patrice grinned. 'Now I'm getting in the lifeboat. If you're lucky, I'll call out the code to you as I leave.'

'What computer? Where is it?' Lucy demanded. She turned to Nina. 'We need to find it, now!'

Lucy ran over to the other side of the deck to look at the lifeboat. The mechanism to lower it into the water seemed to be working.

'The computer's gone,' Marcel cried out, staring wide-eyed at Patrice.

Patrice turned to him. 'Gone? What are you talking about?'

'I gave it to Fabien to take on the small boat with him. I told him to take it back to the house. I didn't know . . . I thought you'd want to keep it safe. You made such a fuss about it, I thought it was important . . .'

'There's room for all of us in the lifeboat,' Lucy said, hurrying back across the deck to rejoin them.

'All but one of us,' Alain said, pointing his gun at Patrice.

'You can't leave me here to die,' Patrice cried out in alarm.

'It's what you were going to do to us.'

'No, I never. I was . . . I thought . . . Look, take me with you and I'll give you whatever you want. Anything at all.' Patrice's eyes blazed with sudden desperation. 'I can make you richer than you ever dreamed possible. No more grafting for a living. Women, booze, whatever you want. Here, take this for a start.' Wrenching his diamond ring off his finger, he shoved it in Alain's pocket. 'Twenty-two-carat gold. You don't see that every day. And the rock is five carats of perfect ice. It's worth a fucking fortune, and I'm giving it to you. And that's just the start. There's a truckload more for you when we get back.'

'You think you can buy my support, you scum?'

With a sudden swipe, Patrice grabbed a set of handcuffs from his pocket and attached his own wrist to Alain's. He looked up and grinned in triumph.

'You think you're clever, but no one gets the better of me. No one! You're not going to leave this boat without me. No one fucks with me and gets away with it. No one!' He raised his arm, dragging Alain's arm up with his own. 'Now you've got to take me with you when you leave. I won't forget any of this, and that's a promise. Once we're back on land, I'll crush you, all of you. I'll make you suffer for what you tried to do to me.' He glared at Lucy. 'You're going to regret the day you stole that film of me, Lucy Hall. Wherever you go, wherever you hide, I'll hunt you down. You'll never sleep in peace again as long as you live. And that's a promise too. If they lock me up, I'll send my boys to track you down, from my prison cell. There'll be no escape for you, as long as you live.'

They were standing by the rail that ran round the deck. As Patrice finished speaking, Alain slipped a spare pair of handcuffs from his own pocket and fastened his other hand to the rail. Turning his head to face Lucy with his one good eye, he smiled.

54

APPALLED, LUCY STARED AT ALAIN AND PATRICE standing side by side against the safety rail. In a few minutes, they would both be blown to pieces along with the boat and there was nothing anyone could do to prevent it. Alain had chosen to give up his own life to ensure Patrice could not survive the explosion. In the meantime, the rest of them had to act quickly or they would be killed along with them. As though the same thought occurred to everyone on board at the same time, the deck erupted into mayhem. Everyone seemed to be yelling at once.

'We have to get off this boat or we'll all die!' Nina yelled, staggering over to the far side of the deck where the lifeboat was still descending. 'Somebody has to do something!'

Lucy ran over to join her and looked over the side. 'It's nearly there!' she called out. 'The lifeboat is almost in the water! How long have we got?'

Patrice was tugging frenziedly at the rail to which he and Alain were fastened.

'Patrice, how long have we got?' she repeated.

'We need to pull this rail out right now!' Patrice was shouting. 'There's no time to work on the handcuffs, so we're going to have to take this with us.'

Alain stood watching calmly as Patrice strained to wrench the railing out of the deck. It did not budge.

'You're wasting your energy,' Alain said after a moment. 'It's not as if there's any point. What do you expect to happen? There's no way you're going in the lifeboat with this.' He slapped the top of the rail with his hand. 'It'll sink us all. And if you manage to throw yourself overboard while you're attached to it, you might as well be tethered to an anchor. There's no point even trying to detach it from the deck. It's over, Patrice. You're a dead man.'

He turned to Lucy and spoke rapidly.

'It's time for you to leave us, Lucy. Oh, don't look so miserable. There's no way back for me now, but your life's just beginning. There's only one thing left for me to do now, and that's to see my job through, which means helping you to get out of this in one piece. Lucy, listen to me. You've got the will and the courage to help others, and do your bit to make the world a better place. I was like you once, full of hope for the future. All that's left for me now is to make sure you have your chance.'

Dragging Patrice's hand up with his own, he held out the ring he had been given. Cold and fiery, the diamond sparkled between them.

'Here. Take this.'

Lucy drew back, shaking her head. 'Whatever it is, I don't want it.'

'You don't have to use it. Take it to remember me by. Please. It's no use to me where I'm going.'

He lunged forward and thrust the ring into her pocket. It was hard to believe that only a week had elapsed since Jérôme Meunier had slipped his tiny camera into that same pocket.

Alain smiled at her. 'You can give it back to me when I see you again. Now, it's time for you to leave.'

'First we have to get you free of all this. Has Nina still got that pen clip?'

'There's not enough time. You have to go now!'

Muttering a curse, Patrice stepped forward and kicked Marcel. 'Don't just lie there, you fucking idiot. Get up and help me.' He held out his hand that was attached to Alain's. 'I don't give a fuck how you do it, but you need to get me free of him. It can't be that difficult. Come on, you're not a complete moron. You heard what he said. There's no time to pick the lock. Just hack through his wrist. You can leave his other hand chained to the rail.' He spat at Alain. 'Don't think for one minute we're taking you with us.'

Patrice kicked Marcel again.

Groaning, Marcel staggered to his feet and grabbed Lucy by the arm. 'Take me with you,' he pleaded, grimacing with pain. 'Take me with you. I don't want to stay here and be blown up. Take me with you!'

Patrice let out a cry of rage. 'Never mind whining to that whore. Do what you're told!'

'Fuck that. I don't want to die.'

'Have you forgotten who I am? And what I know about you? Where are the rest of my gang? After all I've done for them, where the fuck are they when I need them?'

'The others have all gone,' Lucy said. 'Now, how long have we got?'

No one answered. She grabbed Nina's hand and led her over to the other side of the deck. They only had to climb down the steps and they would be in the lifeboat.

'Go on, get in,' Lucy urged her.

Nina nodded nervously. Clinging to the handrail, she lowered one foot over the side and felt for the top rung of the ladder. Before she had disappeared from view, Lucy turned back and nearly crashed into Marcel who was standing right behind her, blubbering and begging. Lucy nodded and stepped aside. With difficulty Marcel began shuffling across the deck towards the ladder, moaning as every step jolted his shoulder painfully. Lucy dashed back to Alain, who was watching from the far side of the deck. Nina called out to her but she did not answer.

'Save us!' Patrice begged, his face contorted in fear.

Meanwhile Alain was standing completely still, watching Lucy. He looked quite peaceful.

'Come on, Lucy,' Nina shouted, climbing back up the ladder, 'we've got to get away. The boat could explode at any moment. Lucy! Do you want to stay here and be blown up?'

Lucy turned to look at Nina, her face streaked with tears. 'We can't just leave Alain here.'

'Look, I don't like this any more than you do,' Nina yelled back, 'but there's nothing we can do about it. We can't take him with us. If there was any way we could get him off the boat, we would. But it's impossible, and we've got to go. Now!'

'We can't abandon him.'

For the first time, Alain seemed to register her words. 'Don't be so bloody stupid,' he said. 'If you don't get off this boat right now, you'll be blown up.'

'*You're* not getting off.'

'For a very good reason.' He raised his hands, as far as he could. 'There's nothing can be done to prolong my miserable life, but at least I'll have the satisfaction of knowing I've done the right thing at last.'

Lucy knew he was thinking about his brother.

Before she could respond, Alain called out to Nina. 'For God's sake get her into the lifeboat and as far away from here as possible, before you're both blown to smithereens.' He turned back to Lucy. '"It is a far, far better thing that I do", and all that. I can't remember the rest of it.'

'"It is a far, far better thing that I do, than I have ever done; it is a far, far better rest that I go to than I have ever known." It's from

A Tale of Two Cities, the last words a man from Paris says before he sacrifices himself to save a woman from London.'

'That's the one.' He gave Lucy a crooked smile from the un-injured side of his face. 'You might not understand why I'm doing this. I'm not even sure I understand it myself. But I know I'm doing the right thing. Goodbye, Lucy Hall, and good luck.'

55

THROUGH LUCY'S TEARS, Alain's face was just a blur. Blinking, she saw his one eye gazing levelly at her. Before she realised what was happening, Nina seized her by the wrist and began dragging her across the deck.

'What are you doing?' Lucy yelled. 'Let me go!'

'Come on, Lucy, we need to get off the boat before we're all blown up. We have to get out of here. Please, Lucy, I don't want to die!'

For an instant, Lucy felt as helpless as Patrice chained to the railing. Then a wave of panic flooded through her as her regret was swallowed up by the fear that she would be too late to escape. Alain had chosen to die. She wondered if he was regretting his choice, but it was too late to help him.

She was scared of being left behind, knowing she had only a few minutes left to breathe in the fresh, salty sea air. She wanted to see the stars and watch the moonlight glistening on the water. She wanted to face the challenges that lay ahead of her. More than anything, she wanted to live.

Nina disappeared over the side. Lucy scuttled after her. In her hurry, she missed her footing on the slippery ladder. Slithering down the last few rungs, she tumbled into the lifeboat where

Nina was waiting for her. Marcel was standing with his back to the yacht, staring out to sea. As Lucy fell, she collided with Nina who crashed into Marcel, sending him hurtling over the side. Bellowing, he landed in the water with a momentous splash. Then there was silence. Lucy dashed to the side expecting to see him thrashing around, yelling, but there was no sign of him. Below her, black water churned and bubbled between the yacht and the lifeboat.

'Come on, there's no time to waste!' Nina shouted. 'The bomb's going to go off! We've got to get away from here!'

Nina was right. They needed to put as much distance as possible between themselves and the yacht if they did not want to be blown up, or sunk by debris from the explosion.

Abandoning her search for Marcel, Lucy turned her attention to the lifeboat. She was not going to give up trying to save herself and Nina after all they had endured in order to escape. She had to guess what to do. At her third attempt, the engine sparked into life and they sped away across the water. They were only just in time. With a roar that rang inside Lucy's ears for a long time, the yacht burst into a massive ball of fire. Blinding flames were obscured by thick smoke that rose, billowing, into the sky. Lucy blinked. When she opened her eyes, the yacht had gone. Only a pall of black smoke hung in the air, marking the place where it had been rocking on the waves a moment before. The wash from the explosion reached the lifeboat, which pitched violently for a few moments.

Clutching the tiller, Lucy broke the silence. 'Make yourself comfortable, Nina, this could take a while.'

'Do you think we can get a signal out here?' Nina asked, taking out a mobile phone.

'Bloody hell, how did you manage to hang onto that?' Lucy asked.

'I didn't. I took it from Marcel's pocket.'

'We need to get rid of it,' Lucy said. 'It might attract unwanted attention.'

She took the phone from Nina and fiddled with it for a moment before tossing it into the sea. Nina let out a wail of protest, but it was too late to retrieve it. Nina stared miserably into the distance without speaking.

Lucy broke the silence. 'The English Channel is just under twenty miles across, so assuming we're heading in the right direction we should reach England in a few hours. It's difficult to tell how fast we're travelling.'

'*Assuming* we're heading in the right direction?' Nina repeated. 'What if we're not? We could be going the wrong way, or going round in circles.' Her voice rose in panic. 'And we're going to run out of fuel soon!'

'We'll be fine.'

'How can you be sure?'

'I checked the compass on Marcel's phone and noted the position of the sun before I chucked the phone away.'

'That was clever,' Nina said.

'Give me some credit,' Lucy answered.

She was pleased that her lie had comforted Nina. The truth was she had no idea where they were heading. In any case, the sun would soon be setting.

'Lucy? Are you awake?' Nina asked after a while.

'Yes.'

'I thought maybe you'd fallen asleep. Do you want me to take over so you can have a rest?'

'I'm fine.'

'Lucy?'

'Yes?'

'I'm sorry about Alain.'

Lucy stared down at the dark water. 'We only just met, I can't remember when, exactly. I feel as though I knew him for years, although it can't be much more than a week. I know it sounds strange, but we established a kind of connection.'

'I know what you mean. When you've been through a lot with someone, you can bond really quickly. I hardly knew him either. I still can't work out what to make of him, but I'll never forget him.'

'Nina?'

'Yes?'

'I'm sorry I got you involved in all this. I had no idea . . .'

Nina let out a sigh that was like a sob. 'It's hard to believe it happened. But it wasn't your fault.' There was a pause before she added, 'I still don't understand what it was all about.'

'I know. Anyway, who cares? Patrice is history now,' Lucy said, smiling grimly. 'He's not going to be causing any more problems.' Lucy stopped talking because Nina was snoring gently.

They voyaged on through the darkness. Sooner or later they would find land. It was not as if they were lost in the middle of a vast ocean. They were only trying to cross the English Channel. There were a couple of flares in the bottom of the lifeboat, so they could send up a distress signal if they spotted a ship. Lucy stared out over the black water. Apart from the steady chugging of the engine, there was no sound. The whole world seemed to be at peace. She lay back on her seat and gazed up at the sky. If only she had known how to identify the individual stars and constellations, she could have steered them back to England, the sky was so clear.

Removing Patrice's ring from her pocket, she squinted at it. The diamond glowed up at her in the moonlight. It did not really belong to her, but there was nothing to stop her keeping it. Alain had given it to her. No one else knew she had it. In any case, she could not pass it on to his family because she had never thought to ask his real name. She supposed she could discover his identity from the real Alain Michel, but it no longer mattered. To her, the man she had known would always be Alain. She hesitated before replacing the ring in her pocket. Somehow she would find a worthwhile use for it. She did not need anything to help her remember the man who had sacrificed himself to keep her safe.

They travelled on through the night. Drowsing, Lucy almost missed the lights of a ship in the distance. Leaning forward, she picked up a flare and set it off. The light rose high above them, tracing a brilliant arc in the sky. A moment later a powerful searchlight swept across the waves. When it found them, the ship's hooter boomed across at them. Soon a small boat was heading towards them and an English voice hailed them through a loudspeaker.

Before the boat reached them, Nina woke up. Breaking down in tears, she thanked Lucy.

'What are you thanking me for?'

'For saving my life.'

Remembering how she had been responsible for dragging Nina into their ordeal in the first place, Lucy shook her head. Overwhelmed by regret, she could not speak. Alain had believed it was worth sacrificing a single human life to save countless others. She would never have a chance to convince him that he was wrong. However gratifying it was that Patrice could not cause any more suffering, the cost had been too high.

'Lucy?' There was a catch in Nina's voice. 'They will be able to sort out my face, won't they?'

'Of course they will.'

'Do you think I'll have to wait long?'

Feeling the diamond ring in her pocket, Lucy smiled through her tears for Alain. 'You won't have to wait at all.'

'There's no way I can afford to have it done privately. Plastic surgery costs a fortune.'

'Trust me, you'll be able to get it done as soon as you like. And that's a promise.'

Lucy knew Alain would have approved of her decision.

Acknowledgements

I am deeply indebted to my inspiring editors Emilie Marneur and Sophie Wilson for their perceptive guidance, and for the kindness they have shown me. It is a privilege to work with such talented editors. I am very grateful to the whole team at Thomas and Mercer for all their support. I would like to thank my agent, Annette Crossland, for her unwavering enthusiasm and advice. Finally, I am grateful to all my friends in Paris, especially Kim, Helen and David, for their interest and help.

About the Author

Leigh Russell is the author of the internationally bestselling DI Geraldine Steel and DS Ian Peterson crime series, both of which are currently in development for television; *Girl in Danger* is the second of her Lucy Hall series, following *Journey to Death*. She studied at the University of Kent, gaining a master's degree in English and American literature. After many years teaching English at secondary school, she now writes crime fiction full-time. Published on both sides of the Atlantic, as well as in translation throughout Europe, Russell's books have reached top positions on many bestseller lists, including #1 on Kindle and iTunes. Her work has been nominated for a number of major awards, including the CWA New Blood Dagger and CWA Dagger in the Library. As well as writing bestselling crime novels, Russell appears at national and international literary festivals and runs occasional creative writing courses across Europe.

86567951R00186

Made in the USA
Columbia, SC
16 January 2018